The Wife's Irish Secret

BOOKS BY SUSANNE O'LEARY

Sandy Cove Series

Secrets of Willow House

Sisters of Willow House

Dreams of Willow House

Daughters of Wild Rose Bay

Memories of Wild Rose Bay

Miracles in Wild Rose Bay

Starlight Cottages Series

The Lost Girls of Ireland

The Lost Secret of Ireland

The Lost Promise of Ireland

The Lost House of Ireland

The Lost Letters of Ireland

The Lost Mother of Ireland

Magnolia Manor Series

The Keeper of the Irish Secret

The Granddaughter's Irish Secret

The Girl with the Irish Secret

The Widow's Irish Secret

The Book of Irish Secrets

The Road Trip

A Holiday to Remember

Susanne O'Leary

The Wife's Irish Secret

Bookouture

Published by Bookouture in 2025

An imprint of Storyfire Ltd.
Carmelite House
50 Victoria Embankment
London EC4Y 0DZ

www.bookouture.com

The authorised representative in the EEA is Hachette Ireland
8 Castlecourt Centre
Dublin 15 D15 XTP3
Ireland
(email: info@hbgi.ie)

ISBN: 978-1-80550-386-6
eBook ISBN: 978-1-80550-385-9

ONE

On the long flight from Sydney to Dubai, Marian Fleury found herself telling a complete stranger the story of her life. It wasn't what she would do under normal circumstances, but after all the stress and heartbreak she had been through recently, she felt an urge to talk to anyone with a sympathetic ear. Unable to sleep, she had wriggled around in her seat, trying to find a comfortable position when her neighbour, a man with a friendly voice and warm smile, had suggested they order a glass of wine.

'It might help us sleep,' he said. 'Or we could watch that documentary about the rivers of South America that's on offer on the tiny screen in front of us.'

'I prefer the wine,' Marian said and waved at a flight attendant who was just passing by. 'Two glasses of red wine,' she said. 'Or would you rather go for white?' she asked the man.

He smiled. 'No. I had the red with dinner. It was surprisingly good for aeroplane plonk.' He spoke with a slight Irish accent laced with a touch of something else. French or Italian, she surmised, taking in his nearly black hair with grey streaks, and brown eyes.

'Red then,' Marian said to the flight attendant. Then she

shot the man a tired smile and held out her hand. 'We didn't introduce ourselves. I'm Marian Fleury.'

'Fleury?' he said, looking intrigued. 'That sounds French, but I know there are a few Fleurys in Ireland.'

'Fleury is a Huguenot name from way back,' Marian said. 'They fled from France in the seventeenth century, due to persecution or something, I think.'

'After the annulment of the edict of Nantes,' he said and took her hand and shook it. 'Sean Pierre Duvivier, and yes, I'm originally from France. I left a little later than your ancestors, though. I've lived in Ireland for a few years.'

'You sound both Irish and French,' Marian remarked.

He nodded. 'Oh yes. I have a foot in both camps. My father wanted to call me Jean-Pierre, but my mother stuck to her guns and I was called Sean and then Pierre, after both grandfathers. I went to school in France and spent my summers in Ireland. And I've just spent two months in Sydney for work. How about you?'

'I've lived in Queensland for seven years,' Marian said, sensing that he didn't want to talk any further about his background. 'I'm from Ireland. Dublin, to be precise.'

'What brought you to Queensland?' he asked.

'My husband,' Marian replied. 'He's from there.'

'Is he the Fleury or did you keep your birth name?' he asked, looking intrigued.

'I'm the Fleury,' Marian said with an amused smile. 'His name is Watson but, well, I didn't feel like giving up my birth name when we got married.'

'Quite wise,' Sean said. 'Fleury is such a nice name. So now you're going back to Dublin for a visit?' he asked.

'Not quite. I'm going to Kerry for my sister's wedding,' Marian replied. 'And possibly to stay for a while. I have family there.'

'Oh.' His eyebrows shot up. 'Actually, I'm going to Ireland

too. But first London, for a meeting and then on to Dublin, and then I'll drive west. I have Irish roots, you see. My mother came from the southwest coast, and now I'm going there because she left me a cottage in her will. She died two months ago. ' His tone was casual but Marian could see a dart of pain in his eyes, gone as soon as it had appeared.

'Oh, I'm sorry,' Marian said. 'So hard to lose your mother, isn't it?'

He nodded. 'Yes. Very hard. We were quite close. But then we kind of drifted apart when I started working as a journalist. She lived alone in France after my dad died twenty years ago. Never wanted to move back to Ireland, so I had to go over regularly, which was expensive, but nice all the same. I hadn't been there for two years when she passed away. Made me feel guilty, I have to confess.'

'Not your fault,' Marian soothed. 'But I know how you must feel. I had a similar experience a while ago. It's difficult to deal with all the emotions when someone close to you has passed away.'

'Thank you. That's kind of you to say. Was it your mother who died?' he asked.

'No, my great-aunt. She was all we had after my parents died in a car accident and I should have been to see her more often. I felt awful about not going home while she was ill.'

'I know. It's a horrible feeling. But here's our wine now,' he said when the flight attendant arrived with two glasses and a little basket with crackers and cheese.

'Let me know if you need anything else,' she said and disappeared down the aisle to answer another call.

'She works hard,' Marian remarked. 'I wouldn't want to be a flight attendant.'

'It's fun if you like to travel, I can imagine,' Sean said and lifted his glass. 'Here's to an enjoyable journey. Cheers.'

'Cheers,' Marian said and sipped her wine. 'Well, it's more

enjoyable now than when we got on board. You didn't look like you wanted to talk then.'

'I wasn't going to,' Sean said. 'I don't usually talk to people on flights, other than "hello" and "how are you".'

'Me neither,' Marian confessed. 'Before you know it, you have to listen to someone's life story which can be pretty dreary.'

He smiled and nodded. 'Exactly. I wasn't going to start a conversation with you. But then I thought you looked as if you needed cheering up, so I thought I'd make an effort.'

'That was kind,' Marian said. 'And you're right. I do need cheering up.'

'Not looking forward to the wedding?' he asked.

'Oh, no, it's not that,' Marian protested. 'I'm very much looking forward to the wedding. My sister and I are very close. It's something else. Relationship issues,' she added.

Sean drank some wine and looked at her curiously. 'I see. Well, then no need to tell me. I'm sure you don't want to share your personal life with a stranger who just happened to sit beside you on a plane.'

'Well, actually...' Marian started after another sip of wine. *A stranger on a plane might be the perfect person to share my story with*, she said to herself as she met his kind eyes. 'You don't know me or anyone in my family, so why not?' she quipped.

'True,' he said. 'And it might feel good to unload your problems to someone with a sympathetic ear. So, if you want to talk about it, go ahead.'

'Well...' Marian hesitated. 'Maybe it wouldn't be fair to burden you with my misery. But oh, it would be good to talk.' He kept looking at her with that empathic gaze which encouraged her. Marian took a deep breath. 'So, I'm on my way to Ireland to my sister's wedding, like I told you. I've lived in Queensland for seven years. In Surfers Paradise, to be precise.

My husband and I run a shop that sells surfboards and wetsuits and everything to do with water sports.'

'Seems like the perfect place for it,' Sean remarked.

'Yes, of course,' Marian said with a sigh. 'But there are many such shops there so it was a bit of a struggle at times to get it off the ground. But now it's doing really well and my husband is happy.'

'But you're not?' Sean asked.

'No.' Marian put her empty glass on the tray in front of her. 'I was never really happy, to be honest. I tried my best to put down roots, but I never felt at home in Queensland. Theo, my husband, loves it, though.'

'Theo?' Sean asked. 'Is that short for Theodore?'

'Yes,' Marian replied. 'His full name is Andrew Theodore, but everyone in Surfers Paradise knows him as Theo. He's from around there so it's home to him. He grew up on the beach, surfing and swimming. He's in his element in that environment.'

'He would be,' Sean remarked. 'So how did an Aussie surf dude and an Irish colleen meet?'

'We met on a beach in France, actually,' Marian said as the memories of that meeting over thirty-five years ago flooded into her mind.

She had been in Biarritz for the summer, working as au pair with a French family. Theo had been there with a group of friends to surf on the windswept beaches of the French Atlantic coast and had spent a few weeks in Biarritz, famous for its high waves. Marian had been on the beach with the children she was minding and when Theo was wading into shore carrying his surfboard, she had admired his toned body, blond hair bleached by the sun and salt water, and his deep tan. He in turn had, as he told her later, been struck by her tall slim figure, fair skin and reddish blonde hair. 'Not to mention your lovely blue eyes and gorgeous smile,' he had explained later. The little boy Marian was minding had stared at the young man and asked if the surf-board was heavy. Theo had stopped to talk to him in his bad French and then sat down on the sand to chat with the children, while shooting Marian such admiring glances that it made her blush. Then he had asked her to come to the bar at the beach that evening for a drink, and 'the rest was history', Marian told the man sitting beside her on the plane.

'I can see how that happened,' he said. 'Sunset on the beach, a lovely young Irish colleen and an Aussie beach boy, what could be more romantic?'

She laughed suddenly. 'Sounds a bit clichéd, but yes, it really was. We stayed on the beach drinking beer and eating hamburgers until well after midnight,' she said wistfully, remembering the feel of the wind in her hair and the stars in the dark sky that night – and that handsome young man kissing her until she was breathless. 'And then we met every day until I had to leave. I was at university in Dublin, studying marketing and business. But I never finished my degree.'

'He followed you there and then you were married?' Sean asked, looking amused.

'Yes, he did,' Marian said with a smile as she remembered Theo arriving out of the blue after three weeks' separation. 'We missed each other so much when I had to go back to college so he decided to come to Ireland. And then, when I met him at the airport, he got down on one knee and proposed. Talk about a whirlwind romance. We were married three months after that. And then Theo got a job with a plumbing firm that was just starting up and I got pregnant very soon after our wedding.'

'So you stayed on in Ireland?' he asked.

'Yes. Theo liked Ireland a lot and he had a good job as a qualified plumber. Then my parents died in a car crash and I had to look after my sister, who is five years younger than me, so that was an added reason to stay.'

'How terrible,' Sean said. 'You've had a lot of sadness.'

'Yes, I have,' Marian agreed, trying not to let her sorrow show. 'But I wasn't alone. My sister and I were very close which helped a lot. And then we had our auntie Rachel who was always there for us. And, of course, Theo. We had another baby shortly afterwards. We both wanted the kids to grow up in Ireland, so we stayed on until the children were grown and flew the nest. Then Theo wanted to move to Australia and set up shop in Surfers Paradise and get back to that beach lifestyle he used to love so much.' Marian drew breath and looked at the fresh glass of wine that had been put on her tray while she talked.

'I ordered another one,' Sean said and lifted his own. 'Cheers.'

'Cheers,' Marian said and took a sip. 'So where were we?' The wine relaxed her and made her feel less shy. It was good to talk.

'You moved to Australia. And now you're on your way to Ireland for your sister's wedding,' Sean reminded her. 'And also because you needed a break? Something happened to make you feel that your husband was not as supportive as he should be? Just guessing.'

'You're right,' she said and leaned her head against the head-rest, staring into the dark night outside. She felt suspended in time and space, on her way to nowhere, everyone around her asleep, except the man beside her who, with his kind eyes, seemed to want to hear her story. 'I found something that made me wonder if Theo truly loved me. Or if he married me on the rebound from the break-up with another woman.'

'That must have been painful,' Sean said, his voice gentle.

'Yes,' Marian whispered as a wave of pain and sorrow hit her. What she had found had shaken her but it left so many questions. She knew she should have had it out with him and asked what it all meant, but she couldn't bear to speak to Theo about it, feeling that he might tell her things she didn't want to hear. But she had told him that they would have to talk about his behaviour towards her and how they were not on the same page any more. She added that he didn't seem to want to spend time with her and always found reasons to go out in the evenings with his friends. Theo had accused her of being picky and resentful, which to Marian looked like a very guilty conscience. Added to her enormous homesickness that seemed to get worse with every year, and the disenchantment with their marriage, Marian felt this was the last straw. Instead of making plans for them both to travel together, she had booked a single ticket to Ireland, telling Theo she was going to her sister Claire's wedding on her own and wouldn't be back for some time. They had parted on a sour note, neither of them willing to take the first step towards a reconciliation.

'Fine,' he had said and turned his back to her. Then he had gone to the beach and stayed there all day while Marian packed her suitcase with tears streaming down her cheeks. Theo had arrived back just as the taxi pulled up outside their house. He had given her a quick peck on the cheek and said, 'Bye, then. Have a good trip. Text me when you arrive. Take as much time as you need. And then we'll talk when you come back.'

'Okay,' she had whispered, tears welling up yet again. *If I come back*, she had thought as she got into the taxi. Then she had turned to look at him through the back window, but he had already gone inside.

'It was very painful,' she said to the man beside her. 'But I don't want to talk about it.' It was suddenly too much and she knew if she started to tell him, she would burst into tears.

'Of course not,' he said. 'We'll change the subject.'

'What will we talk about?' Marian asked, relieved that he had understood. She had felt initially that she wanted to tell him everything but then she shied away from what had happened. She didn't want to go back there just yet.

'How about the Fleury family?' Sean suggested. 'I bet they have an interesting history.'

'Oh yes,' Marian said. 'They certainly do. My branch of the family lived in Dublin and we knew nothing about "the other Fleurys" as we used to call them. We only knew that something terrible had happened about a hundred years ago that split the family apart.'

Sean sat up and looked at Marian with excitement in his brown eyes. 'How fascinating. So what was that terrible thing?'

'We had no idea. It was a big secret and we were never to even ask about it,' Marian said. 'Then, about two years ago, my sister Claire came across an old diary after our great-aunt died and it contained a bit of the story. So Claire decided to go to Kerry, where the other Fleurys lived.'

'Where?' Sean asked. 'In Dingle?'

'Just outside the town,' Marian replied. 'In this big house called Magnolia Manor that was built by a Fleury ancestor over two hundred years ago.'

'Wow, this is getting to be really fascinating,' Sean said, looking excited.

'It's better than any movie,' Marian said. 'I was following it step by step through FaceTime with my sister. She was an amazing detective.'

'I hope you're going to tell me,' Sean said. He sat back and closed his eyes. 'I'm ready. I want to hear the whole story, even the tiniest detail.'

Marian laughed softly. 'Okay. I'm wide awake anyway.'

'Me too,' he said, shifting in his seat to get more comfortable. 'Let me hear it.'

Marian nodded and leaned her head on the headrest. 'It all started at a ball in nineteen ten,' she said. 'And ended more than a hundred years later...'

Then, once she had started, she couldn't stop, and during the two hours that followed, Marian told Sean the story of the Fleurys of Magnolia Manor, not leaving out a single thing. Not even the family secrets that she wasn't supposed to reveal.

TWO

Someone tapped Marian on the shoulder. 'The plane has landed in Dubai,' a voice said in her ear. 'Time to get off if you want to catch your connecting flight to Dublin.'

Marian blinked and stared, bleary-eyed, at the flight attendant. 'Oh. I must finally have fallen asleep.' The seat beside her was empty and she saw that most of the passengers had already left the plane. Marian started to gather up her bag and jacket and stood up, feeling both stiff and groggy. 'Where's the man who was sitting beside me?' she asked, looking among the last remaining passengers at the door of the aircraft.

'He left very soon after we landed,' the flight attendant replied. 'He was in a hurry to catch his flight to London. Important meeting, he said.'

Marian nodded. 'Okay. I just thought I'd say goodbye. We had a nice chat before I fell asleep.'

'He asked me to say goodbye to you,' the flight attendant said. 'And to say thank you for a very interesting conversation.'

'Interesting?' Marian said. 'I think I just blathered on about my family.' She tried to remember exactly what she had said, but all she knew was that she had felt a lot better about everything and drifted off, finally getting the rest she had craved after all the upsets before she left Brisbane. She had probably unloaded all her problems onto the poor man. But she did have a feeling he had been very kind and listened to her woes without interrupting.

'Maybe you'll meet again?' the flight attendant suggested.

'I don't think so,' Marian said as she shuffled to the door in the wake of the last passenger. 'It was a case of ships meeting in the night, never to cross paths again.'

'Happens a lot on these long-haul flights,' the flight attendant remarked.

'I'm sure,' Marian agreed. 'Anyway, goodbye and thank you for all your help during the flight.'

The flight attendant smiled. 'You're welcome. Have a good trip home.'

'Home,' Marian said. 'Yes, Ireland is home to me and always will be.' She shot the flight attendant a tired smile and left the plane, thinking about where she was headed: a part of Ireland she had never been to. But her family had originally come from Kerry and her sister, Claire, had gone there over a year ago to unite the two branches of the Fleury family that had been apart for a very long time. Her darling sister, the baby of the family, had managed to do what generations of the family had failed: to find out about the feud that had caused such heartbreak. What Claire had found had united them once more. She had also fallen in love with a man who had helped her during her journey and now they were getting married. Claire had been through a painful divorce from her first husband, from which it took her a long time to recover. And now she was getting married again, to a man who seemed to be the complete oppo-site to her ex-husband: kind, caring and sweet. 'Like a comfy armchair with a soft blanket to wrap around you,' Claire had said with a laugh when they planned Marian's trip through FaceTime. 'Just wait till you meet Pierce. You'll love him.'

'Will I tell him you said he's like a comfy armchair?' Marian had asked.

'Well, maybe not,' Claire had said with a giggle. 'I'm not sure he'd like it.'

Then Marian had happily started to plan her trip, looking forward to meeting all the Fleurys of Magnolia Manor. Theo had initially planned to go with Marian and even suggested that she stay for a few weeks after the wedding while he went back to Australia to look after the shop with the help of an additional assistant. Marian had thought him very generous and understanding. Until she found the letter. What it contained, along with his reaction to her homesickness and their subsequent row, made her realise that Theo wasn't as committed to their marriage as she had thought. The argument had mostly been about her failure to settle into life in Australia and his lack of understanding, which had been so upsetting. Thirty-five years of happiness seemed to have suddenly gone up in smoke and Marian left for Ireland feeling as if part of her life was over.

Many hours later, after an uneventful flight to Dublin and a scramble to get onto the connecting flight to Farranfore, the airport that served south Kerry, Marian fell into Claire's arms, laughing and crying at the same time. 'I can't believe I'm finally here with you,' she sobbed, looking at her sister's cute freckly face, the green eyes and the wild curly hair, so like her own, apart from the colour. Claire's hair was dark auburn, while Marian was a strawberry blonde.

'It's like a dream come true,' Claire said, hugging her sister tight. 'It's been so long since we've been together.'

'Far too long,' Marian agreed, dabbing her eyes. 'But now I'm here and will stay a long time.'

Claire pulled away and looked at Marian. 'How long?'

'I'm not sure, but I'd like to stay for a while,' Marian said.

'You can stay as long as you like. But what about Theo?' Claire asked, looking worried. 'Won't he miss you?'

'I don't think so,' Marian said, fiddling with her handbag to avoid looking at Claire. 'We're going through – something. I'll tell you later. Right now, all I want to do is sleep.'

'Of course,' Claire said. 'You must be horribly jetlagged. Come on, let's get going. My car is not far away. I'll soon have you tucked up in bed in my little flat. Just wait till you see it.'

'I'm so excited,' Marian said. 'Oh, to be at Magnolia Manor at last. What a treat.'

'We'll be a bit squashed in my part of the house,' Claire said with a laugh. 'The place is tiny. A one-bedroom flat in the attic that feels quite separate from the manor. But I just got a sofa bed for the living room and you will sleep in the bedroom.'

'No,' Marian protested. 'I'll take the sofa bed.'

'You will not,' Claire argued when they had reached the car. 'I'll be grand in the sofa bed. You have to take the bed the first few nights and then we'll take turns. In any case, it's only two weeks until the wedding and then you can have the flat all to yourself as long as you want. Pierce and I have bought the cutest little bungalow near Ventry. I can't wait to show it to you once it's been done up.'

'Lovely. I'm so looking forward to meeting Pierce,' Marian said and then got into the car and fell asleep as soon as Claire had left the car park. She slept all the way past Killarney and only woke up an hour later when they were driving down a street along a harbour lined with houses painted all the colours of the rainbow. 'This is wonderful,' she exclaimed. 'Where are we?'

'Dingle town,' Claire said. 'Isn't it beautiful?'

'Amazing,' Marian said and rolled down the window to get the full effect of this gorgeous little seaside town. She breathed in the air from the sea laced with the smell of salt and seaweed and felt the soft wind on her face. This was so different to the seaside of Australia with its harsh sun and tropical heat. Here the sunlight felt warm and soothing and the wind fresh. The ocean sparkled in the sunlight and seagulls glided above them letting out a screech now and then. 'I love it already,' she said.

'Wait till you get to Magnolia Manor,' Claire said. 'It's even better than here.'

'Oh, I can't wait to see it.' Marian stared out the window as they left the town and drove across a little bridge and down a country lane until they reached a set of tall iron gates with a lovely little gatehouse standing just inside it.

'Cousin Vi and her husband, Jack, live here,' Claire said. 'I think they went to the beach with their boys today as it's Saturday, but you'll meet them at Sylvia's Sunday lunch tomorrow.'

Marian thought of Sylvia Fleury, who had been married to her grandfather's first cousin Liam, and the stories she'd heard from Claire about the impressive old woman: the way she'd led her three granddaughters, Lily, Rose and Violet, through such difficult times. 'I can't wait to meet the famous Fleury matriarch,' Marian said.

'She'll be excited to meet you too,' Claire said. 'In fact, you'll be introduced to everyone then. I hope it won't be too scary but they all want to get to know you.'

'I'm sure I'll cope with that after a night's sleep,' Marian said with a huge yawn. 'I'm really looking forward to seeing them all in real life, actually. I've heard so much about them and seen all the photos you sent, so I feel I know them already.'

'I still can't believe the family is together at last,' Claire said.

'Neither can I,' Marian said. 'I remember how we thought they were so glamorous when we were growing up.' Marian cast her mind back to the old days, when they had not been told why or how the two families split apart after a long-ago row. The Dublin Fleurys never met the Kerry Fleurys until Claire had found out that their great-grandfathers had been twins and had had a huge row, splitting the two sides of the family tree across the country. And that Claire and Marian's great-grandfather was the one who should have inherited Magnolia Manor all those years ago, a secret that had been kept within the family ever since, never to be told.

They pulled up in front of a large building that Marian recognised from photos. She looked up at the imposing Georgian façade, the many windows that glinted in the late-evening sun, the massive double entrance doors and the huge magnolia tree beside the front steps. She couldn't believe she was here at last, at the manor house that had been built by one of her ancestors over two hundred years ago. 'A dream come true,' she whispered.

'That's what I felt, too, the first time I came here,' Claire said. 'It was like seeing something from a fairy tale.'

Marian kept staring up at the house, feeling overwhelmed with the fact that she was here at last and that she would be living here for a while. How long that would be, she had no idea, but it felt good to know she could stay as long as she wanted. She needed time to herself, and also time to get to the bottom of who Theo was involved with. She knew from the letters she had found that he had been serious about a woman some time ago, but not when or where she lived. That was something she needed to find out – but not yet. Right now, she wanted to meet her relatives and simply drink in the atmosphere of this magical place.

'Come on,' Claire urged. 'Let's get your stuff upstairs. I have lasagne waiting; it only needs to be heated up. We'll have a glass of wine and then you can have a bath and go to bed. How does that sound?'

'Heavenly,' Marian said with a happy sigh. 'It was a very long trip.'

'I know,' Claire said. 'I did it once, remember? When I came to visit you and then I slept for what seemed like days.'

'You were like a zombie,' Marian said with a laugh. 'But then you perked up when the kids got you to come to the beach.'

'Oh, yeah,' Claire said, smiling. 'They tried to teach me to surf but I kept falling off that dratted surfboard. And that was when we were still on the beach. Surfing – forget it. I was too old even then to try it.' She paused and shook her head. 'Anyway, how are the kids?'

'Oh, they're fine,' Marian said. 'All grown up, or so they say. Rebecca is trying her hand at journalism at a magazine in Sydney and Conor has just qualified as an engineer and is working with a firm in London. He's on holiday in California right now, so he can't come to the wedding.'

'That's a pity,' Claire said. 'But I understand why it would be difficult to change his plans.'

'Yes, he couldn't rebook his ticket,' Marian said. 'They're at the age when they only keep in touch with parents when they're in trouble, or need money. I miss them terribly.' Her eyes filled with tears as she thought about her children, who seemed to have grown up so fast. 'I miss us being a family,' she said. 'You know, that routine of picking them up from school, doing homework at the kitchen table, picnics on the beach and watching them playing soccer and doing Irish dancing, all that stuff that seemed so tedious then.'

'I know what you mean,' Claire said. 'Even if I never had that. But now, I'm involved with the Fleury grandchildren and I try to help out when they need me. There are six of them, so I'm often asked to babysit or to pick up from school or preschool. That way I get a little bit of family life and it's lovely.'

'I'm really looking forward to meeting them,' Marian said, cheering up at the thought.

They got out of the car and took out the luggage, carrying it into the house. Marian looked around the huge entrance hall with its black and white floor tiles, the vast fireplace and the antlers on the walls. It was grander than she had imagined and it oozed the atmosphere of years gone by. Then they used the lift to get to the second floor and had to lug the bags up the remaining flight of stairs.

'They only got the lift that far,' Claire explained. 'The attics seemed unimportant, so anyone wanting to get any further has to work hard. But wait till you see my little flat. It's really lovely and I've been so happy up there.'

'Will you miss it?' Marian asked as they arrived at the door.

'In a way,' Claire said. 'I'll miss living at the top of Magnolia Manor. It's such a special place.'

'I can't believe I'm here,' Marian said. 'It's like being in a movie.'

'And tomorrow you'll meet all the stars,' Claire said with a grin. 'But they're wonderful and they'll love you. Rose said only yesterday that she was looking forward to getting to know you. And Naomi and Sophie, Lily and Rose's little girls, said they want to meet my big sister.'

'I still can't believe we're like one big family,' Marian said. 'Auntie Rachel would be so pleased.'

'I know,' Claire said and took a key from her pocket. 'It's so fabulous. But now, let's get you and your stuff inside.' She unlocked the door and then opened it wide to reveal a tiny hall that led into a cosy living room. 'Here we are. Small but perfectly formed.'

Marian walked through the hall and into the tiny but bright living room, looking around at the window with stunning views of the gardens and the bay beyond, the kitchen alcove with a round table and two chairs and the bedroom that she could glimpse through another door. The rooms were not spacious but charming with bright yellow walls, cream curtains and a colourful rug in front of the miniature fireplace. There was a sofa in front of the window that folded out into a bed, which Claire said was very comfortable.

'So where is Pierce?' Marian asked.

'He still lives in the granny flat behind my boss Karina's house,' Claire explained.

'Oh, yeah, she's his sister as well,' Marian said, remembering what Claire had told her.

'That's right. Pierce comes here occasionally but he finds the place too small for us both. And now he's camping in the new house while it's being done up.'

'So I didn't push him out?' Marian asked.

'Not at all. In any case, he felt we needed to have girls' night in when you arrived.'

'That's was kind of him.'

'That's the way he is,' Claire said with a happy sigh. 'Oh, and the bathroom is off the bedroom if you want to have a shower.'

'Oh, lovely,' Marian exclaimed. 'I'll have quick wash and get into my pyjamas, if you don't mind.'

'Of course not,' Claire said. 'I'll get into my jammies too and then we'll eat and catch up and then you can go to bed when you feel like it.'

'Like the old days,' Marian said. 'When I was fifteen and you were ten and refused to go to bed if I was still up.'

'So you'd pretend to get ready for bed,' Claire said. 'Only to get dressed again to go out with your friends when I was asleep.'

Marian laughed. 'Oh yes, I did. But it didn't fool you. Lucky we had Auntie Rachel to mind you when our parents were away.'

'We were blessed to have her,' Claire agreed with a fond smile. 'And then she was there for me when Mum and Dad died. But hey, let's get our jammies on and I'll heat up the lasagne.' She carried one of Marian's bags into the bedroom and put it on the bed and Marian followed with the rest of the luggage. Then Marian had a shower in the tiny bathroom and when they were both in their pyjamas, they sat on the sofa and ate the lasagne accompanied by a glass of red wine.

Claire held up her glass. 'Here's to our reunion. I can't tell you how much I've missed you.'

Marian clinked glasses with Claire. 'I missed you like crazy, too, darling Claire. I'm so happy to be here with you. It seems like a dream that I will finally meet all the Kerry Fleurys at last.'

Claire took a sip of wine. 'They're really lovely. And they will love you too.'

Marian finished her mouthful of lasagne. 'So Sunday lunch tomorrow? What time?'

'Around one o'clock,' Claire replied. 'But first we'll go to mass in Dingle town and then we'll have coffee with Pierce and Karina at the little café near the church. Then lunch and then we might go down to the beach with the kids if it's warm enough. I hope that's not too much for you.'

'Oh, I'm sure it'll be fine,' Marian said. 'I just want a good night's sleep and then I can cope with anything.'

'You do need it,' Claire said and drained her glass. 'Gosh, this is nice. One of Pierce's best. Do you want another glass?'

'No, I'm fine,' Marian replied. 'One glass is enough for me right now. I feel a bit wobbly after the trip.'

'Then just finish the food and you can go to bed,' Claire said, getting up from the sofa. 'Karina made the lasagne; she really is the most incredible chef. I'll have another glass and then I think I'll watch a movie on my computer. It's only eight o'clock, so I'm not sleepy yet.'

Marian laughed. 'Interesting role reversal. I'm going to bed and you're staying up.' She finished her helping of lasagne and pushed the plate away. 'That was delicious. Karina is a very good cook.'

'She's brilliant,' Claire said. 'And I love working for her. We get on so well.'

'And the Fleurys?' Marian asked, more interested in her distant cousins than Claire's boss. 'Do you get on with them all?'

'Oh yes, absolutely,' Claire said. 'They're terrific. We're

very close all of us and fiercely protective. We never reveal any kind of secret to outsiders. What happens in the family stays in the family, if you see what I mean. All the Fleury secrets I found out have never been told to anyone in town. Nobody in the family shares anything remotely confidential to anyone.'

'I like that idea,' Marian said. She yawned. 'I'm sorry, but the jetlag is catching up with me.'

'Off to bed with you,' Claire ordered. 'I'll clean up.'

Marian rose from the sofa. 'I'll just brush my teeth and then I'll cuddle in under that lovely duvet.'

'Night, night,' Claire said and threw Marian a kiss. 'Sleep tight.'

'Night,' Marian said, smiling at her sister. 'See you in the morning light.'

Then she went into the bedroom and sent a quick message to Theo that she had arrived safely. That done, she closed the curtains and after brushing her teeth, sank into bed, and put her head on the pillow. She could hear faint birdsong through the open window and, in the distance, the gentle sound of waves against the shore. She drifted off to sleep, the long, tiring trip slowly receding from her mind. She thought briefly of what Claire had said about the family, that they closed ranks against the outside world if anyone was in trouble, and... *what happens in the family, stays in the family...* Which Marian had understood meant that nobody revealed what was confidential.

Her conversation with the stranger she had met during the flight to Dubai suddenly popped into her mind. She had told him the story of the Fleury family and he had seemed very interested. Had she revealed any important facts or secrets? she wondered. She couldn't quite remember exactly what she had said. She had been sleepy after two glasses of wine and possibly rambled on for a while before she went to sleep. He had probably drifted off, too, while she droned on. *Oh no,* she thought, suddenly panicking. *Did I tell him things that should be kept in the family?* Then she dismissed the idea, feeling slightly less worried. *Even if I did, I'm sure he forgot all about it,* she said to herself. *I'll never meet him again, anyway.* Then sleep finally took over and she slept soundly all night, dreaming about Magnolia Manor, the family she was yet to meet and the Fleurys who had built this beautiful house.

THREE

Marian woke up to a beautiful summer's day with the sun streaming in through the half-open curtains. She got out of bed and opened them wide, enjoying the view of the garden with shrubs and trees in full bloom. The velvety lawns were a deep green and she could see a mix of subtropical plants and palm trees which made the gardens look lush and greener still. It was early June, the beginning of winter in Australia but nearly full summer here in the southwest of Ireland. Marian sighed happily and leaned her elbows on the windowsill, taking in all the beautiful sights and feeling the soft breeze from the sea against her face. She looked further away and saw the ocean glittering seductively in the distance. A noise at the door made her turn around to discover Claire with a tray.

'Good morning,' Claire chanted. 'Isn't it a fabulous day? Did you sleep well?'

'I slept like a log,' Marian said. 'And yes, it's a gorgeous day. What time is it?'

'Eight o'clock,' Claire replied. 'I heard you get up so I made breakfast. Tea and toast and some homemade granola with strawberries from Lily's kitchen garden.'

'Wow,' Marian said, her stomach rumbling at the sight of the breakfast. 'But can't we eat together at that cute little table just off the kitchen?'

'Of course.' Claire turned around and went back out. 'I thought we'd go for a swim before we go to mass.'

'Do we have time?' Marian asked.

'Yes,' Claire said as she put the tray on the round table. 'Mass is at eleven o'clock.'

'Oodles of time, then,' Marian said and sat down at the table with a contented sigh. 'Oh, this is so fantastic. Irish summer weather. Not too hot or too cold. And swimming in the Atlantic. Heavenly.'

'You don't miss the tropics?' Claire asked as she joined Marian at the table.

'Not a bit,' Marian said. 'I always had to hide from the sun. I was always like a wet rag with that humid heat. But Theo loves it, so...' She paused and sipped her tea to hide her distress. 'I just put up with it. I was too lonely to be positive about anything, I suppose.'

'You were homesick?' Claire asked gently.

'All the time,' Marian said. 'I tried my best to get used to everything but it was so hard. The heat, the sun, the huge insects, the snakes... And then the threat of sharks in the sea. I always felt I had to be on the lookout for things that would either make me sick or actually kill me.'

'I know what you mean,' Claire said. 'I remember all that from my visits to you. But I thought you'd get used to it after seven years.'

'I don't know,' Marian said with a sigh. She dug into the granola. 'I don't think I ever did.'

'Maybe it was Conor and Rebecca settling down elsewhere? Knowing they'd never live near you?' Claire asked.

'Yes, that could be it. Sometimes I...' She paused, wondering if she could say out loud something she had been feeling in her heart for months now. 'Sometimes I feel like I lost my whole family as soon as I moved there.'

'I had no idea you were so sad and lonely.' Claire looked saddened, putting her hand out to hold Marian's. 'Did you tell Theo how unhappy you were?'

'No,' Marian said. 'He was so happy to be back home, and I didn't want to upset him. I didn't want to look like a wimp who couldn't cope. He was trying to make the business get off the ground and had a lot of stress associated with that. I think he forgot about me during that time. It was only when things improved that he looked up and noticed me. But then it was too late.'

'In what way?' Claire asked. 'Had something happened?'

'Yes. I found something that made me realise that he doesn't care about me as much as I thought. A letter from a woman he seems to have corresponded with for a long time.'

'A letter?' Claire asked. 'How old fashioned. Don't most people communicate by text or email these days?'

'It was an old letter, written years ago. He must have kept it and read it many times.' Marian paused and picked up a strawberry. 'But I don't want to talk about it now. There are pieces I need to put together to get the whole picture. In any case, I want to enjoy this day when I will be meeting your fiancé and our cousins and get to know the house and the area. And then there's your wedding in two weeks. I want to help you with the preparations and do everything I can to make it a wonderful day.' Marian drew breath and smiled at Claire. 'I just want to be happy for a little while.'

Claire looked at Marian with sympathy. 'Of course you do. I'm sorry to be asking all those questions. I want to make your first day here fun.'

'It already is,' Marian said as she finished the last of her toasted soda bread. 'Let's go down for a swim. I can't wait to see that little beach.'

'There's a jetty and a raft to swim out to,' Claire said. 'And I'm sure we'll meet Tricia and Cillian there. That's the girls' mother and her partner,' she added as she put the cups and plates into the dishwasher.

'I know,' Marian said. 'You told me all about them. Tricia seems like an interesting person, who's been through a lot.'

'She has,' Claire agreed. 'She was widowed twice and now she's with a very nice man. I think you'll like her. She's in her early sixties and very youthful and fun.'

'My generation, then,' Marian said.

'Yeah, but you're only fifty-five,' Claire said. 'So she must be about five years older or more.'

'Oh, whatever,' Marian said. 'Who cares about age these days? I don't.'

'Nor me,' Claire said. 'Anyway, let's get ready for the beach. Did you bring your togs?'

'I have a whole wardrobe full of them in Australia,' Marian said. 'I brought two of them as I know swimming here must be so great.'

'It is,' Claire said. 'Especially now in early summer.'

Marian finished her breakfast and got up. 'I'll go and dig out the togs and take the towel you gave me, if that's okay.'

'Of course,' Claire said. 'I'll get ready too and we'll walk down to the jetty. I prefer it to the beach because I don't really like getting sand everywhere.'

When they were ready, they walked together down the gravel path through the garden that was just as lovely as it had looked from the bedroom window. Marian peered up at the leafy canopy of oaks and beech trees that had to be several hundred years old as they made their way to the shore. 'This garden is amazing,' she said. 'Like some enchanted place in a story.'

'I love it,' Claire said. 'Summer or winter. I love to imagine the trees looking down at us and rustling their leaves to wish us a nice day.'

'What a lovely thought,' Marian said and put her arm through Claire's. 'I'm so happy to be here with you at last.'

'Me too,' Claire said and squeezed Marian's arm.

They arrived at the wooden jetty that stretched out into the bay. Marian could see a raft further out which she assumed was the one Claire had described. Someone was sitting in a deck chair on the shore, reading a book. She turned around and smiled as they approached. 'Hi, Claire,' she said. 'So your sister arrived?'

'Hi, Tricia,' Claire said. 'Yes, this is Marian, who came yesterday.'

The woman got up and smiled at them both, holding out her hand. 'Welcome, Marian, I've heard so much about you.'

Marian shook the woman's hand and smiled back at her. Dressed in denim shorts and a white T-shirt, she had short blonde hair, sparkling blue eyes and a wide smile. 'Hi, Tricia. I've heard loads about you too.'

'Then we know each other already,' Tricia said. She looked years younger than her age and seemed genuinely pleased to meet Marian. 'But of course you're third cousins with my daughters, so you're family.' She peered at Marian for a moment. 'You're quite similar to Claire but not as Fleury-like as she is.'

'Marian doesn't have the freckles,' Claire said. 'Isn't she lucky?'

'I wouldn't say that,' Tricia protested. 'I think freckles are gorgeous.'

'You're very kind,' Claire said. 'Where's Cillian?'

'In the cottage, working,' Tricia said. 'I'm a happy pensioner these days, so I can enjoy the fine weather whenever I like. But you should get your swim as the tide is in. The water is lovely.'

'We'll dive in so,' Claire said. 'We won't stay long as we're going to mass later.'

'So am I, come to think of it,' Tricia said, and started to gather up her book, towel and swimsuit. 'I got lost in this novel and forgot about the time. A really good read, I have to say.'

'Which book is it?' Claire asked.

'It's called *A Baker's Dozen*, by this new author I've just discovered.' Tricia showed the book to Claire and Marian. 'It's a thriller and it's set in France. Riveting, actually.'

Claire looked at the cover that had a design of a very French-looking house with a broken window. 'Looks interesting,' she said. 'I've never heard of John Peters.'

'He's getting to be quite famous and some of his books have been very high in the Amazon charts,' Tricia said.

'Oh?' Claire turned the book around to look at the back of it. 'I don't have to time to read much. Here's his photo.' She showed the book to Marian. 'Do you know this author?'

'John Peters? No,' Marian said and glanced at the photo on the back of the book. Then she blinked and stared at it in shock. She had seen that face in real life recently. But where? She kept looking at the face of a man with greying dark hair, brown eyes and a wide smile. Then it hit her. Of course. It was *that* man... The man who had been sitting beside her on the flight to Dubai. The man who had listened so intently to her as she told him the story of the Fleury family. And every single confidential detail.

FOUR

Still shocked by that photo, Marian swam to the raft in Claire's wake while all kinds of thoughts whirled around in her mind. *Is that really him? Maybe it's just someone who looks like him? People have doubles sometimes. But that name – John Peters... That would be his first names, Sean Pierre, translated to English. But how could the man on the plane be an author whose books are so popular in Ireland?*

'Come on.' Claire's voice interrupted Marian's thoughts as they reached the raft. 'We haven't got all day.' She heaved herself up and sat on the raft, dangling her legs in the water. 'You must still be tired,' she said. 'You usually beat me by several metres.'

'Yes, I am a bit tired,' Marian said, breathing hard as she got up on the raft. 'Your swimming has improved too.' She sat beside Claire and looked into the crystal-clear water where she could see fish flitting in and out among the rocks. 'This is a wonderful place to swim. The water is so clean and fresh. Beats the swimming in Queensland, I have to say.' She lifted her head and gazed across the bay, enjoying the feel of the sun on her skin and the salt-laden breeze, forgetting for a moment her confusion about the author and his photo. 'This is such a peaceful place. I feel that I can relax and forget all my troubles even if it's just for a little while.'

She thought again about that author and what she might have said, but then pushed it all away. He might not have listened that intently and had probably gone to sleep as she rambled on about the Fleurys and their manor house. Marian decided not to worry about it and try to enjoy the next few weeks. Claire's wedding was looming and she was determined to do everything she could to make it a very special day. Then there was Theo and what she had found that had made her feel their marriage was over. But even that shouldn't ruin her stay in this beautiful place, she decided. So when Claire jumped into the water, Marian, feeling suddenly light-hearted, jumped in after her and swam with strong strokes faster than before, and managed to arrive at the jetty several lengths before her younger sister.

They ran up the path and into the manor, racing up the stairs, laughing like teenagers, and arrived on the top landing, breathless. Then they took turns to have a shower, dried their hair and quickly dressed before they descended the stairs again, this time more demurely.

Mass gave Marian a chance to sit down and relax as she half listened to the sermon. She gazed at the beautiful stained-glass windows over the altar, the images of the stations of the cross on the walls that were not as garish as in some churches but depicted the path to the cross in a gentle, subtle way. There was a statue of the Virgin Mary beside the altar that Claire later said was mediaeval and had been found in the ruins of a church nearby.

When mass was over, Marian walked out into the warm sunshine and was introduced to Father O'Malley, with whom she shook hands as he told her she was welcome in Dingle and asked if she could sing at all, as the choir needed more singers.

'I'm afraid I can't sing to save my life,' Marian had to confess. 'So I wouldn't be a good addition to the choir. In any case, I'm not sure how long I'm going to stay.'

'A very long time, I hope,' Claire piped up beside Marian and then pulled at her arm and made her turn to come face to face with an older lady with white hair and beautiful brown eyes. 'Marian, this is Sylvia Fleury.'

Marian felt her heart beat faster as she shook hands with the old woman who was tall and slim with a ramrod-straight back. 'Hello,' she mumbled nervously. 'How nice to meet you, Mrs Fleury.'

'We're family, so please call me Sylvia,' she said as she squeezed Marian's hand in a tight grip. 'I'm very happy to meet you, too, Marian. Claire has been so excited about your arrival. I hope you're comfortable in that little flat? A bit of a squeeze for two people, I imagine,' she added with an amused smile.

'Yes, but we're so happy to be together,' Claire said, smiling at Sylvia. 'And after the wedding, Marian can have the flat for as long as she wants. I've checked with Rose and as I've paid the rent until the end of July, she said it was fine.'

'That's good,' Sylvia said. Then she looked around. 'Where's Pierce? I thought he would be here with you today.'

'Well, he's not much of a church person,' Claire said. 'He'll meet us at the café.'

'I see,' Sylvia said. 'I suppose you can't force anyone to go to mass. I'm not going to the café, so I'll see you both at lunch. As it's a lovely day, we will be eating on the terrace and have a barbecue. I think the children will be happy about that. And then they can run wild in the garden if they feel like it.'

'Great idea,' Claire said. 'We'll see you later, so.' Sylvia smiled at them both and moved away to greet another old lady who was just coming out of the church.

'So now you've met our own grande dame,' Claire said when Sylvia was out of earshot. 'Magnificent, isn't she?'

'The epitome of elegance,' Marian said. 'Is that a real Chanel suit she's wearing?'

'Yes, but it's many years old,' Claire said. 'She has the most amazing vintage wardrobe. I'd say she'll change into something more casual for lunch. Casual for her, that is,' she added with a grin.

'She sounds like an interesting woman,' Marian said. 'Maybe she had a lot of adventures when she was young.'

'Not as far as I know,' Claire said. 'She grew up in Kerry and was married quite young and then she's lived here all of her adult life.'

'Her husband was our grandfather's first cousin, wasn't he?' Marian asked. 'Liam Fleury, I mean.'

'That's right,' Claire replied. 'Sylvia often talks about how she and Liam met on a train and fell madly in love at first sight.'

'A train going where?' Marian asked, her interest in Sylvia increasing. Until now she had just been a rather formidable old lady, the matriarch of the Kerry Fleurys. But now that she had met Sylvia in real life, Marian realised that she must have been a stunning woman in her youth. That tall figure, the lovely eyes and thick hair that would have been dark some years ago, all added to the image of someone who had both class and style. Something that could not come from spending her entire life in Kerry.

'I don't know,' Claire said, looking confused. 'She never said where this train was going to. Just that it was a long journey and that they talked and talked late into the night, forgetting the time until they arrived at their destination.'

'No train journey in Ireland is very long or late at night,' Marian remarked. 'So it must have been either in England or the continent.'

'I never actually wondered about where they were at the time,' Claire said. 'I only thought that it was so romantic.'

'Yes, that's true,' Marian said. 'It sounds very romantic.' She started to walk away from the forecourt of the church. 'Anyway, we'll forget about Sylvia and her interesting past for the moment. I want to go and meet your lovely future husband.'

But her thoughts were not on Claire's fiancé, but on that train journey in the 1960s, where Sylvia had met her husband. She looked thoughtfully at Sylvia's retreating figure as they walked away from the steps of the church.

A woman with an interesting past, Marian thought to herself. *But maybe there is a reason she will never reveal where that train journey took place...*

FIVE

Claire linked arms with Marian and they walked together down the street to a café that had a small garden at the front with two round tables, one of which was occupied by a tall man with fair hair dressed in a bright green Kerry football T-shirt and blue shorts. He was reading a book but shot up from his chair as they approached. 'Marian,' he said, holding out his hand, 'we meet at last.'

Marian shook hands with Pierce, noticing his very blue eyes behind horn-rimmed glasses, and his warm smile. 'Hi, Pierce, I've been dying to meet the man who's captured my sister's heart.'

'And she captured mine,' he said and pulled out a chair. 'But sit down so we can get to know each other. Not that there's much I haven't heard from Claire. She's been telling me all about you for weeks.'

'She's been talking about you ever since you met,' Marian said as she sat down.

'There you go,' Claire said and sat down on Pierce's other side. 'Now we can talk about other things except yourselves. I saved you the trouble.'

'I ordered coffee and a Danish for us all,' Pierce said. 'We're both addicted to a good Danish, you see,' he explained.

'But it's only allowed on Sundays,' Claire filled in.

'She keeps an eye on my figure,' Pierce hissed in Marian's ear.

Claire patted Pierce on his slight paunch. 'Yes, I do, or your waist would increase so much your stylish wardrobe would have to be replaced.'

'She's always teasing me about my clothes,' Pierce said. 'Could you tell her to stop, Marian? You're the older sister after all.'

'Stop teasing Pierce about his clothes, Claire,' Marian said.

'I'll try,' Claire said and kissed Pierce on the cheek. 'Sorry, darling.'

'You're forgiven,' Pierce said, taking Claire's hand and kissing it.

Marian noticed how Pierce held Claire's hand whenever he had a chance and how they couldn't take their eyes off each other. They looked very much like a couple deeply in love. *Just like Theo and me when we were first married,* Marian thought, feeling a dart of pain. *What happened to us? When did we lose all that?*

Pierce turned to Marian. 'So, how does it feel to be here?'

'Wonderful and strange,' Marian said. 'I can't believe I'm really in Kerry at last.' She turned to look down the hill at the harbour where an array of boats swayed on the glittering waves, and then further out, where the sea met the horizon. 'And the fantastic views everywhere take my breath away. It's so stunning, especially on a lovely summer's day like today.'

'It's a grand morning,' Pierce agreed as a waitress appeared from the door of the café with a tray. 'And here's our coffee and pastries now.' He got up to take the tray and thanked the waitress in a charming way. Then he put the tray on the table and told them to dig in.

They continued to chat as they ate the pastries and drank the coffee, Marian telling Pierce how strange it was that she felt so at home here already, even though she had only just arrived.

'That's wonderful,' Pierce said and wiped his mouth on a paper napkin. 'I was going to ask you, though, what you're going to do while you're here.'

'I'm not sure yet,' Marian said. 'Obviously, helping Claire with the wedding preparations is going to take up a lot of my time, but after that, I might look for a job nearby.'

'Are you planning to stay long enough to need a job?' Claire asked, looking surprised.

'Yes,' Marian replied. 'I'm thinking I might stay until the end of the summer at least. So I'd love to have some kind of job.'

'Doing what?' Pierce asked. 'I'm curious because Claire said you studied marketing and business before you were married.'

'Yes, but I never finished my degree,' Marian said. 'So I don't think any firm would take me on doing something like that. In any case, college was over thirty years ago so anything I learned then would not be valid today with all the digital marketing and the Internet and stuff.'

'You might get a job in a shop,' Claire suggested, draining her cup. 'You have great experience selling surfboards and sports equipment.'

Marian nodded. 'Yes, I might look into that. There are plenty of such shops in Tralee.'

Pierce looked at Marian thoughtfully while he chewed on the last bite of his Danish. 'Or you might get a job with me,' he said. 'I need someone to take over some of the secretarial tasks in my office in Karina's house. I'm getting more jobs marketing and publicising new books after Karina's book launch last year. Could be good training in modern marketing for you. So if you think you might be interested in that, give me a shout.'

'That's a great idea, darling,' Claire exclaimed. 'I know you need help to keep the office tidy and Marian is the queen of organisation. If it wasn't for her, I would have sunk under a mountain of clothes and mess when we were growing up. She taught me everything when it comes to being clean and tidy, and everything to do with paperwork and bank accounts.'

Pierce raised an eyebrow. 'Really? But you're so good at that now. Karina couldn't do without your organisation skills. And your sister taught you all that?' He turned to Marian. 'You sound like the perfect candidate for the job. Would you be interested?'

'Well...' Marian hesitated. She wasn't sure she wanted a secretarial job. Working in a shop seemed easier. In any case, she wasn't sure yet how long she was going to stay in Ireland. But the thought of going back to Australia filled her with panic. She knew she couldn't go back there, even if Theo begged her. 'What would I be doing?' she asked.

'Just about everything,' Pierce said with a broad smile. 'Filing, typing, helping me pick photos for publicity campaigns, talking to book bloggers and journalists, not to mention sharing any marketing ideas, which I'm sure you could come up with. You'd also have to read some of the books I market. So if you're into reading, that would be an added bonus.'

'I love reading,' Marian said. 'I always had my nose in a book when I was younger.'

'That's true,' Claire chipped in. 'And you used to make up stories for me when I was little. I always thought you'd be an author one day.'

'Well, that was a bit of a pipedream,' Marian said. 'But I read a lot now, too, whenever I have the chance. There's nothing like getting lost in a story to escape reality.'

'So true,' Pierce agreed. 'Except sometimes you get pulled in by a story and can't stop. Like this one,' he said, holding up a paperback.

Claire took the book from him. 'Wow, this is the same one

Tricia was reading at the beach. By this new author, John Peters. She said it's a thriller.'

'Not quite,' Pierce said. 'It's actually literary fiction but it has a little bit of a thriller aspect, that's true. Someone in the family is a spy, but we don't know who yet. The hero is trying to figure it out.' He turned the book and showed them the back. 'Amazing writer. Self-published too. He's extremely successful all on his own. Don't know how he did it.'

'Must be good at creating that word-of-mouth thing that sells,' Marian said and glanced at the photo, again feeling that jab of recognition. Yes, it really was the man from the plane. How amazing. *And how worrying,* she thought. She tried to remember exactly what she had revealed. But it was a blur of a rambling conversation that didn't seem to make sense like this, in retrospect. She hoped he would have forgotten it too.

Suddenly, Marian was pulled out of her trance. 'You sound perfect for the job. When can you start?' Pierce asked.

SIX

Marian thought for a while, trying to settle her thoughts. 'Not until after your wedding,' she replied after a long pause. 'I want to be free to help Claire organise it.'

'And help me pick a dress,' Claire chimed in. 'And choose the flowers for my bouquet and for the party. And the food, and...'

'Yes, but maybe you could mind the shop, so to speak, while we're on our honeymoon?' Pierce suggested. 'I could give you a crash course beforehand. I just need someone to answer the phone and to check emails, nothing complicated.'

'We're only going to be away a few days,' Claire cut in. 'It's the busiest time of the year for Karina's catering business, so she needs all hands on deck. Pierce just needs someone to keep an eye on things for a short time. Otherwise, he'll be on the phone checking stuff when we're supposed to be together.'

Marian smiled. 'Oh, okay, I accept the offer. It will be a lot more interesting than standing in a shop selling equipment to surf dudes.'

Pierce beamed at Marian. 'Brilliant. Thank you so much. I

think you'll like the job. It's very varied and I'm not a demanding boss, really.'

'I'm sure you're not,' Marian said, smiling at his enthusiasm. 'But can we agree that it's only a temporary position? I know I said I'd like to stay until the end of the summer, but I'm not quite sure about anything right now, to be honest.'

Pierce nodded. 'That's fine. We don't need to sign any contracts, just an agreement to keep it temporary, like a summer job or something.'

'Brilliant,' Marian said.

'Oh, I'm so happy that's settled,' Claire said. 'But now we have to get going or we'll be late for Sylvia's lunch. Drinks at twelve, followed by the best lunch in Kerry, cooked by Arnaud, Granny's fiancé.'

'Can't wait to meet everyone,' Marian said as Pierce paid the bill and they all walked down the street together. 'Are you coming with us, Pierce?'

'Yes,' he replied. 'I'll squash into the back seat and let you girls sit together and natter.'

'We don't natter,' Claire said and gave Pierce a push. 'We talk about serious things.'

'Of course,' Pierce said, winking at Marian. 'Very serious.'

'No, you sit in the front with Claire,' Marian protested. 'I'll be fine in the back. It's such a short trip anyway.'

Marian sat in the back seat and stared out the window during the short drive back to Magnolia Manor. The job offer from Pierce had come as a surprise but now she felt it was a good idea. It would take her mind off everything that was bothering her and maybe even give her a fresh start doing something new.

It didn't take them long to drive back to Magnolia Manor, where the drinks were already being served on the back terrace. Sylvia, who had changed into a pale green silk dress and slingback shoes with very high heels, greeted them warmly and asked what they wanted to drink.

'We have champagne to celebrate Marian's arrival,' she said. 'Help yourselves to that, or something non-alcoholic if you prefer.'

'Thank you, Sylvia,' Marian said. 'That's very kind of you. I don't usually have anything alcoholic before dinner, but champagne is so special, so I can't resist.'

Pierce offered to get Marian a glass of champagne and Claire went with him to say hello to everybody gathered around the table with the drinks and nibbles. Marian smiled at Sylvia. 'They're so sweet. And so blissfully happy.'

'Very much in love,' Sylvia agreed. 'It's wonderful to see Claire so happy after all she's been through.'

'Oh, yes,' Marian agreed. 'Love your dress, by the way. That colour is fabulous on you.'

'Thank you,' Sylvia said with a warm smile. 'It's just an old thing I've had for years. But if you buy quality, it lasts forever.'

'Very true,' Marian said. Sylvia's dress was truly exquisite in its simplicity, with tiny details that said it had been very expensive, even if it had been bought a long time ago, possibly in the sixties. It also seemed to be from some kind of haute couture designer of that era. This was very mysterious. How come Sylvia had had the means to buy such clothes when she was very young? And where had she learned to walk so gracefully on very high heels, even at her age?

'Claire told me you have a lot of vintage fashion in your wardrobe,' Marian said, hoping Sylvia wouldn't think her too nosy. 'Where did you find them?'

'Oh,' Sylvia said airily. 'You know, here and there, in boutiques and vintage shops. Now, I must go and see about lunch. I think the barbecue is hot enough for the meat. We'll chat later,' she said and glided away across the terrace and in through a French window on the far side.

'Marian,' Claire called. 'Come and meet everybody.'

Marian turned her attention away from Sylvia and walked to the edge of the terrace, where a group of people were waiting to meet her. She was introduced to her third cousins Lily, Rose and Violet, and their husbands. The children running around on the lawn below the terrace ranged in age from ten to two years old. They were called to say hello to their new cousin and shook hands before they ran off again, chasing each other and shouting at the top of their voices.

'I hope they don't disturb the tenants,' Rose said, looking concerned. 'They're making a lot of noise.'

Marian knew that some of the rooms on the first floor had recently been converted to apartments for seniors which had been a huge success. This, with the addition of the Regency garden and café, had made it possible to earn extra funds to run the estate.

'I think a lot of them are out,' Lily said. 'I saw that there were only two cars in the car park. The nice weather must have lured a lot of the tenants out to the beach or up the mountains.'

'Or to be with their grandchildren,' Rose suggested. 'Anyway, most of them are used to kids.'

'They'll calm down when they get food,' Dominic, Lily's husband, said. 'Is Arnaud doing sausages for them? With ketchup?'

'Of course not,' Vi said with a laugh. 'He thinks children should learn to eat good food as early as possible. So they're going to get the same as we are. Chicken or beef skewers with Arnaud's special barbecue sauce. He thinks they should grow up knowing real, good food, like French kids do.'

'We just throw ours a pizza or hamburger at the weekend,' Violet's husband, Jack, said. 'Easier that way and nobody complains.'

'They're too small to complain,' Vi said. 'After all, the twins are only two and a half. They'll eat whatever is going, thank goodness.'

Rose looked across the lawn at all the children running around. 'They're having such fun. But they're growing up too fast. Just look at Naomi with her long legs. She's nearly ten but soon she'll be a teenager and Sophie is not far behind.'

'We'll have trouble then,' her husband, Noel, said. 'But not yet, so let's enjoy them being kids for a while longer.'

They turned around and started to help themselves to drinks and nibbles, while the mouthwatering smell of barbecued food wafted around them.

Marian stayed at the wall of the terrace looking at the children, remembering her own son and daughter at the same age. They had been just like this, running, jumping, playing, blissfully ignorant of what was going on in the adult world: war and suffering, politics and climate change and everything they would have to worry about when they grew up. It was such a safe, happy period that had only lasted a few years, if they were lucky. Marian felt glad that she had been able to give her children that kind of childhood and that it had given them a good start in life. They were both very grounded and confident in their chosen careers. She missed them and thought about them every day and hoped they were well and happy. But she didn't want to interfere, so she tried not to call too often, leaving it up to them to contact her if they wanted to. And they did. Whenever they called, even if it was just to ask for 'a little extra cash', they always had a nice chat, which Marian loved, even if she had to pretend she didn't miss them.

But then there was the problem with Theo... Marian sighed as she thought of him and the way they had parted. She only partly figured out what had caused their marriage to head for the rocks. He had not fully understood her terrible homesickness and had thought she'd get used to living in Australia with time. But after seven years, she still felt like an alien in a country where the climate, flora and fauna made her feel like she had landed on a different planet. She had longed for the soft rain, the fresh breeze and the green hills of Ireland and nothing could heal her sadness. He hadn't loved Ireland as much as she did, but had settled in very well and been quite content with the Irish lifestyle.

The reason they had moved to Australia was partly because Theo was homesick, and also because his father had been ill and needed his son to take over the business. Then his father had died and now there was no practical reason to stay in Queensland, except for Theo's love of surfing – and that he felt so happy being back home. He had sold the family firm and opened the shop in Surfers Paradise, so he could indulge in the sport he loved. Marian had thought they would come to some sort of agreement about going back to Ireland – or at least spend more time there. But lately, Theo seemed to have forgotten what they had decided and everything had been about him. Marian had felt more and more left out.

'There you are,' Claire said in Marian's ear. 'Come and meet Arnaud and have some of the delicious food.' She handed Marian a plate. 'Here, help yourself. There are some fabulous steaks, or chicken skewers.'

Suddenly hungry, Marian pushed away the sad thoughts and followed Claire to the barbecue at the far side of the terrace where a good-looking man with white hair was putting steaks and skewers on a platter. He smiled at them as they arrived and proffered the platter. 'Hello, Claire. Is the lovely lady your sister?'

'Yes, this is Marian,' Claire replied. 'Marian, meet Arnaud, the five-star chef of Magnolia Manor.'

'Hi, Arnaud,' Marian said and held out her hand.

'*Bonjour*, Marian. Can't shake hands, but I'll greet you the French way instead,' he said and kissed Marian lightly on both cheeks. 'So nice to meet you at last, *ma chère*. Claire has been telling us how much she has missed you.'

'I've missed her too,' Marian said, charmed by this nice man who looked like a French version of Cary Grant. 'This looks delicious,' she said and picked up a steak with the fork Arnaud handed her.

'I hope you'll like it,' Arnaud said. 'It's medium rare, so I hope that will be okay. Please help yourself to Béarnaise sauce, garlic butter or relish, whatever you prefer. It's all out on the long table so you'll have to pass it around when you sit down. And there's potato salad and beans and all kinds of vegetables as well.'

'Fabulous,' Marian said and joined Claire at the long table that had been laid with plates, cutlery and glasses on an embroidered tablecloth. She found herself sitting between Rose and Karina Flavin, Claire's boss, who shook hands and apologised for her late arrival.

'So you're the big sister?' Karina said, studying Marian for a moment. 'You look only faintly alike. Claire is such a Fleury, but you're a little different.'

'I'm not as colourful as Claire,' Marian remarked. 'I have the strong jaw but not the freckles and my hair is straight and a shade or two lighter even though it has auburn streaks.'

'And you have fair skin that I guess burns easily,' Karina said, smiling. 'Just like me. I burn to a crisp if I'm not careful. How on earth did you manage the Aussie sun?'

'Well, as they say down under: slip, slop, slap,' Marian said. 'Slip on a T-shirt, slop on sunblock and slap on a hat.'

Karina nodded. 'I've heard of that slogan. Very sound advice, I have to say, and it should be everywhere, even here.'

'Yes,' Marian agreed. 'It really should. But here I feel you can still sit in the sun for a while without fear. It's positively dangerous in Australia, especially in Queensland. It gets very hot there, even in the winter.'

'Not a real winter, I assume. So how long do you plan to stay?' Karina asked.

'Oh, I don't really know,' Marian said. 'I'd like to stay for a long time. I want to get to know the area and the family. I've actually just agreed to help your brother in the office for a bit as he needs someone to organise all his various jobs.'

'He certainly does,' Karina said drily. 'And if you're as disciplined as Claire, he's lucky to get you on board. But his messy ways might drive you crazy. He never seems to get his paperwork in order.'

'I think I'll cope,' Marian said. 'I'm used to disorganised men. My husband is a bit like that. Messy, I mean. He's more interested in surfing than office work, so I did most of that stuff.'

'Won't he miss you if you're away so long?' Karina asked.

'No, I don't think he will,' Marian said, feeling a wave of sadness wash over her. 'He'll get someone to help him. We're kind of separated,' she added after a moment's reflection. She hadn't been sure how to explain it, but now it came out and she felt suddenly that it was the right way to describe what was going on between them. 'Separated' sounded like halfway to divorce but it was less final.

Karina put her hand on Marian's. 'I'm so sorry, I shouldn't have asked. That was very rude of me. I hope things will improve between you, though.'

'Thank you,' Marian said. 'I wasn't offended by your question anyway. You weren't to know what was going on.'

'Good,' Karina said, looking relieved. She raised her glass of champagne. 'But let's not dwell on it and enjoy this marvellous day and the fabulous food. Cheers for Claire and Pierce, too. I couldn't ask for a nicer sister-in-law.'

'Or a better brother-in-law, in my case,' Marian said and clinked glasses with Karina. 'I like Pierce already.' She looked down the table at Claire and Pierce chatting and laughing with the Fleury family and smiling at the children who were now enjoying the food. Sylvia and Arnaud sat together, talking in hushed voices in what seemed like a very private conversation. How happy they all looked with their spouses and partners. Marian felt envious of them all and wondered if she would ever find happiness again. It didn't seem very likely at this moment and that thought made her sad again.

Karina put her hand on Marian's arm. 'I'm sure you're looking forward to the wedding. It's not a church wedding as they have both been married before, so it'll be at the registry office in Tralee. But then the party will be here, in the ballroom afterwards and it'll be fabulous. The Fleurys and the O'Farrells together again.'

'Again?' Marian asked.

'Yes. Sylvia is an O'Farrell by birth,' Karina explained. 'She and our mother were first cousins. She married Liam in nineteen sixty-two, only six months after they met.'

'On a train,' Marian filled in. 'At least that's what Claire told me.'

Karina smiled. 'Yes, that's right. So romantic.'

'Where was this train journey taking place?' Marian asked.

Karina frowned. 'You know, I have no idea. She never said. Could have been anywhere. I know Liam travelled a lot in those days.'

'Travelled where?' Marian asked, intrigued.

'Oh, everywhere. In Ireland and Europe and Scotland, too, I think. For the family business when he was young.'

'And Sylvia?' Marian asked. 'Did she travel a lot too? Before she met Liam Fleury, I mean.'

Karina thought for a moment. 'I think she did. She went somewhere on the continent at some stage to study, and she was in London during the swinging sixties, she says. But I don't know much about her life before Liam, so to speak. Way before my time. If you want to know, why don't you ask her yourself?'

'Yes, maybe I should,' Marian said as she looked across the

table at Sylvia. 'But I have a feeling she wouldn't tell me much. There is a mysterious air about her.'

Karina nodded. 'Yes, she keeps her cards close to her chest, that's for sure. That's what makes her so fascinating.'

Marian nodded, gazing at Sylvia, who was smiling adoringly at Arnaud. There was something about her that seemed slightly at odds with her official image of a matriarch, a much-loved grandmother and a countrywoman born and bred. She watched the elderly couple, still engrossed in their intimate conversation, and wondered if Arnaud knew Sylvia's whole story.

SEVEN

A week after that Sunday lunch, Marian found herself sucked into the wedding preparations with Claire. She had been in Pierce's office yesterday to familiarise herself with what she would be doing while Pierce was away. It didn't seem to hard to answer calls and emails but she would have more things to do when he came back. She had texted Theo a second time in order to test the waters but there had been no reply. He seemed to be still sulking and Marian wondered if they would ever get back what they had lost. But she pushed all those thoughts away while she concentrated on Claire's wedding preparations.

They had a fun afternoon in Cork where they scoured the shops for the perfect outfit. 'Not too blushing bride or matronly,' Claire said during their drive. 'Something in between those two would be great.'

'Hmm,' Marian mused as she considered the problem while they drove down the winding road to Cork city. 'How about a big hat and a suit? I mean a jacket and skirt. I saw an old photo of Mick Jagger and Bianca when they were married in St Tropez in the early nineteen seventies. She wore a big hat and a suit. All white, but you could pick another colour, like pale green to go with your eyes. I know it sounds weird, but I think that would...'

'Yes,' Claire exclaimed, looking briefly at Marian with shining eyes before she concentrated on the road again. 'I love that idea. So classy and ageless. But where would we find such an outfit?'

'We'll start with the hat,' Marian said and picked up her phone. 'I'll google hat shops in Cork to see if I can find something. Then we could go to Brown Thomas and look for that kind of suit. I know it might cost an arm and a leg, but it's your special day.'

'And I can wear the suit at other occasions afterwards,' Claire said. 'Marian, you're a genius.'

'We haven't found that suit yet,' Marian remarked. 'But when we do, I'll accept the compliment.'

'Ah, we will,' Claire said with a grin. 'I can feel it.'

They drove through the winding streets of Cork and miraculously found a parking spot near Patrick Street, where all the best shops were to be found. Then, as Marian hadn't managed to find any hat shops, they walked the short distance to Brown Thomas, hoping they also had hats among their large and fashionable stock. As they walked towards the department store, Claire suddenly stopped dead, so suddenly Marian nearly fell over.

'Look,' Claire squealed, pointing at a poster in the window of a bookshop. 'That author everyone in Dingle is talking about is doing a book signing next week.'

'Oh?' Marian stared at the poster with the cover of a book depicting a meadow full of wildflowers with the title *A Stranger Comes Home* written in large letters across it. Then there was a photo of that face that was now so familiar to her. 'The same day as your wedding,' she said to Claire.

'What a pity,' Claire said. 'I'd have gone to get a signed

copy, if I could. But hey, let's go in and buy that book. It's his latest and nobody in Dingle will have read it yet.'

'Okay,' Marian said and followed Claire through the door of the shop. She had to confess that it would be interesting to read his latest book and find out what all the fuss was about. 'I'll have time to read it while you're away,' she said.

'And then I'll read it,' Claire said. 'Oh,' she said, looking around, 'what a lovely shop.'

Marian had to agree. The bookshop was more like a cosy library than a shop, with bookshelves painted green and colourful rugs on the wooden floor. There was even a fireplace with two leather easy chairs beside it and an arrangement of dried flowers on the mantelpiece.

'You just want to pick a book and sit down and read for a few hours,' Marian remarked.

'I know. It's very cosy. But here's the book,' Claire said and picked up one of the copies from a stack on a table by the door. 'Hi,' she said to the shop assistant at the till. 'Is this the latest novel by John Peters?'

'That's right,' the shop assistant said and pushed her glasses up her nose. 'He's signing here next week.'

'We'd come if we could,' Claire said. 'But we have something else on.' She handed the assistant the book. 'So we'll buy this copy and come to the next book signing, whenever that is.'

'Soon, I hope,' the assistant said as Claire paid. 'He said he's working on something new that will be finished in a month or two. He publishes his own books, so he can get them out quite quickly, depending on how much time he has.'

'If he's self-published, how come you're promoting his book like this?' Marian asked. 'With a book signing and a poster and everything.'

'We don't usually stock self-published authors' books,' the shop assistant replied. 'But he's so popular and we sell an enormous amount of his books, so we make an exception. And the owner is a personal friend of John Peters. This is an independent bookstore, so we're not in a chain and can do what we like. I don't think Easons would be as willing to do that as we are.'

'Long live independence, in that case,' Claire said.

'Oh yes,' the shop assistant agreed. 'Independent bookshops are a lot more interesting.'

'I love books,' Marian said, looking longingly at the well-stocked bookshelves. 'If I had the time, I'd stay here and browse.'

'But we don't,' Claire said, pulling at Marian's arm. 'Come on, we have to find that perfect outfit.'

'She's getting married in about a week,' Marian said to the shop assistant. 'But I don't want her to turn into Bridezilla, so we'd better find that suit quickly.'

'How lovely,' the shop assistant said. 'I wish you every happiness.' She picked up a card from a stack on the counter. 'Here, take this. You'll find our Facebook page there and then you can keep up to date with our events and John Peters' next book signing.'

'Brilliant.' Claire took the card and put it in her handbag. 'Thank you so much. We'll do our best to come to the next event, won't we, Marian?'

'Of course,' Marian said.

They said goodbye to the shop assistant and left, hurrying down the street to the department store. 'What a lovely bookshop,' Claire said. 'We must go back next time we're in Cork.'

'We should,' Marian agreed. 'I'll look out for the next book signing. I want to know everything about that author. John Peters, I mean. Everyone around here seems to love his books.'

'You could start by looking him up on Facebook or Amazon,' Claire suggested. 'He probably does his own marketing, so he's bound to have posted everything about himself and his books all over the Internet.'

'Great idea. Why didn't I think of that?' Marian said as they reached the entrance door of Brown Thomas. 'But here we are. Let's go shopping.'

After more than an hour searching through various designers, they emerged carrying two big bags with the famous Brown Thomas logo. One of them contained not the suit Marian had suggested, but a dress Claire had fallen instantly in love with. It was by a new Irish designer in pale green linen with tiny white and pink flowers around the frilly neckline. It suited Claire's complexion and Marian had to agree it was lovely. And then by sheer good fortune, they had found a straw hat with a green ribbon around the crown, which was a perfect match with the dress. 'Like Scarlett O'Hara,' Marian said when Claire put on the hat. 'But it's not exactly what I had planned.'

'Oh fiddle-di-dee,' Claire joked as she did a twirl in the changing room. 'Let's forget Bianca Jagger and say hello to a southern belle. I simply have to have this whole outfit. Pierce will love it.'

'Everyone will,' Marian declared. 'And it will be lovely to watch you dance the first waltz in that dress. And this is my treat,' she continued, taking out her credit card. 'No arguments.'

'I won't argue,' Claire said, looking a little doubtful. 'But can you afford it?'

'Of course I can,' Marian said. 'I haven't touched the inheritance from Auntie Rachel, and I intend to spend it on nice things, like your wedding dress.'

'Oh.' Claire looked relieved. 'That's okay, then. I'm afraid I spent my inheritance on the downpayment for our new house. But I think she would be happy about that.'

'Of course she would,' Marian agreed. 'I can't think of anything better to spend it on.'

'Darling Auntie Rachel,' Claire said. 'How lucky we were to have her.'

'She was such a character,' Marian said. 'And so generous.'

'She was,' Claire agreed. She took off the dress and handed it to the shop assistant who had just appeared. 'We'll take the dress and the hat. And now we must find something for you, Marian. You have to look pretty at my wedding too.'

'Oh,' Marian said. 'I hadn't thought about that. But I did see an outfit I liked on the Pamela Scott website. I'll show it to you when we have lunch. And if you like it, I'll order it and then it'll be sent to Magnolia Manor.'

'Good idea,' Claire agreed. 'We'll just have this packed up and go to lunch somewhere nice.'

'Okay,' Marian said. 'I'm getting hungry. Let's go to that fish restaurant I've heard so much about. Isn't it around here somewhere?'

'You mean Quinlan's?' Claire asked. 'Yes, that's what I thought too.' She stopped and took her phone from her handbag. 'I'll google them.'

They found Quinlan's fish restaurant down a little side street and went inside. It wasn't crowded, so they managed to get a table by the window, where they sat down and started to peruse the menu. Marian picked a shrimp cocktail with Marie Rose sauce and Claire a crab sandwich. 'All freshly caught early this morning,' the waiter told them. They also ordered a celebratory glass of white wine and then sat back, smiling at each other while they waited for the food to arrive. Marian showed Claire the outfit on the Pamela Scott website: a light blue linen shift dress with a matching jacket. She clicked on the order button and put in her credit card details when Claire said she loved it.

'Where's that book you bought?' Marian asked. 'I'd like to look at the blurb and see what it's about.'

'I put it into the bag with the dress,' Claire said and searched among their shopping that they had put on a free chair beside them. 'Here it is,' she said and pulled out a brown paper bag and gave it to Marian. 'You'd better have it as you're going to read it first.'

'Thanks.' Marian turned the book over and read the short blurb. 'It's about a man who has been away from his hometown in County Clare for a long time and how he is finding his roots.'

'A bit like us,' Claire remarked. 'Except it was our great-grandfather's roots in a place we had never been to.'

'Yes, but that's a different kind of story,' Marian said.

'Yes, that's true,' Claire said. 'A real mystery with a happy ending.'

'Exactly,' Marian said. 'I was so excited about your journey and your quest to find out the truth about that family feud when our great-granddad left Magnolia Manor and never came back.'

'It was such a nerve-racking time,' Claire said. 'Sneaking into the family archives when nobody was looking and pretending to be someone else. Telling lies and trying to keep calm all through the months before I revealed everything to the family. I don't know how I coped. But I was obsessed. I just had to find out what happened.'

'You went undercover like a real-life spy,' Marian said, still feeling huge admiration for her sister, who had never given up despite having to lie to everyone.

'I know.' Claire grinned. 'I found out I was quite good at lying.'

They were interrupted by the waiter bringing them their food and wine. 'Shrimp cocktail and crab sandwich,' he said, putting their orders in front of them.

They dug into the delicious seafood accompanied by a glass of crisp white wine, followed by a cup of coffee and slice of apple tart that they shared. Then Claire sat back and picked up her phone. 'I'm just going to send Pierce a text and then look up a few emails for Karina. Hope you don't mind.'

'Of course not,' Marian said. 'I can look up that author and his website. He seems like an interesting man.'

'And not bad looking either,' Claire said with a wink.

'That's not an issue,' Marian said, trying to look stern. 'It's the quality of his work that matters.'

'Of course,' Claire said with mock seriousness. 'Absolutely.' Then she busied herself with her messages while Marian made a face at her.

Marian laughed and pulled her phone from her pocket, thinking how nice it was to be so close to her sister again. They had been apart for such a long time and had missed each other very much. She turned her attention to her phone and googled John Peters, looking up the website as it came up. And there he was again, in a different photo, standing against the backdrop of green hills with the glint of the sea at an angle. Possibly that village he had mentioned during their chat on the plane. He was dressed in a white polo shirt which clung to his muscular torso with a dark blue sweater across his shoulders. His smile was wide and charming and Marian felt a dart of recognition. That was the attractive smile he had beamed at her during the trip. And then those brown eyes and the crinkles around them, the dark hair with a sprinkle of grey... He was indeed very hand-some and she remembered his deep voice and slight French accent mixed with an Irish lilt. All very attractive, of course.

But as she had said to Claire, it was his novels she was more interested in. She saw that he had published ten in the past five years, which was impressive. The first five were in the thriller genre, but then he seemed to have switched to literary fiction, which were the ones that had sold the most copies, mainly in ebook format, even though the printed books were also quite popular, especially in Ireland. His new book was at the top of the list, and then there was another one, soon to be published, with a link to preorder for the ebook. The novel had the title *Family Secrets* and it would arrive as soon as it was published into the reader's Kindle, if they had an account. Marian, despite having both an account and a Kindle, preferred nevertheless reading what she called 'a real book' that she could hold in her hand. Despite this, she clicked on the preorder button for the Kindle edition and then proceeded to read the description of the book. It was quite short but what it contained made the blood drain from Marian's face.

EIGHT

A family in a country manor with secrets that will shock and surprise their friends and neighbours. A gambling debt from the past. A family feud that lingered for a hundred years. But most of all, a beloved grandmother whose disreputable past will cause huge scandal if it is ever revealed. But who is the legal heir to the estate?

'Oh no,' Marian whispered as she read the brief description.

Claire looked up from her phone. 'What's happened? You're as white as a sheet.'

Marian shook her head. 'Oh, nothing. Just an item I saw on the news that was a bit startling.'

'Like what? The weather report? Is it going to rain on my wedding?' Claire asked, looking worried.

'Yes,' Marian lied. 'I thought I saw something about rain on that day in the long-term forecast.'

'What? No, that's not possible,' Claire said, looking concerned. 'I'll look up the Met Éireann app. Hold on...' She studied her phone for a moment while Marian tried to compose herself. 'Well, they say it's going to be a mixture of cloud and sunshine, so that's what I'm going to believe.' Claire smiled at Marian. 'So now all we can do is keep our fingers crossed.'

'I must have made a mistake,' Marian mumbled and put her phone on the table. She was still shaken by the description of the book that would be published at the end of the summer, a book the plot of which appeared to be based on what she had revealed about the Fleury family to that stranger on the plane. Had he recorded what she said on his phone? Was that why he had got off the plane while she was still asleep? She had to try to get in touch with him somehow and ask him to – what? Change the plot of his new novel?

I have to stop it before it comes out, Marian thought. *Maybe he'll be willing to change some of the story, especially the details about the grandmother, who has to be Sylvia... he must have found out something in her past all by himself. But he might not have been interested if I hadn't started talking about the Fleurys...*

'Okay, that's all done,' Claire said and put away her phone. 'I think we should get back home before the rush hour. The traffic in Cork can be horrific around five o'clock.'

They paid the bill and gathered up their shopping and then walked back to where the car was parked while Marian kept thinking about what she had read in the book description. She had to look up the website again and see if there was an email address she could use to contact the author.

'You're very quiet,' Claire remarked as they went through the suburbs of Cork city. 'What are you thinking about?'

'Oh this and that,' Marian said vaguely. 'Just letting my thoughts wander.'

'That's okay,' Claire said. 'I'm sure you're thinking about Theo and what's going to happen with your marriage. But I won't ask. Tell me if you need to talk. I've been through that stuff, too, you know.'

'Thanks.' Marian nodded, staring out the window at the

green hills and meandering rivers, fields with cattle and horses and old farmhouses. She had tried not to think about Theo, as he hadn't been in touch, but Claire's words brought it all back. 'I don't want to talk about Theo right now. I just want to look forward to the wedding and be there for you,' she said, remembering Theo's sullen face as she left for the airport. She hadn't said anything to either of the children, not wanting to upset them. 'What's next on the agenda?' she asked, wanting to turn her thoughts away from her marriage problems.

'Flowers,' Claire said. 'For our bouquets. Yours, mine and Naomi's and Sophie's. They're so excited to be flower girls. Little Liam is going to carry the rings on a tiny cushion and Freddie will be carrying a lace hanky, just so he won't be jealous of Liam.'

'I love how the boys are called after Sylvia's husband and son. So sad those two men weren't alive to see those grandchildren.'

'Sad for them too,' Claire said with a sigh. 'But there is a little bit of their father and grandfather in every one of those children. In their looks and smiles and gestures. That's what Sylvia said, anyway, and I think it's such a lovely thought.'

'It is,' Marian agreed, thinking of their own parents, who didn't live long enough to see their grandchildren either. Then she let her thoughts drift again, to that man she had met and told all kinds of secrets that should never have been revealed to anyone outside the family. She felt like traitor to cousins she was only beginning to get to know and it was like a niggling pain that wouldn't go away. She had been so happy to have this extended family and had looked forward to meeting them. But now it all seemed tainted by her own carelessness and that made her sad.

That last sentence in the book's description kept echoing through her mind. *A beloved grandmother whose disreputable past will cause huge scandal if it is ever revealed...* That had to be Sylvia. But what did he mean? She hadn't said anything about Sylvia's past, simply because she didn't know anything about it. She had just said that Sylvia was an interesting woman but she didn't know her at all. Had he found out something in Sylvia's past that could be in any way shocking? What could it be? She remembered vaguely that he had said something about being good at research and digging into the past, but she had thought that was about journalism and politics. But now she wondered if he had found out something shocking about Sylvia.

Marian had felt that there was something mysterious about Sylvia from the moment they met for the first time a few days ago. She wasn't at all the cosy grandmother or countrywoman Marian had expected. Sylvia had such poise and style, unusual for someone who had spent her whole life in a small country town. It would also have seemed odd for a sophisticated man like Arnaud to fall for a woman who wasn't familiar with fine wines, haute cuisine, art and literature. They seemed so in tune with each other, which spoke of a shared interest in everything to do with a cultured lifestyle. *Sylvia is hiding something,* Marian thought. *Something that this author must have somehow found out. But how? And what?* She simply had to get in touch with him as soon as possible. It could be that he had made up a story about Sylvia that would fit into the plot of his novel. He was probably going to put in a disclaimer saying that the story was fictional and that there was no connection to anyone in real life. Well, that was all quite correct but if the family in the story were anything like the Fleurys, the gossip would start with embarrassing consequences. The family was well known. And everyone in Kerry was reading his novels.

'Daisies and pink roses,' Claire said. 'For my bouquet. And then the same colours in the wreaths the flower girls will wear in their hair. What do you think?'

'Lovely,' Marian said, pushing the worries about the novel away. She had to forget about it for the moment and concentrate on the wedding. There was still plenty of time to find the author before the novel was published in August, which was nearly two months away. 'They could carry little posies with roses and baby's breath, just to match the colour scheme.'

'That sounds perfect,' Claire said. 'And then we'll have pink peonies and a twig of baby's breath on the tables.'

Marian nodded. 'That'll be really nice.' The wedding was only a week away and there was so much to do. She felt happy that she was able to be here to help out and support Claire. 'I hope my outfit will arrive in time,' she said.

'It will,' Claire reassured her. 'They are usually really quick. Should get to you in a day or two.'

'Oh, good,' Marian said. She sat back, relaxed her shoulders and began to look forward to the wedding. It was wonderful to see Claire so happy. She deserved it after the heartbreaking time when her first husband had suddenly left her for a new life in Spain. Marian had never really liked him, despite his good looks and charm. She had felt in her bones that he wasn't right for Claire and that he would one day make her miserable. She had been right, but now it felt ironic as her own marriage was heading for the rocks. But at least she was back in Ireland and in a place where she had never been to but which had oddly felt like home the minute she stepped inside the ancestral house her great-grandfather had left over a hundred years ago. She relished the thought that she would live at Magnolia Manor even if it was only for a short time. She had no idea what she would do after the summer but it didn't seem to matter right now.

'Don't worry about the future,' Claire said as if reading Marian's thoughts. 'Everything will sort itself out eventually.'

'Maybe,' Marian said with a deep sigh. 'It's just that the road to that eventual sorting out, as you put it, will be steep and rough and full of obstacles. I'm just looking forward to your big day right now. Nothing is more important than that. Then I'll get a grip and try to sort out my life.'

Claire shot Marian a smile. 'You're wonderful. I'm so happy you're here at last. My wedding day wouldn't be the same without you. But you have to promise me that you will put yourself first when you settle things with Theo. Don't let him call all the shots. And whatever you do, don't go back to Australia if you're not a hundred per cent sure.'

'That I can promise you,' Marian said with feeling. 'From now on, everything will be on my terms.'

That thought cheered her up and as they pulled up outside Magnolia Manor, she looked up at the beautiful building and felt its magic giving her the power to go on. She knew in her bones that this was where she was meant to be. For how long, she didn't know but whatever happened, this was where her ancestors came from and it felt like a fortress, protecting her from anything that could hurt her. Even an author using her story for a novel that might expose the family. And also from the husband she felt she had run away from. But all the talk about weddings had brought Marian back to that time in her own life. She especially remembered when they had bought their first little house in Dublin and Theo carried her across the threshold.

'Put me down, you fool,' Marian had giggled. 'Remember that you're carrying not one but two people here.'

Theo laughed and gently put Marian on the sofa in the tiny living room. 'There. Safe and sound, both of you.'

'Thank you, my gallant hero,' Marian said and looked adoringly at her husband of only two days.

He smiled and sank to his knees and put his arms around her. 'I will always try to be your hero, Marian. I know you've given up a lot, your independence, your studies, the future you had planned. But I'll make it up to you, I swear.' He looked into her eyes. 'I just want you to be happy.'

'I *am* happy,' Marian had whispered back, touched by his words and the tears in his eyes. 'We're having a baby; what could be happier than that?'

'Maybe more furniture?' he had suggested.

'Well, maybe that, too.'

Marian looked around the room that, apart from the sofa, was bare of furniture. They had only been able to afford to buy this saggy second-hand sofa, a bed and a kitchen table after lodging the downpayment for the little house on the north side of Dublin. The house was tiny but it was theirs and a start on the property ladder, Theo had said. They were so in love and so happy to be in their first home and having their first baby that material things didn't matter. They were together, a team, and they would work hard to improve their lifestyle, they had vowed. When Theo had carried her into the house and she had felt his strong arms around her and looked up at his handsome face, Marian had felt such love and happiness she thought her heart would burst. Nothing could ruin their love for each other, she had thought. Nothing could break them apart.

But now, as she remembered how she had felt then all those years ago, she wondered if she would ever be that happy again.

NINE

A month later, Marian wondered where time had gone when she and Claire looked at the wedding photos, sitting on the sofa in the living room of the flat on a balmy evening in the middle of July. The wedding had been lovely and just as romantic as Claire had wished. But it had felt sad for Marian as she watched Claire and Pierce exchange their vows, bringing her back to her own wedding thirty-five years ago, and the sad state of her marriage that had once been so happy. Theo hadn't been in touch since she left, and had not replied to her texts. She knew he was still sulking, as he usually did after any kind of row and she had to leave him alone until he was ready to talk. It was hard to accept but she just had to try to be patient, even though she knew he was in the wrong. She felt as if he was drifting away, along with all the happy memories of their early years together. It was as if it had happened in another life and all that was left was a feeling of resentment and suspicion. Marian realised she needed to let go and move on and try to settle into her new life in this wonderful part of Ireland where she felt so at home already. In fact, she wanted a holiday away from all the heartache.

Easy to say but oh so hard to do, she thought.

Then there was the issue of that novel, the publication of which now loomed even closer. She had tried to get in touch with the man she had met on the plane, but he had not replied. She had looked at his photo on the Internet so many times, she knew it by heart: his brown eyes, his wide smile and his deep voice that all combined into the image of a charming, flirtatious man that was hard to resist. But now that she had found out what he had done, she tried to fight the attraction she had felt that night on the plane when she had been so sad.

'The wedding seems like it happened only yesterday,' Claire said as she opened the beautiful leather-bound album, her voice cutting into Marian's musings.

'It was like a dream,' Marian said.

'I know,' Claire said. 'And the honeymoon just flew by. I only just got this from the photographer, who put it all together.' She opened the album and pointed at the group photo on the first page. 'Look at everyone all dressed up. And the flower girls with their bouquets and pretty dresses.'

'And Scarlett O'Hara in her hat,' Marian teased. 'You look like the cat that got the cream.'

'That's how I felt,' Claire said. 'And I still do. I never knew being newly married felt like this. With Hugh, it was so different. Pierce is so considerate and always asks me how he can make me happy. Hugh took for granted that I was over the moon to be married to a hunk like him.'

'I don't think you should compare them,' Marian said. 'Just forget Hugh and count your lucky stars that you got it right the second time.'

Claire nodded. 'Yes, you're right. Why do I keep harping on the past?' She turned and looked at Marian. 'You look great. The rest has been so good for you.'

'I know.' Marian smiled. 'I've had the best few weeks. Working for Pierce hasn't been too hard. He only really needs me in the mornings and then when I've gone through all the messages and straightened up the paperwork, I mostly have the afternoon free. I've been spending a lot of time on the beach with Tricia, actually.'

'You seem to get on so well,' Claire said. 'I'm glad you've made friends with her.'

'She's been so nice and introduced me to some of her friends,' Marian said. 'And she has included me in her book club. We met last night at Tricia's house.'

'What book were they reading?' Claire asked.

'That book we bought when we were in Cork,' Marian said. '*A Stranger Comes Home.* It's really good. Very moving. You should read it.'

'I will when I get the time,' Claire said. 'You seem to have liked it.'

'I did.' Marian had enjoyed that book enormously and been swept away by the story. She had started reading it out of curiosity, but then found she couldn't put it down. The writing was beautiful and the story very moving. It had opened her eyes to John Peters' wonderful prose and descriptive style. He was truly a remarkable writer. But while she read it, she had thought about his forthcoming novel and wondered why he hadn't replied to the email she had sent him two weeks ago. She remembered every word she had written.

Dear John Peters – or should I call you Sean?

I hope this finds you well. You might remember me, the sobby woman in the seat next to you on the Qantas flight from Sydney to Dubai about a month ago. You asked me to tell you my story, so I did with knobs on… Not only my story, but the story of my family, going back over a hundred years. I was tired, sad and had drunk a lot of very bad aeroplane wine, which must have gone to my head. I revealed things that I wish could be unsaid and I thought that you might have forgotten the whole thing.

When I arrived in Dingle, where my family lives, I discovered to my amazement that you are in fact an author and very popular around here. Your books are being read and discussed everywhere – in pubs and book clubs and cafés and people's living rooms and wherever else reading and chatting about books take place. I imagine that you will be delighted to hear this.

But now I come to your next book, Family Secrets. I discovered it by accident on Amazon and maybe you might imagine the horror I felt as I read the description. It seems to me that you somehow remembered every detail about my story, and then added your own frills to that. Especially details about Sylvia Fleury that I didn't even mention, as I knew nothing about her past and still don't.

I have just arrived here and am beginning to get to know a family I never knew. Every one of the Fleurys have been remarkably kind and helpful to me ever since I arrived. I feel so welcome and so part of the family in a place that is finally home. There is only one thing ruining my sense of mental wellbeing that I need during this very hard time in my life and that is your forthcoming novel. I would like us to meet so I can talk to you about this, and maybe persuade you to make changes to the characters and plot in order not to embarrass my family.

Hoping to hear from you soon,

Marian Fleury

She had sent it off, hoping that he would reply soon afterwards. She had checked her emails nearly every hour since then, but there had been no reply. It worried her so much she found it hard to sleep. She was glad she had the job with Pierce and could turn her mind away during the hours she spent in his office. It was a fun and interesting job, covering all aspects of publicity and marketing, and she had learned a lot about advertising online and using social media to get attention for a book.

Despite her sorrow about Theo's behaviour, she secretly enjoyed this period of me-time ever since Claire's wedding. The little flat at the top of the manor was a true haven and Marian loved opening the windows wide on warm evenings as she had dinner looking at the beautiful views of the gardens with its meadows with wildflowers in full bloom, and beyond across the treetops to the ocean. She had a pair of binoculars on the windowsill and could spot the birds flying high in the blue sky, gannets diving for fish and seagulls gliding just above the waves.

The air was so pure and fresh, bringing with it that special smell of salt and seaweed. It made her heart sing and healed her soul. If only she could get in touch with John Peters and get him to make changes to his novel, all would be perfect. But as he hadn't replied to her email, she didn't know what to do next. She had contacted the bookshop in Cork, asking if they had his phone number or address, but they said they didn't give such details to anyone and that she would have to wait until the next book signing and talk to John Peters in person then. *But that will be too late*, Marian thought, feeling fear creeping up her spine like tiny ice-cold darts. *How am I going to stop this novel and avoid scandal?*

'Look at this photo of Sylvia and Arnaud,' Clare said, interrupting Marian's musings. 'Aren't they such an elegant couple?'

'Yes,' Marian said, studying the shot of the two of them clinking champagne glasses and looking into each other's eyes. 'They are truly compatible.' Sylvia had been wearing a long-sleeved green silk dress with a knee-length skirt that showed off her still slender legs. 'Where did Sylvia get that elegance, though?' she mumbled, thinking about what she had read in that book description about the fictional grandmother that must have been based on her own fleeting mention of Sylvia.

'I think she was in Paris at some stage before she met her husband,' Claire said. 'I heard that from one of Pierce's aunts who was at our wedding. Sylvia grew up somewhere near where they lived. This aunt seemed to have known her very well when they were both at Coláiste Íde. That's an all-Irish boarding school for girls here on the Dingle peninsula.'

'I know,' Marian said, her thoughts drifting. 'That's interesting, though. Syvia being in Paris in the sixties, I mean. I wonder what she got up to there?'

'Up to?' Claire asked, looking puzzled. 'You sound as if she did something bad, which I doubt very much.'

'I didn't mean it that way,' Marian protested. 'I just thought it might have been a fun time to be in Paris.'

'I'm sure it was. I never thought of asking her about it.' Claire closed the album. 'I'd better go. Pierce is cooking tonight so I don't want to be late. Oh, and I nearly forgot. We're having a housewarming party in the bungalow in a week or two. We finally finished all the painting and decorating, so we'll celebrate when the smell of paint wears off.' She got up, tucking the album under her arm. 'We'll let you know. I think we might do a barbecue if the weather allows.'

'That sounds like fun,' Marian said. 'I'm looking forward to it already.'

'I didn't want you to see it before all the redecoration and building work were finished,' Claire said. 'But now it's nearly done and it looks fabulous. We've done a lot of the painting ourselves and it's been great fun, if a bit tiring.'

'Can't wait to see it,' Marian said.

Claire said goodbye and Marian turned to her phone to check her email before making herself something to eat. She looked up her Gmail account and saw that there was a new message in her inbox – from John Peters.

Her heart beating, Marian opened the message that read:

Hi Marian,

So sorry for not replying to your email sooner, but I only just found it in my spam folder.

I read through your message and I think we should meet to discuss your concerns. I could come to Dingle tomorrow and meet you at a place that's convenient for you, so please name time and place.

Looking forward to hearing from you very soon.

Best,

Sean

'Finally,' Marian said to herself as she tried to think of the best place to meet him. It had to be in a place where nobody would pay attention to them. She couldn't think of anywhere in Dingle where they could have a private chat without anyone seeing them and then starting to gossip. She had been to practically every pub and café in town with all the Fleury girls, and with Tricia and her gang, too, on many occasions. They had introduced her to anyone they met and now everyone in town knew who she was – one of the Dublin Fleurys. So anywhere in town was out. It had to be somewhere else, where there might be lots of tourists who wouldn't have a clue who either of them was. Then she had an idea and immediately composed a reply.

Hi Sean,

Well, as you might imagine, I have been wondering why you didn't reply. Anyway, I think it's best if we don't meet in Dingle as we might attract too much attention. Everyone knows me by now, and you're the talk of the town. So how about the South Pole Inn in Anascaul for lunch tomorrow at 12.30?

Marian

The reply arrived five minutes later:

That's fine. See you then. I'll put in the phone number at the end of this message, in case of any problems.
    See you tomorrow.

Sean

Marian heaved a sigh of relief. She had finally managed to contact him and now had a chance to make him change, if not the whole story, enough to prevent any rumours to start flying.

Then she felt another wave of panic at the thought of meeting Sean again. How could she persuade him to do what she wanted? It would take a lot of talking and explaining. She had to make absolutely sure that he understood her plight.

If that novel is published, exposing the family and Sylvia, and if they find out who gave Sean the idea, Marian thought, *I will have to leave and never come back.*

But she suddenly realised she had nowhere to go.

TEN

After a sleepless night, Marian got up early, trying to figure out what she was going to say to Sean when they met at lunchtime. She would drive to Anascaul in Claire's car that she had left at the manor for Marian to use, as she now shared Pierce's Peugeot with him. It would take a little over half an hour to get there, so Marian had plenty of time for a leisurely breakfast. But she was so nervous she couldn't eat and darted around the flat, trying to decide what to wear, the butterflies in her stomach making her feel nearly sick with nerves. Breakfast ended up being a slice of toast, a few strawberries and a cup of tea. Not very substantial but she didn't have much of an appetite. Then she got dressed, putting on beige linen trousers and a white T-shirt, an outfit that was bland and ordinary but she felt she had to dress down in order to show she wasn't there to impress anyone. Then she got into the car and drove down the avenue, anticipating her meeting with trepidation.

As she made her way down the avenue, Marian wondered why she had so much to deal with right now. The meeting with that author was stressful enough, but Theo's silence was even worse. The letter she had found in a drawer when she was looking for her passport had been from a woman called Helen and the tone in the letter spoke of an intimate relationship of many years. It had been stuck into a birthday card dated two years ago and it seemed to have been read over and over again, judging by the folds and wrinkles of the paper.

The message was etched into Marian's brain and she remembered every single word.

Dear old friend,

I do miss you and what used to be 'us' so very much even after all the years that have passed. But you fell in love with that blonde beauty and forgot all about me and what we had. We remained friends as I moved from Australia to Dublin with my husband just before you left for Queensland. What a strange coincidence!

Now I treasure our friendship and I was touched by your last message telling me you still want to keep writing to me. I wish you the happiest of birthdays in our faraway land on the other side of the globe. Your wife seems disenchanted with our country, which you told me was so hard for you to bear. You should tell her to get a grip and get used to things. She seems a little spoiled to me and that might be your fault for indulging her. But who am I to judge? Have drink for me and remember the good times we had.

Love and hugs,

Helen

Marian winced as that familiar pain stabbed her in her heart yet again. She gripped the steering wheel harder, stared out at the beautiful view of the ocean and tried to turn her mind away from her sadness. She simply had to try to get over it or she'd be miserable for the rest of her life. She would have to get in touch with Theo herself soon, but now she had to tackle another problem that threatened to jeopardise her stay in Kerry.

Marian took the road out of Dingle and then turned left towards Anascaul. She had heard that the picturesque village, set in the heart of the Dingle Peninsula in the southern foothills of the Slieve Mish mountains, was a walker's paradise. With stunning views of mountains, rivers, lakes, glaciated valleys and the ocean, Anascaul had over a dozen trails to choose from, which Marian had thought would be wonderful to discover. But right now she had other things on her mind.

The road took her up the mountainside with vertiginous views of Dingle Bay and the mountains beyond. The blue sky, the green fields dotted with sheep and the wildflowers in the meadows did not register with Marian as she drove. She was more concerned about the confrontation with the man she had met on the plane, a man that could threaten the reputation of her new-found family, especially the old woman she had come to be so fond of. Her thoughts turned to Sylvia and whatever adventures she had had in her youth. Was it all made up, or had he discovered something in Sylvia's past that could be embarrassing if it was made public? In that case, where had he found it? Was it so shocking that it would make a sensation when the novel came out?

All these questions whirled around in Marian's mind as she parked the car by the little humpbacked bridge near the entrance to the South Pole Inn, the pub that the explorer Tom Crean had built with his own hands over a hundred years ago. She looked at the building for a moment, amazed at the thought that Tom Crean had constructed it himself, brick by brick. What a monumental task it must have been. Then she remembered how Theo had practically built their first home just like that, gutting an old house and making the interior into a cosy little home for them, even though it had been very basic. She thought about how he had worked so hard after a long day at the plumbing firm, coming home, having a quick bite to eat and then getting stuck into building the bathroom and kitchen, while she did the painting and decorating, after which they fell into bed, exhausted. Theo had been so romantic then, so loving and caring, bringing her flowers every Friday and insisting on firing up the barbecue in the tiny back garden, when the weather was warm enough. That house had been a true little love nest.

All those memories went through Marian's mind as she looked up at the old pub. The image of Theo's tender smile and his eyes so full of love as he looked at her over the rim of his glass of wine seemed as if it had happened in another life and now all she had left was the sorrow of what they had lost. She suddenly felt a pang of longing for those days – and for Theo.

Then she pulled herself together and reminded herself why she was here and what she had to do. This was not the time for self-pity. She was here to meet Sean and she had to concentrate on her task.

She watched customers walk inside, as she tried to spot Sean. But there was no sign of him and she assumed he might have arrived already, so she got out of the car and walked through the entrance into the dim interior of the old pub, her heart beating, glancing at the framed photos of the famous explorer and his family but too preoccupied to study them in detail.

She spotted him at the back of the main bar straight away. He was sitting at a table by the window, looking at his phone, so he didn't see her as she walked towards him. She stopped and looked at him for a moment before she spoke. His wavy dark hair was a little longer than when they had been together on the plane, but apart from that he looked the same. Then she took another step forward which startled him and he shot up from his chair as she approached.

'Hello, ahem... Marian,' he said and held out his hand. 'Nice to see you again.'

'Yes, well,' she started, suddenly stuck for words. 'Nice to see you too.'

They shook hands awkwardly and then he gestured at the chair opposite. 'Why don't you sit down and we'll order lunch?'

'Okay.' Marian sank down on the chair and picked up the menu. 'I've heard the fish and chips are good here,' she said without looking at the list of dishes.

'That sounds fine,' he said. 'We'll have that.'

'Okay. Let's order, so.' She nodded and glanced around the room to see if any of the staff were around and then waved at a waitress approaching them.

'Hello there,' the waitress said with a smile. 'What would you like?'

'Fish and chips for us both,' Sean said. 'And a glass of Guinness zero for me. How about you, Marian?'

'The same,' Marian said.

'Anything else?' the waitress asked as she scribbled down the order on her pad.

'No, that's fine,' Marian said.

'Great.' The waitress nodded and left.

'So,' Sean said as he met Marian's gaze. 'We meet again. How strange.'

'Very,' she said.

'You look great. All tanned and rested.'

'I feel good,' she said. 'But I would feel a lot better if it weren't for what's in that book description.'

His eyes darkened. 'Let's get to the main point of our meeting, then. I take it from your email that you want to try to make me change the plot of my new novel?'

'Well, maybe not the whole plot,' Marian started. 'Just some of the details that make it so obviously about my family. Like the name of the house, for example. Rhododendron House? I mean that's too like Magnolia Manor. And it's set in Kerry and there are three granddaughters and a grandmother who has this shady past that she tries to hide behind a respectable façade.' She stopped and glared at him while she waited for an answer.

He looked back at her before he spoke. 'I'm flattered that you read every detail of the description.'

'Of course I did, so please don't try to joke about it – or me,' she snapped. 'I suspect that you somehow recorded everything I said during that plane journey, which was really sneaky, I have to say.'

'Well, I couldn't resist such a fascinating story,' Sean remarked. 'And as an author I always look out for a good plot. Yours inspired me to write it into the book I had nearly finished. I wanted it to be about a family that was respected and admired in the area where they lived. And then behind that façade lurked quite a lot of secrets that were never to be told.'

Marian leaned forward, glaring at him while a seething anger began to build. 'And it never will be. How dare you use me in this way? Don't you understand how damaging this will be to all the Fleurys? How devastating and hurtful? Especially the bits about the gambling debt and the rightful heir, not to mention the hints about Sylvia, which I think you've made up all by yourself. All this will spark off gossip that will never end, and then everyone will start second guessing and create other stories that aren't true. All based on whatever you heard from a tired, slightly sloshed woman on a plane.' She leaned back with a feeling of hopelessness as she noticed a tiny smile hovering on his lips. He looked both smug and arrogant and she began to feel that it was no use. He was never going to rewrite his novel no matter how much she pleaded with him.

'Well,' he said. 'That was quite a speech. You're more eloquent than the last time we met.'

'I was quite eloquent even then, apparently,' Marian said sourly. 'Enough to inspire you, as you said.'

He nodded. 'Yes, that's true. And maybe it was a little underhand of me to use my phone to record you when you thought you were talking to some random stranger with a sympathetic ear.'

'But instead you were an author looking for a juicy story,' Marian filled in. 'Why didn't you tell me?'

'You didn't ask,' he said with an ironic twist to his mouth.

'Very funny.' Marian was about to continue when the waitress arrived with their drinks.

He lifted his glass of Guinness. 'Well, cheers, anyway.'

'To what? Your forthcoming novel?' Marian asked, taking a long sip of her Guinness without clinking glasses as he seemed to expect.

'Let's calm down and discuss the problem when we've got our food,' Sean suggested.

'I'm perfectly calm,' Marian said.

'No, you're furious,' he countered. 'But maybe we can come to an agreement. Please relax and stop looking at me as if you want to throw that drink in my face.'

'And waste a glass of Guinness?' she said, beginning to see a ray of hope. If she pleaded with him, he might agree to change some of his story, or at least rewrite the description, which would be a good start. She was suddenly livid with Theo for making her feel so sad, which had made her start talking about the Fleurys just to forget her sorrows about their marriage. 'I'm very tempted,' she said. Then she took a sip and started to enjoy the rich taste. 'But I don't want to make scene.'

He laughed suddenly. 'Well, that would be a pity. Not to mention the mess it would make of my white shirt. And then people would stare at us and wonder what was going on. And then someone would recognise one of us and then the word would be out that Marian Fleury was on a date with this author whose books they're all reading. We can't have that, can we?'

'No.' She took another sip and then put her glass on the

table, trying not to be pulled in by his charm and good humour, not to mention those flirty brown eyes and the dimple that appeared beside his mouth when he smiled. But then she wondered what Theo would think if he saw her now, half-flirting with another man, the idea making her sit up straighter.

The waitress arrived with two plates of fish and chips, which smelled delicious. 'Let me know if you want anything else,' she said as she put the plates before them.

Marian forgot her distress as the fragrance of freshly caught fish in golden batter hit her nose. The chips were hand cut and the sauces looked freshly made. 'Wow,' she said without thinking. 'I've heard this pub serves the best fish and chips in Ireland and now I'm beginning to believe it.'

'Well,' Sean said and lifted his knife and fork, 'let's dig in, then, and see if it's true. I take it the green goo in the little pot is the famous mushy peas. And then there's the tartare sauce. All according to tradition.'

'And all fabulous,' Marian said as she dipped a piece of fish into the tartare sauce and felt it melt in her mouth.

'I have to agree with you,' he said, devouring the fish and taking sips of Guinness in between bites. 'Too good to have an argument over.'

'I feel less argumentative with every bite,' Marian said, smiling at him, the food making her feel more positive.

'You have a little foam on your lip,' he said. 'And it suits you.'

'And you have some green stuff between your teeth,' she countered, dabbing her mouth with her napkin.

He squirmed. 'Do I?'

'No. I was joking.' Marian patted her mouth with her napkin again and looked at her empty plate. 'I can't believe I finished it.'

'You look much better for it,' Sean said. He leaned back and studied her. 'In fact, you look a lot better than the last time we met. It seems that Kerry is good for you.'

'That, and a good rest and having space and time to think,' Marian said, looking away from his warm gaze. 'And I even managed to get a job.'

'Already?' Sean looked impressed. 'Doing what?'

'Marketing. I'm working for my brother-in-law, who runs a publicity and marketing firm. I'm really enjoying it.'

'I bet you're good at it,' he said.

'I'm not sure about that. I'm learning a lot, anyway. But that's not what I came here to talk about,' Marian remarked.

'I know,' he said with a tiny sigh. 'So let's talk. About my book and the problem you have with it. I've been thinking about it while I was enjoying the amazing food.'

She looked expectantly at him, feeling a dart of hope. 'Yes?'

'I'm not going to change anything in the story. The plot is too good. But I could change the description a little and maybe change the name of the house. But that's all I'm willing to do.'

'It's a good start,' Marian said, feeling calmer. 'I'm amazed that nobody in Dingle has read the description and made the connection. But then most people would be waiting for the paperback, so they wouldn't look at the Kindle preorder and read the blurb.'

'No, I suppose not. I get the impression that my readers around here want what they refer to as "real books".' He looked thoughtfully at her for a moment. 'A good start? So you think you'll convince me to rewrite a lot of the book so nobody will point the finger at the Fleury family?'

'Maybe you would if I tell you that they – or, in any case, Sylvia – will sue you for defamation or slander or something like that. Her granddaughter's husband is a solicitor so that's not out of the question. I don't think she'll take kindly to a made-up juicy story about whatever you say in your book she was up to in her youth.'

'Well, they can sue if they want. But that kind of thing would only hurt them, not me. It would give me great publicity and make everyone want to read this roman à clef, as it's known in French. Win-win for me, I think.'

'Yes, but you'll still be telling lies,' Marian argued. 'About Sylvia Fleury, I mean. I didn't say anything about her to you. How could I? I hadn't even met her yet.'

'No, but I have found out from other sources what she was involved in,' Sean argued. 'And it was quite shocking.'

'I don't believe you,' Marian said with a snort. 'You're making it up.'

'I'm not.' Sean leaned forward across the table and lowered his voice. 'I've heard from a reliable source that Sylvia changed from the demure convent girl she was when she left Dingle and turned into quite the femme fatale when she was in Paris. If anyone around here had found out, it would have caused a huge scandal. She could never have been able to show her face here again.'

'You can't prove that,' Marian argued, shaken by his words. 'If you're telling lies, you will pay dearly for that.'

He lifted one eyebrow. 'Lies? You think it's a made-up story? But what if it isn't?'

ELEVEN

Marian nearly stopped breathing as she took in what he had just said. 'You mean it's true?' she said in a near whisper when she had found her voice. 'Whatever is in your new novel? Sylvia did something scandalous in Paris all those years ago?'

'Scandalous then, not so much now,' Sean replied. 'But yes, in Paris in nineteen sixty. If that had come out then, she would have had a very different life in what used to be holy Catholic Ireland, that's for sure.' He winked.

'What did she do?' Marian asked, nearly dizzy with shock. 'And how did you find out?'

He shook his head. 'No, no, Marian, that will have to remain a secret until the novel is published.' He leaned forward and whispered, 'Did you think that I'd tell you the secret just like that?' Then he straightened up and grinned at her. 'Sorry to disappoint you.'

Marian bristled. 'I see.' She picked up her handbag. 'I'd better leave as you don't seem to understand the situation you're putting me in. I know you found out about Sylvia on your own, but I started the whole thing by revealing some of the family secrets which inspired you to put it all into your novel.'

'What situation?' he asked. 'Who's going to find out that you were the one who told me the story of the Fleurys? Only we know.'

'It says "inspired by a true story" in the blurb,' Marian remarked. 'So anyone would wonder what true story that was and then make the connection. It wouldn't take them long.' Feeling fed up and annoyed, she got up from her chair. 'But this is leading nowhere, so I'll say goodbye.'

'As you wish.' He rose and held out his hand. 'Let's not be enemies and shake hands. It was nice to see you again, even if you're angry with me. Lunch is on me, of course.'

She reluctantly shook his hand. 'Okay. Not enemies, but absolutely not friends. Not ever. Thanks for lunch. Goodbye, Sean.'

'Goodbye, Marian,' he said and held her hand in a tight grip for a moment while he looked into her eyes. 'Pity we can't be friends. You're a very attractive woman and I liked talking to you.'

She tried to look away from those velvety brown eyes. She knew she was attracted to him despite their differences. But she was married, even if separated, and she couldn't let herself be swept away by a pair of lovely eyes and a devastating smile. In any case, what he had done and his refusal to rewrite the parts of his novel that might be damaging to the family had hurt her feelings. There was a hard core of selfishness about him which was not very endearing. *I'd better stay away from him from now on,* Marian thought as she walked out of the pub, confused about her feelings for both Sean and her husband.

'Oh, Theo,' she whispered, 'why did you have to behave the way you did?' She felt so sad and lonely as she thought of him and how they had parted, wishing that she had told him about the letter she had found. She should have asked him to explain what that woman meant to him. They might have had a row, but it could have cleared the air and she wouldn't have left believing he didn't love her. If Theo had given her a plausible explanation, she would not have been as eager to talk to a stranger on the plane. One thing had led to another, like a game of dominoes, and the result had been this awful mess with Sean's novel. All because of her own need for a shoulder to cry on.

Then Marian went back over the conversation in the pub just now and another idea hit her. Maybe she should tell Sylvia about the novel that was due to be published in about a month? Marian had become very fond of Sylvia during the time she had been here. Sylvia was fun to talk to and her take on everyone often made Marian laugh. She was so good at assessing people and she seemed to see through every attempt at pretence. Marian would forget about Sylvia's age as they chatted over a coffee or a glass of wine, simply enjoying the older woman's wisdom and wonderful sense of humour. It was an odd friendship, but very sweet for Marian, who felt she had found a kind of mother figure that she had been missing ever since Auntie Rachel died.

Yes, Marian thought, *I must warn Sylvia about the novel that is due to be published soon. It would be better for her to be prepared than horribly shocked when the gossip starts to spread.*

She didn't need to reveal her own part in the story, just that she feared that John Peters' novel could damage Sylvia's reputation. With that decision firmly in her mind, Marian got into the car and drove away, feeling slightly better, at least about how the novel might be received. Her sorrow about Theo was another matter that she had to deal with, but right now, it was better to try not to think about it at all.

A week later, which had been busy and stressful with a lot of deadlines and publicity work to get through, Marian decided to schedule a meeting with Sylvia. John Peters' novel would be published soon and it was only by sheer luck that nobody in Dingle had made the connection between the fictional grandmother mentioned in the description and Sylvia. It was high time to warn her, Marian thought, and sitting at her desk in Pierce's office, she rang Sylvia's private number.

She answered straight away. 'Hello? Is this Marian? How are things with you?'

'I'm fine, thanks,' Marian replied. 'Everything is great here at the office. How are you?'

'I'm very well, thank you,' Sylvia said, her voice warm. 'I hope Pierce gives you a little time off to enjoy the lovely summer weather we're having at the moment.'

Marian smiled. 'We're very busy with a lot of books being published right now. But I do get time off, too, of course and I've been swimming from the beach and doing lots of hiking with Pierce and Claire nearly every Sunday.'

'Wonderful,' Sylvia said. 'I'm so glad you're settling in so well. I'm sorry if I haven't been in touch for a while, but I've been so busy. So what can I do for you?'

'There's something I need to talk to you about. Would you be free to have coffee with me in my flat this afternoon?' Marian asked. 'Pierce gave me the rest of the day off because he has a meeting with a local author and doesn't need me.'

'I'll check my diary,' Sylvia said. 'I think I'm having lunch with someone today, can't remember with whom, though.' She laughed suddenly. 'I have to write everything down or I'll forget my own name. That's the problem with old age, among other things. Not that you'll know anything about that for a very long time.'

'I'm not exactly a spring chicken,' Marian remarked.

'Compared to me, you're a teenager,' Sylvia said. 'But where were we... Oh yes, this afternoon. Just let me check.'

'Take your time,' Marian soothed, not wanting to push Sylvia to do anything in a rush.

'Back in a minute,' Sylvia said.

Marian rehearsed what she was going to say to Sylvia while she waited. She would have to simply read out the description of the novel and see what Sylvia said. There was no need to say anything about what had happened during the journey on the plane. Only Marian and Sean knew about her role in what had sparked his interest in the family. The Fleurys were well known enough for him to have heard about them from some local talking to him in a pub. The fact that all the other secrets were also a large part of the plot could be revealed to Sylvia later on. Right now, she just needed to be warned about whatever she had been doing in Paris that would have been so shocking at the time.

'I can see you at four o'clock,' Sylvia said, her voice cutting into Marian's musings. 'Would that suit you? I need a little snooze after lunch, you see. Maybe we could meet in my study on the ground floor? I find the stairs a little hard on my knees.'

'Of course,' Marian said. 'No problem at all.'

'Wonderful,' Sylvia said. 'See you then, dear girl.'

'Bye for now,' Marian said and hung up. There. It was done and there was no going back. All she had to do now was to warn Sylvia that there would soon be a novel by a popular author who seemed to have found out some deep, dark secret from Sylvia's youth. Some people were bound to make the connection between the fictional and real family that it was based on. Marian only wished she could undo her own part in what had sparked the author's interest in the Fleury family.

Why did I have to open my big mouth? she thought. *I only started to tell him about the Fleurys to distract him from my problems with Theo. Why didn't I just tell him about what was going on with me?*

She knew she had wanted to turn her own mind away from the sorrow of her break-up with Theo and talk about other things. She had babbled on about the Fleury family, about

Cornelius and how he had gambled away the property and how he had married his twin brother's girlfriend. Then there was the necklace that had been given to Rose that had turned out to be fake. All family secrets that Marian had sworn not to reveal outside the family. But then she had been careless while sad and tired and she had told someone who turned out to be an author.

Oh, what a mess, Marian thought, feeling her stomach tighten at the thought of Sylvia finding out. But all she would be told right now was about what had happened in Paris in 1960 and that had nothing to do with Marian. *Except I sparked off his interest in the family. He wouldn't be writing this story if it weren't for me.*

Marian's phone pinged, startling her. She looked at it and gasped as she saw who it was from.

Marian, I need to talk to you. I'm in Ireland, on the way to Kerry. I'll be in Dingle tonight and I've booked into a B&B. I feel we need to meet so we can decide what to do. Let me know where you are and when we can get together. Love, Theo.

Marian stared at the message. Theo was on his way here. This was all she needed on top of everything else. She was surprised that Theo had decided to come to Kerry. Did he think he could convince her to come back to Queensland? She knew she wanted to stay here at Magnolia Manor where she felt so at home. There was no way she would go back, no matter how much Theo pleaded.

She thought about him for a moment, trying to assess her feelings for him. She still loved him, even if she had recently also been resentful of the way he had taken for granted that she would stay with him and work in the shop and be his assistant as well as his wife. She was also hurt that he hadn't understood how homesick she had been ever since they had first arrived in

Australia. And she suspected that he wanted to stay there, in his hometown, where he had grown up. But she would never feel at home there. She had never told him this, though, and perhaps it was time she did.

Then there was the letter she had found in his desk, a letter from a woman called Helen he appeared to have been writing to for a long time. He seemed to have poured out his feelings to her, telling this other woman how frustrated he was with Marian, how he couldn't understand why she didn't make an effort to settle down in Queensland. That letter had hinted at a relationship that was quite close and Marian had understood from what Helen had written that she had been Theo's girlfriend before he met Marian. That had made her suspicious of their current connection, but as Marian remembered the wording of the letter, she realised that it didn't look as bad as she had feared.

Then, when she started to analyse things further, Marian began to see it from another angle. Theo had been quite happy in Ireland for many years. Then they moved to Australia and the relationship between them soured as Marian couldn't get used to life in a country so far away from home, where the tropical climate was difficult to cope with.

I must have been such a pain to live with, Marian thought. *Suffering in silence like some kind of martyr. No wonder Theo needed a friend to confide in, just as I felt like unburdening myself to someone with a sympathetic ear who happened to sit beside me on a long plane journey. I'm as much to blame as Theo – or even more,* she said to herself with a shiver.

She suddenly knew that Theo had also been feeling unhappy for a long time without telling her. How stupid they had been not to confide in each other.

'Marian?' Pierce, having just walked through the door, looked at her with concern. 'Are you okay?'

Marian pulled herself up. 'Yes, I'm grand. I was just trying to reply to a text message I just got. But I'll do the emails and then check through the press release for Karina's new book first. Shouldn't take long.'

'Great.' Pierce looked at her for a moment. 'It was just that you looked a little upset there for a moment.'

She smiled at him. 'Not really upset. Just preoccupied with some private stuff. But no big deal.'

He nodded. 'Okay. It's getting a little less busy so if you want to take this afternoon and even tomorrow off, I'll manage on my own. I have just one new client to deal with tomorrow and a few bits and pieces. Then it's the weekend and we can all relax.'

'Sounds good,' Marian said, thinking what a nice man he was. And such a great boss. 'I do like working for you,' she said. 'It's all so interesting and varied. And I love how flexible the working hours are.'

'I think we're a good fit,' Pierce said. 'You're good at the marketing stuff too. I'm so glad you're happy.'

'Who's the new client?' Marian asked.

'A self-published author,' Pierce said. 'Someone who's done so well promoting on his own. But now he needs help with all that so he can concentrate on his writing. I think you might have heard his name. He's very popular around here.'

Marian's heart sank. She knew who that author was. 'Are you talking about John Peters?'

TWELVE

'How did you guess?' Pierce asked.

'Because everyone is talking about him,' Marian said. 'I just read his latest book. He's a good writer, I have to say.'

'He's amazing,' Pierce agreed. He walked across the room and sat down in his easy chair by the window and then swivelled around to face her. 'So we have to do our best for him. I'd like to see if we can't get him on *The Late Late Show* and that morning radio show on Newstalk. Then we have to contact *The Irish Times* and all the major newspapers to get them to review the book. Create a buzz around it, if you see what I mean. You could do that when I've spoken to the author.'

Marian nodded. 'Yes, of course.' She tried her best not to show the turmoil his announcement had caused. *There will be plenty of buzz once the book comes out,* she thought bitterly. *More buzz than anyone might wish for, especially Sylvia.*

It seemed so ironic that Marian, who was trying her best to stop the rumours that might spread, now would be working with the very author whose book would be the source of those rumours.

'In any case, he's coming here for a chat with me tomorrow,'

Pierce continued. 'And after that, we'll just communicate by email and texts. We'll draw up a plan and contact the media and then wait and see. Pity he contacted me so late. He is going to publish the new novel in late August, only a month away. We'll have a job trying to get any kind of TV or radio slots.'

'That's true,' Marian said, beginning to see a ray of hope. Maybe they could delay the publication of this novel somehow? 'They have everything booked months beforehand. But maybe we could convince him to change the publication date? Like two months later or something? I mean, he is self-published, so he can pick any date for the book to go live.' She looked expectantly at Pierce, waiting for his reaction. She saw a chance to buy time so that she might convince Sean to rewrite parts of his novel. Two months would give her a window of opportunity to make it happen.

Pierce looked thoughtful. 'You have a point there. Of course we need more time. I'm going to get onto my contact at RTÉ and *The Irish Times* this afternoon. I'll see what they say and then if they give me an idea if they can do anything and when they can do it. And I can then suggest to John Peters he hold the publication until the mainstream guys are ready.'

'He just has to change the date on the preorder,' Marian said. 'And then tell the bookshop he'll be signing at the beginning of October instead.'

'Exactly. I don't think that will be a problem.' He smiled at her. 'Brilliant, Marian. Thank you for your very helpful suggestions.'

'You're welcome,' Marian said. 'Happy to be useful.'

'Useful? You're a lot more than that. You really have a knack for marketing. And all the media people you've been in touch with like you a lot. This past month has probably been the best period for me since I set up my agency.'

'That's wonderful.' Marian smiled at him, wishing she could tell him everything, but that wouldn't be wise.

'I think you can go home now,' he said. 'It's nearly lunchtime anyway.'

'What about these emails?' Marian asked, gesturing at the computer screen. 'Don't you want me to deal with them?'

'I'll do them,' Pierce replied. 'I have to look at John Peters' new novel on Amazon and read the description and so on as well. Off you go and enjoy the beautiful day.'

'You're going to look at the new novel on Amazon?' Marian asked, beginning to panic again. 'And you'll read the description of the Kindle preorder?'

'Yes. Why do you look so startled?' Pierce asked, confused.

Marian tried to look unperturbed. 'I'm not startled, just excited at hearing we'll be promoting the most popular author around here.'

'Yes, so am I,' Pierce agreed. 'I'm thrilled that he wants us to do his publicity. I have no idea how he found us. We have only done publicity for cookery books and self-help books until now. I'm ready to try something new, though.' He paused. 'But go and have your lunch. Oh, and before I forget, Claire is going to get in touch with you about our housewarming that's finally happening. We just decided and it's going to be on Sunday afternoon. Barbecue on our new deck. But she'll fill you in on the details soon.'

'That sounds like fun. Looking forward to it already,' Marian said as she got up from the desk. 'I'll go and have some lunch now. I have an appointment with Sylvia later today, so I'd better not delay.'

'Maybe you could tell Sylvia about our housewarming party?' Pierce asked. 'I know she likes gold-edged invitation cards, but this is a family affair and very casual.'

'I'll tell her to expect an invitation,' Marian said. 'I'll just say this is a save-the-date kind of thing.'

'Perfect,' Pierce said. 'You know your way around older women.'

'Well, as I am one myself, it's not too hard,' Marian quipped.

'Older than what?' Pierce enquired. 'Aren't we roughly the same vintage?'

'"Roughly" is the word,' Marian said. 'Give or take five years or so. But now I'm off.'

'See you Sunday. I'll keep you posted about John Peters and his reaction to your suggestions.'

'Just don't tell him it came from me,' Marian said as she walked to the door.

Pierce smiled. 'Of course not. I have all the brilliant ideas around here. Officially.'

Marian said goodbye and left the office and got into her car that was parked outside. Then she took out her phone and composed a text for Theo. She knew they had to meet and talk, but it was so hard to figure out what she was going to say. She desperately wanted to see him, now that she had realised that they had both been at fault. They needed to talk about their innermost feelings again, the way they used to when they were first married. They had been so close then, but with time had drifted apart, each in their own world, which seemed so wrong now. Marian thought for a moment before she started typing her reply.

Hi Theo, I was surprised to find out you were on your way here, but I'm at the same time delighted. Of course we need to talk. I'm staying in Claire's old flat at Magnolia Manor, only a few minutes' drive from Dingle town. Call me when you've arrived and we'll decide where to meet. See you soon, Marian.

Was that too cold? Too unfriendly? Did it send all the wrong signals despite her saying she was delighted to hear from him? Well, whatever, she didn't want to give him false hope, she decided, and hit send and immediately regretting not having added at least an x or two. Then she added a heart as an afterthought.

That done, she threw her phone into her bag and started the car, trying to forget about her crumbling marriage, and turned her mind to her meeting with Sylvia. How could she explain to the old lady that the sins of her youth that she had kept secret were about to be revealed? Marian felt her stomach churn at the thought, and she hoped with all her heart that Pierce would manage to get Sean to delay the publication of his novel. Then she would try to meet him again and plead with him to somehow change his story so that it would no longer be obvious that it was about the Fleury family – or apparent where the story had come from.

Marian rolled down the window, having realised that it was indeed a beautiful day with clear blue skies and brilliant sunshine. She stopped outside a little café on the Strand with views of the bay and decided to have lunch there before she headed home. There was an outside seating area with small round tables which would be a nice place to have a sandwich. She pulled into the last parking space just up the street and then walked down to the café and bought a ham sandwich and a bottle of water at the counter before settling down at the last available table outside. Once seated, she unwrapped the sandwich, took a big bite and a swig of water and looked out at the stunning view of Dingle Bay, enjoying the warm sunshine. A soft sea breeze played with her hair and caressed her face, making her close her eyes for a moment and feeling a sense of peace. Then she opened them again as a seagull's plaintive call woke her out of her trance and all her worries tumbled into her mind, reminding her that she would have to face Theo very soon.

Marian had tried to push all thoughts of her marriage out of her mind ever since she arrived without success. Despite the heartache, she had enjoyed having time to herself but now she felt as if her break away from him and their problems had come to an abrupt end. It had been such a treat, to reunite with her sister, get to know their new-found family and settle into life in this beautiful part of Ireland.

Marian had fallen in love with Kerry during the very first few weeks here. It was not only the fields of brilliant green, the waterfalls in hidden woodlands, the winding rivers through the beautiful landscape, or the majestic cliffs that towered over the wild ocean. All that was a mere backdrop to the welcome of the people she had met every day. Her kind brother-in-law who had offered her an interesting job was another reason she felt so happy here and she knew she would never leave. The only way she and Theo could heal together was if he could agree to settle here with her. It seemed selfish and harsh to demand that he give up his country for her, but those would be her terms.

Marian also knew from phone conversations with her daughter, Rebecca, that she would be very keen to come back to Ireland and reconnect with her old friends in Dublin, where she had gone to school. Rebecca had confessed that although Sydney was a great place to start her career, she yearned to come back home. If her daughter settled in Dublin, they could see each other often, Marian thought with a dart of happiness.

But now she had to tackle Sylvia and prepare her for what might be a huge shock and the start of a lot of nasty gossip. Marian was sure that, although Sylvia was greatly admired in town, there were also a lot of people who would be jealous of her status and would revel in the chance to take her down.

Having finished her lunch, Marian drove to Magnolia Manor and her meeting with Sylvia that was sure to be difficult.

Marian parked in the courtyard at the back of the manor, near Sylvia's entrance door that led to the hall and the study beyond the kitchen. But when she got out of the car, Sylvia opened the entrance door and told Marian to meet her on the terrace outside the big dining room as it was such a lovely day. 'We can sit in the sun and look at the roses that have just come out in full bloom,' she said. 'I'll bring coffee and cake.'

'Great idea,' Marian said and got back into her car. 'I'll park on the other side, so. See you in a minute.'

When she had parked the car, Marian made her way around the house and walked along the lawn to the terrace where Sylvia had just arrived carrying a basket. She looked, as usual, very elegant in blue linen slacks and a pale pink shirt. Her hair was brushed back from her lined but still beautiful face and her brown eyes were warm as she greeted Marian. Sylvia moved with astonishing grace, probably due to all the exercise she was doing, Marian assumed, admiringly. *I hope I'll be as fit and healthy when I reach Sylvia's age*, she thought. *Maybe it's also due to a loving relationship with a man who appreciates her?*

They sat down at a table near the railings which faced the rose garden, where red, yellow, pink and white roses were adorning every bush in the little garden inside a well-tended hedgerow. There was a heady floral scent in the air that competed with the salty tang from the sea. A slight humming sound from bees, too, which, combined with birdsong, made the terrace even lovelier.

'What a gorgeous place this is,' Marian said, admiring the sight of all the flowers.

'My favourite place in the summer,' Sylvia said as she took a thermos and mugs out of her basket. 'In the winter, not so much.'

'I can imagine,' Marian said. 'I haven't been here in the winter yet, but I'd say it can get wild.'

'That's an understatement.' Sylvia poured coffee into the mugs and pushed one of them across the table. 'Sugar or milk? Or both?'

'I take it black,' Marian said.

'So do I.'

'Before I forget,' Marian started, 'Pierce asked me to tell you that they are giving a housewarming party on Sunday and that they'd love you and Arnaud to come.'

Sylvia nodded, smiling. 'That sounds like fun. Tell him we'll be there, even though he didn't ask me himself.'

'They should have sent you a card, but I think it was a spur-of-the moment idea,' Marian explained.

'I see, well, everyone is so casual these days.' Sylvia took a plate with two slices of fruitcake covered in clingfilm out of the basket and handed one of them to Marian. 'Maura, who works for Karina, made these for a tea party tomorrow and she gave two to me to taste. Her famous barmbrack, just like my mother used to make it.'

'Oh, wonderful,' Marian said and took a bite. 'I haven't had barmbrack since I left Dublin to go to Australia. This one is delicious. So moist.' She took another bite, relishing the rich taste of dried fruit with a hint of orange peel. She took a sip of coffee, which made it even more tasty. 'What a treat to have it with you in this beautiful spot.'

Sylvia smiled. 'I agree. You're very good company, Marian.' She leaned forward. 'But you have a weary look in your eyes, I have to say. Are you worried about something?'

'Lots of things,' Marian said with a sigh. 'But I don't want to trouble you with—' She stopped, not knowing how to go on.

'With what?' Sylvia said, confused. 'Is there something you need to tell me? Something that has to do with me? Or the family?'

'Mostly you,' Marian said. 'But the family too. Oh, I don't know how to explain it.'

'Maybe you could try?' Sylvia said softly. 'I'm good at figuring out things even if they're a little cryptic.'

Marian nodded, her heartbeat beginning to race. 'The best start would be to read you something from the Internet.'

Sylvia nodded and sat back. 'That sounds mysterious. Go on.'

'You see, there is this novel that will be published soon,' Marian started, as she fished her phone out of her handbag. 'By this very popular author called John Peters.'

'I've heard of him,' Sylvia said. 'But what does that have to do with me?'

'Well, you see, his new novel is going to cause a lot of trouble for you.'

Sylvia raised an eyebrow. 'Really? Why?'

'Because, even though it's fiction, the story seems to be about Magnolia Manor, this family, and – you.' Marian drew breath.

'Me?' Sylvia's eyes widened. 'In what way?'

'I'll read the description to you,' Marian said and unlocked her phone. After a little bit of searching, she found the page. 'It's called *Family Secrets*. And here is the description of the plot.' Marian read the blurb out loud. She finished and drew breath, looking at Sylvia, who had turned very pale.

'Oh,' Sylvia finally said. 'That's quite a story.'

'Ring any bells?' Marian asked.

'A whole carillon,' Sylvia said. 'It's about us, isn't it?'

'Very thinly veiled, I'm afraid,' Marian said. 'But that's not the worst bit, is it?'

'No,' Sylvia replied, meeting Marian's gaze. 'It's the part about me.'

'Yes,' Marian said.

'I fear that part in the description could start a lot of rumours,' Sylvia said. 'But as it's fiction, will anyone believe any of it? I mean, "a beloved grandmother whose disreputable past will cause huge scandal if it is ever revealed". That could be any grandmother, couldn't it?'

'Yes, of course it could. It's probably all made up anyway,' Marian soothed.

'Or maybe not.' Sylvia looked thoughtful. 'Nobody would be able to prove it's true, anyway. Whatever it is, I mean.'

'Could it be based on real facts?' Marian asked. 'I mean, is there anything in your past that might be worth gossiping about?'

'Plenty,' Sylvia said with a sudden laugh. 'But I'm not going to tell you. I'll just say this: I have never done anything that I'm the slightest bit ashamed of. But if it came out, it might be misinterpreted. The past is the past and one's youthful adventures should stay there.'

'Of course,' Marian said. 'I agree a hundred per cent.'

Sylvia nodded, looking happier. 'Good. Now, what I would like to know is, who in the family has been talking about things that we have all agreed should stay in the family? Do you have any idea?'

Marian squirmed, trying to think of something to say. She felt terrible, and she didn't want to tell a lie. Should she admit to Sylvia that she was the one who spoke to Sean?

'The family is growing and it's difficult not to let something slip in conversation,' Sylvia said with a little sigh. 'It only takes a hint or two and the story is out there, getting more and more fantastic with time. Then, if the person listening is an author or maybe even a friend of one, it's so inspiring they have to put it into a book. Then people begin to wonder where the author got this story from and start to make connections. A feather becomes a whole hen and then there's no stopping the tales that are told by people who like to gossip.'

'I'm sorry?' Marian said, staring at Sylvia in confusion.

Sylvia laughed. 'Now you'll think I've gone completely bonkers. I was referring to a fairy tale by Hans Christian Andersen that we read as children. A hen loses a feather and jokes that she did it to make herself more beautiful. Then another hen tells another hen about it, then more and more hens talk about it, and every time the story is told, it's embroidered to make it more interesting. And the hen who had lost the little loose feather naturally doesn't recognise her own story when it comes back to her because it is now the story of five hens who have plucked out all of their feathers in vanity, and then pecked each other to death. As she was a respectable hen, she says, "I despise such hens, but there are many of that kind! Such stories should not be hushed up, and I'll do my best to get the story into the newspapers. Then it will be known all over the country; that will serve those hens right, and their families, too." And it gets to the newspapers, and it is printed. And that's how rumours begin and are told over and over again, growing each time. One little feather grows until it becomes five hens.' Sylvia drew breath and looked at Marian.

'That's a brilliant story,' Marian said, smiling. 'Very true to what happens once gossip starts.'

'Yes. That book might be a result of just one little lost feather,' Sylvia said. 'It will, in time, become a whole hen once the gossipmongers get hold of it. But what can we do about it other than ignore it and look as if we don't care?'

'Is that what we should do?' Marian asked.

'That's what I'm going to do anyway,' Sylvia said. She sipped her coffee, looking at Marian over the rim of her mug. 'You have to decide for yourself.'

'Oh, I won't comment at all,' Marian said. 'Even if they ask. I'll just say it's a work of fiction and as such it's all made up.' She took another bite of the barmbrack as she tried to gather up enough courage to ask Sylvia a question she had wanted to ask ever since she saw the description of that novel. 'You seem to have had quite an exciting time way back in the early nineteen sixties,' she said, hoping it would make Sylvia say something about what she had been up to before she was married.

'Oh yes, I did,' Sylvia said with a wistful smile. 'I managed to escape oppression for a while and have fun without anyone knowing about it.'

'Oppression?' Marian asked.

Sylvia nodded, running a finger around the rim of her mug. 'That's how it felt anyway. Ireland, I mean. My generation of women were brought up to be wives and mothers, you see. I was lucky to go to a school where women were taught to be independent and opinionated. Coláiste Íde was a wonderful place of learning and the women who taught us so inspirational. But out there in the real world, it was a different story. The Catholic church, the nuns and priests, were strict and forbidding. There were so many rules about behaviour and what a young girl should and shouldn't do. I was expected to perhaps go to college but then, after that, I was to marry someone suitable and become a housewife. So I...'

'You ran away?' Marian asked, excited at the thought.

'No, not quite,' Sylvia said, shaking her head and smiling. 'I asked if I could go abroad for a year instead of going to college. I wasn't really interested in studying at university anyway. I wasn't very academic. So my parents agreed to let me go to France to work as an au pair for a year, which was a new concept then. They thought I would be safe living with a family minding children and going to French classes on my days off.'

'So you went to Paris?' Marian suggested. 'For a whole year?'

'Yes,' Sylvia said. 'That year changed my life in so many ways. I met young women who had taken charge of their lives and done amazing things. One woman in particular.'

'Such a contrast to life in Kerry in those days, I'm sure,' Marian remarked.

'It certainly was,' Sylvia agreed. 'Just as much of a contrast to Ireland as Australia, I can imagine. A different world.'

'That's for sure,' Marian agreed, amazed at how Sylvia had so elegantly turned the spotlight away from herself.

'You must have thought you had landed on another planet,' Sylvia suggested.

'Oh yes,' Marian said. 'That's exactly how it felt. Everything was upside-down: the seasons, the constellations of the stars, and the flora and fauna so strange and new. I never got used to the intense heat either. And I was more and more homesick as time wore on.'

'Was that why you left?' Sylvia asked with great sympathy in her eyes. 'I'm assuming you don't want to go back.'

'No, I don't, actually,' Marian confessed. 'But it wasn't only that. It was also...' She stopped, wondering if she should reveal the troubles of her marriage. It would feel so good to confide in someone wise and kind like Sylvia. Marian felt a sudden urge to unload everything on the old lady, but then changed her mind. It wouldn't be fair to burden Sylvia right now, when she might be worried about what was going to be in that book.

'It was also about your husband?' Sylvia asked gently.

'Well, yes,' Marian said, tears welling up as the memory of their parting caused a wave of sadness. 'We were having problems. He didn't understand why I was so homesick. He thought I'd snap out of it but I never did.'

'Snap out of it?' Sylvia asked. 'How can you snap out of missing your home country? That's in your heart and soul. I could never leave Ireland and settle somewhere else, despite how women were treated when I was young. I went abroad for a break from all of that. But I never felt that I wanted to stay away for good.'

'I didn't think it was going to be for good,' Marian said. 'I thought we'd live half the year in Ireland and the other half in Australia. That's what I thought we had agreed, anyway.'

'But he had other ideas?' Sylvia said disapprovingly.

'I think he was hoping I'd come around to liking it.' Marian sighed deeply. 'But I never did. Oh, it wasn't the fault of the people I met; they were all so nice to me. The Aussies are lovely and it's a beautiful country, if you like constant sunshine and practically living on the beach. That's what Theo loves anyway. I did enjoy working in the shop that sells surfboards and sporting equipment. That was fun and I was good at marketing. But we drifted apart. I was very unhappy in the end.'

'So you left and now he's over there trying to cope without you?' Sylvia looked at Marian as if she couldn't quite decide if she approved.

'No, not quite,' Marian said quietly. 'He is actually on his way here. I'll arrange to meet him tomorrow.'

'Well, that's good, isn't it?' Sylvia said. 'It'll give you a chance to talk. Maybe he'll come around and you can start again, living in both places like you originally planned.'

'I'm not sure about that.' Marian's shoulders slumped.

'Do you still love him?' Sylvia asked.

Marian sighed. 'Sometimes I think I love him so much I might burst into flames. But I've suppressed so much of myself for so long. And he hasn't been honest with me. I don't know if I can trust him the same way again. If the relationship we had in the early days will ever come back.'

'It might,' Sylvia suggested. 'If you both want it to.' She put a hand on Marian's arm. 'You've lost the joy of loving, of being together, that "us against the world" that is so important. If you want it again, you have to fight for it. Both of you. I hope you get it back, I really do.'

'Thank you, Sylvia,' Marian said. 'I'll remember that.'

Sylvia patted Marian's hand. 'Good. You know there is no such thing as a blissfully happy marriage, not all the time, I mean. There are happy moments and then there is contentment and harmony. But there are also differences and wishes and dreams that clash with each other.'

'But you and Liam were very happy, weren't you?' Marian asked.

'Most of the time,' Sylvia said with a sad little smile. 'But he didn't completely understand that I sometimes felt stuck in this role of housewife running this big house. That I'd like to go off on my own and maybe see my old friends, the ones I met in

Paris. That little bit of freedom I had was gone forever when we got married.' She looked across the garden with faraway expression. 'Arnaud understands it. But French men have different attitudes to women. They're closer to their feminine side, I think.'

'Arnaud is a lovely man,' Marian said. 'Everyone is so fond of him.'

'I know. That makes me so happy.' Sylvia started to gather up the mugs. 'But now I have to go. I have a meeting with the Tidy Towns committee at five thirty, so I have to change.'

'But what about the book and what it might say about you?' Marian asked. 'What are you going to do about it?'

Sylvia got up. 'Nothing for the moment. I need to think about all of this for a while. The secrets, the scandal, the betrayal. Who could have shared all this?'

Marian shivered. Should she admit it was her? But before she could consider it properly, Sylvia picked up her basket, waved and left, gliding across the terrace in the graceful way Marian found so amazing.

Marian sat there for a while feeling slightly shellshocked after her conversation with Sylvia. She had given Marian much to think about, especially concerning Theo and their relationship. But then, when she went through everything from start to finish, she began to wonder if all that might have been a smokescreen to cover up Sylvia's youthful misdemeanours. She had cleverly turned the conversation to Marian and her marriage and there had been no more mention of what she had done in Paris all those years ago.

Sylvia said that what happened in the past should stay in the past, Marian thought. *But I have a feeling it won't.*

FOURTEEN

Theo called later that evening when Marian was stepping out of the shower.

'Hi,' she said with a laugh as she grabbed a towel from the rail. 'Why does the phone always ring when you're in the shower?'

'Telepathy,' he said. 'How are you?'

She froze at the sound of his voice. She hadn't heard it for such a long time she had forgotten its dark timbre and that Aussie twang that always gave her butterflies. 'Fine,' she said, her voice shaking with nerves. 'And you? How was your flight?'

'Good,' he said. 'When can we meet? I have a car and I could get to you in a few minutes.'

'Oh, eh... Just let me get ready and then...' She wracked her brain for a place where they could meet. She didn't want him to come to the flat just yet. It was too small and intimate. She needed space and air around her, so she could back away if their arguments got too heated. 'Come to the entrance of Magnolia Manor and we can go for a walk through the gardens down to the beach,' she said. 'There'll be nobody around. It's such a lovely evening, so we can sit on the bench by the jetty and look at the sea. And it'll stay bright until ten o'clock.'

He didn't argue, which surprised her. 'Okay,' he said. 'I'll be there in about twenty minutes. Okay with you?'

'Perfect,' she said. 'See you then.'

Marian hung up and looked wildly around the bedroom. What should she wear for this meeting with her estranged husband? Her hair was still damp from the shower and her face devoid of make-up. She didn't feel she had to dress up for Theo, but she still needed a little power dressing to feel confident. She finally decided on a pair of jeans, a light blue shirt and her new Adidas trainers. Then she quickly blow-dried her hair that had grown to shoulder length with blonde streaks from the sun.

She applied a tinted moisturiser and blusher and a touch of mascara and stood back, looking at herself in the bathroom mirror. There was no hiding the fact that the rest, the new job and the time to herself had made her look and feel years younger, the many hours of swimming and walking giving her a wonderful glow.

It's the lack of stress, the feeling of belonging and the peace I've found here that has made me feel so good, Marian thought. *I don't want to give that up, whatever he says. In any case, my first question will be about the woman he has been writing to.*

She stuck her phone in her pocket and ran down the stairs, her heart beating at the thought of meeting Theo here at Magnolia Manor, where she felt so at home.

He was waiting just below the steps, looking up at the imposing façade. 'Hey,' he said when Marian came through the massive entrance doors. 'This is some pile.'

'Beautiful, isn't it?' she said as she walked down the steps to meet him.

'Incredible,' he said. He looked tired, his blond hair in need of a cut and his normally clean-shaven face had a dark stubble. His grey eyes were weary and Marian could see that he had lost weight. But he was still handsome and still looked so like the young man she had fallen in love with over thirty-five years ago that she felt a familiar dart of attraction.

She kissed him lightly on the cheek. 'Hello,' she said. 'You look exhausted.'

'Jetlagged.' He ran his hand over his face. 'I only landed in Dublin yesterday. I've been on the road since early this morning. Didn't know it would take so long to get here.'

'Yeah, I know. And I bet you got stuck in Adare,' she said. 'Such a pain.'

'Yes, it is.' He studied her for a moment. 'You look great,' he said as if he didn't like it.

'Thanks,' she said, his slightly sour look making her feel awkward. 'I've had a good month or so here.'

'Six weeks,' he corrected. 'I've missed you. Where can we talk?'

'Let's walk down to the beach,' she said, avoiding his eyes that were full of pain and resentment. 'We can talk there.'

He nodded and they started to walk, side by side, down the path that wound through the beautiful garden with its flowerbeds, shrubs in full bloom and tropical plants. The sunlight through the foliage of the trees threw a dappled light on the path and the breeze from the sea was soft and comforting.

'Lovely gardens,' he said, looking around. 'So well kept.'

'Yes,' Marian said. 'I love this walk.'

Then they could glimpse the water through the arch formed by the branches of the trees and as they came closer, the vista of the open sea became visible. Theo stopped and stared at the glimmering blue water of the bay, the green hills, the sky meeting the ocean at the horizon and the seagulls gliding above them. 'Wow,' he said. 'What a gorgeous view. Breathtaking.'

'I know,' Marian said, pleased that he was so impressed by all the beauty around them. 'I was just as stunned the first time

I came here.' She walked ahead and sat down on the little granite bench beside the jetty. 'Let's sit here for a while and talk.'

'Okay.' He joined her on the bench and they sat in awkward silence for a while until Marian spoke.

'I know you were upset that I didn't come back to Australia after Claire's wedding. But I needed some time to myself. I needed time to think.'

'About what?' he asked.

'About a letter I found in the desk when I was looking for my passport. It was from a woman called Helen and she seemed to know you very well. The letter wasn't very long, but the gist of it was that she thought you should have it out with me, whatever that meant.' Marian glared at him, waiting for his reply.

Theo looked confused for a moment. 'A letter from Helen? Oh, I see. That's an old letter. Just a note, really. Stuck into a birthday card she sent me a few years ago. That's why you were so upset when you left? You thought...' He stopped for a moment, looking distraught. 'Oh God, Marian, that is not at all the way it seems,' he said.

'No?' Marian tapped her foot. 'What way was it, then?'

He sighed. 'Helen is – was – my girlfriend before I met you. She's Australian but lives in Dublin. I went to see her when she came to Brisbane for a visit two years ago, and then she wrote to me with some advice, that's all. But I only saw her a few times. She's a bit of an amateur therapist and has helped me in the past. I told her that you were feeling homesick and I didn't know what to do. I didn't feel she was a great help, to be honest.'

'So you needed help to cope with me?' Marian asked. 'From an ex-girlfriend?'

'I needed to talk to someone and she was willing to listen. Well, things weren't going so well between us,' Theo ended. 'I felt a little helpless, to be honest.'

'And you thought it was all my fault?' Marian asked angrily.

'And then you went to Helen instead of asking me how I was feeling? Instead of discussing it with me?'

'I suppose I should have talked to you,' Theo said. 'But I didn't think you'd tell me what was wrong.'

Marian sighed, feeling an odd dart of guilt. 'I know what you mean. I gave you the silent treatment, I suppose. And you ran away to the beach and your surfing for comfort. What happened to us? We used to understand each other without talking, but I felt that you didn't see me any more or that you didn't care about how I felt.'

'I know,' he said. 'I was selfish and then I felt guilty when I saw how homesick you were. Talking to Helen didn't help matters at all. She said I should try to get you to stop feeling sorry for yourself.'

'Maybe she was hoping we'd break up?' Marian suggested. 'She seems to think you still have feelings for her.'

Theo looked awkward. 'I don't know. Maybe she does.' He shrugged. 'I felt that she didn't really understand the situation. And I don't have feelings for her other than friendship. But I hoped, in time, that you'd get used to things and love Surfers Paradise as much as I do.'

'It's not much of a paradise to me,' Marian said in a bitter tone. 'I did try, but then you were always off to the beach with your mates and seemed to live a different life. I thought you didn't want me around at all.'

He looked at his feet. 'I know what you mean and I'm sorry if I made you feel that way.' He glanced up. 'I just wanted to feel young again. To ride the waves and have no responsibilities. The kids had grown up and had their own lives, so I knew they didn't need us any more. We were so young when we met and had those children, one after another when we were so newly married. I felt I hadn't had a chance to grow up myself. You were so good at running the shop and I thought you enjoyed it.'

'I did,' Marian said. 'That was the best part, running the

shop, meeting customers, making the business run smoothly. But you left me to cope on my own, only coming home for dinner in the evenings. And then you were off again the next morning, catching the perfect wave.'

'I suppose I forgot about us,' Theo said, his voice heavy with guilt. 'I wanted to be free and have some fun, and I suppose I was afraid of growing old. So it was really all my fault that we drifted apart.' He took her hand. 'But then, when you left, I realised that I had thrown away thirty years of a marriage that was happy for a long time. Until I ruined it. And when you left, I realised how much you mean to me. How much I missed you when you weren't there any more.' He looked into her eyes. 'I just want to know if it's too late to mend what I broke?'

'I don't know,' Marian said sadly, pulling her hand out of his grip. She looked at him and remembered how she had been so attracted to him the very first time they met. And that night at the beach when they had talked until the early hours of the morning, sharing their hopes and dreams, their life stories, their likes and dislikes, favourite music, the kind of books they liked to read, and all sorts of little details that had seemed trivial in retrospect but seemed so important at that moment. She remembered looking into his grey eyes and seeing a kindred spirit, feeling that this was it, the special moment when she had met the love of her life. Was all that gone forever? Was thirty-five years of marriage now over? It made her immensely sad to feel that it was. But now it seemed as if it could take a lot of time to get back what they had – if that was even possible.

She hadn't understood his wish to have some freedom from responsibility until now, when she herself had felt free for the first time for many years. The new job, that little flat, connecting with long-lost relatives had everything to do with her and he was not part of that. But she had to give them a chance. He had taken on the blame for the problems in their marriage, but she knew they were both at fault. She hadn't been honest with him.

'Maybe we could try to get to know each other again?' she suggested. 'I mean, who we are now, not who we were back then, if you see what I mean.'

'Like going on dates?' Theo asked, looking hopeful.

'Something like that,' Marian said, feeling more positive towards him. 'How long are you planning to stay here?'

'I said I'd be away for a month,' Theo replied. 'Frank is taking care of the business while I'm away.'

'But it's the busiest time of year,' Marian argued. 'Can you really afford to take all that time off? Can that nephew of yours really handle it?'

'You're more important to me right now,' Theo said. 'And saving our marriage. I trust Frank and he promised to do his best to keep everything going until I get back.'

'A month,' Marian said as if to herself. 'Well, you know what? Let's see where we are at the end of that month.'

He nodded. 'That's a deal. Let's spend time together and find out who we are. Do things we used to enjoy.'

'Yes, we should,' Marian said. 'When I'm not working.'

'Working? You have a job?' He looked at her incredulously. 'Doing what?'

'Marketing,' Marian said. 'Pierce, Claire's husband, needed an assistant to help with the office work, so I said I'd love to help out. I really enjoy it.'

'And you have a flat in the manor,' he said. 'Must say, you've fallen on your feet here, haven't you?' His tone was slightly resentful, which annoyed Marian.

'Yes, I have. I don't see that there's anything wrong with that.'

'I suppose not. It's just that you seem to have settled in here in such a short time when it took you years to even tolerate Australia.'

'That was different.' Marian shook her head. 'I'm not even going to try to explain it. But I think you'll understand when you spend a little time here and meet my family. Claire and Pierce are having a housewarming on Sunday, so you could come with me and meet them.'

'The long-lost Fleury family?' he asked. 'That should be interesting.'

'Yes, it will be if you come,' she said with a teasing smile. 'Let's see how you cope with the Fleury girls all together.'

'Sounds scary,' he said with a pretend shudder.

'You have no idea,' Marian said with a wink, happy that there was suddenly a more positive vibe between them. 'But the scariest of them all is Sylvia, the matriarch. She will be a tough nut to crack.'

'As you know I like challenge,' Theo said with a grin. 'So bring it on.'

'Brilliant,' Marian said, even though she didn't think it was brilliant at all.

What have I done? she thought. *Nobody knows about the letter I found, or how miserable we've been, so everyone will welcome Theo with open arms and give him false hope... But I should bring him so he can get to know the Fleurys and see for himself how kind and friendly they are.*

She got up. 'It's getting late, so we'd better go. You must be tired anyway.'

He rose. 'Yes, I am. I need a night's sleep. I suppose you're working tomorrow, so I'll amuse myself until Saturday. I was thinking I'd go and check out that famous surfing beach nearby. Inch, I think it's called. Have you heard of it?'

'Of course,' Marian said. 'Very popular with surfers. That's a good idea,' she said, not wanting to admit she had the day off tomorrow. She needed a little time to adjust to him being here and she also wanted to be on the alert for a call from Pierce about his meeting with John Peters. 'I'll be in touch about doing something on Saturday. We could go for a drive.'

'Okay.' He started to walk up the path and she fell in step with him. They walked up the path as dusk was falling, both deep in thought. They didn't speak until they were in front of the manor.

Marian turned to face him. 'Goodnight, Theo. Thank you for coming.'

'It wasn't what I hoped, but better than I feared,' he said with sad little smile. Then he took her hand and held it in his. 'I wanted to say something profound but I can't find the words.'

'Me neither.' Marian wondered if her frozen heart could one day begin to thaw. Right now it didn't feel possible but he looked so sad and forlorn she felt a stab of pity.

'It seems so hopeless right now,' he said. 'That's what makes me sad.'

'I know,' she said. On an impulse, she leaned forward and kissed him on the cheek. 'It'll look better in the morning. Sweet dreams,' she whispered before she opened the door and went inside.

As she walked up the stairs, Marian thought about Theo and what they had decided to do. The fact that he had come all this way to see her and try to mend what was broken between them had touched her. Could they reignite that spark they had when they were young? If they tried hard, maybe they could. But did she really want to?

FIFTEEN

The phone ringing woke Marian up the next morning.

It was Pierce. 'Sorry for calling so early,' he said. 'But I need to talk to you about this novel. The one written by John Peters, I mean. Our new client.'

'Yes?'

'Have you read the description?' Pierce asked.

'I have,' Marian said, knowing what Pierce was going to say.

'Did it remind you of anything?' Pierce said. 'Like, any family around here?'

'I know what you mean,' Marian said. 'It sounds very much like us – the Fleury family, I mean.'

'Of course it does,' Pierce said. 'The family feud, the old gambling debt, it's all there. And then the bit about the grandmother with a dubious past, or whatever it was. No idea what that is about but maybe we should warn Sylvia?'

'I already did,' Marian said. 'She was a bit shaken up at first, but then she said not to worry.'

Pierce snorted a laugh. 'Typical of Sylvia. She's as tough as an old boot. Okay, so she knows there is something in that novel that might be about both the family and her own story. All we have to do is to find out what it is.'

'We could ask him if we can read the book before publication,' Marian suggested. 'I mean we're going to do the publicity, so that would be normal, wouldn't it?'

'I suppose it would, yes,' Pierce said. 'I usually look through every book I've been marketing, but this is my first work of fiction. Yes, that's what we should do. And I was thinking about the meeting with the author, actually. I know it's your day off, but could you be there with me? You're so good at marketing and getting on with people. I'd feel better if you were there, too, like a partner or something. It makes the firm look more professional than a one-man band. And now that I've read the description, it's even more important.'

Marian tried not to panic at the thought of meeting John Peters today. He would know that she was the one who suggested a later publication date for his novel. And what if Sean told Pierce where he got the inspiration for his story? She couldn't begin to imagine how disgusted everyone in her new-found family would be when they learned what she had done.

'I see what you mean,' she said, knowing that she would have to be at that meeting in order to prevent what she feared happening. 'I think you could handle it very well, but if you need me, I'll come in. I hadn't planned to do much today anyway.'

'Great,' Pierce said, sounding calmer. 'He'll be here at two o'clock. I will spend the morning trying to talk to my contacts in the media. If I manage to get some good publicity we have a strong case for a later publication.'

'Okay,' Marian said, trying to get her voice not to shake. 'See you later, then.'

Pierce said goodbye and hung up, leaving Marian sitting up in bed, wringing her hands, wondering how on earth she was going to stop Sean revealing her part in his inspiration for the plot of the novel. This, on top of Theo's arrival, was too much to bear. And now she would have to hide all this from Claire, her own sister, who had been so kind to her since her arrival in Kerry. Marian wondered if she should tell Claire what had happened on the plane. No, it was better to leave well enough alone for the moment and try her best not to rock the boat.

Oh what a mess, Marian thought, slowly getting out of bed. *All because of that rambling to a perfect stranger late at night when I was so tired and a little tipsy. And what do I do about Theo? Why did he have to arrive right now in the middle of all this?*

'How did it go?' Sylvia asked Marian when they bumped into each other downstairs just after lunch as Marian was leaving for the office. 'Meeting your husband again, I mean.'

'It was a bit awkward,' Marian said. 'He was tired and sad and I was angry and resentful. So, not the best way to start rebuilding our marriage. But he wants us to go on some kind of date on Saturday, so it might work better then.'

'Bring him to Claire's party on Sunday,' Sylvia suggested. 'Then he'll meet everybody and he'll see why you're so happy here.'

'I already invited him,' Marian said. 'He said yes, but I'm not sure he really wants to come. He's quite shy, really. And everyone at once might be a bit much for him to cope with.'

'Nonsense,' Sylvia argued. 'I'm sure he'll be happy to meet them. And barbecues are so Australian, he'll feel very much at home. Isn't it better to throw him in at the deep end and see if he can swim?'

Marian had to laugh. 'Yeah, barbies are very Australian. That should make him feel more at ease. He might even take over the cooking.'

'I don't think Pierce would mind that,' Sylvia said. 'Oh, go on, bring him,' she urged, which to Marian sounded more like an order. 'So we can all meet this Australian hunk, as Claire calls him.'

'I know she does, just for fun,' Marian said. 'But okay, I'll bring him. Might be a good way to break the ice.'

'Of course it is.' Sylvia smiled, then went through the door and waved. 'Must rush. The library committee is waiting. See you at the party.'

Marian waved back. 'Bye for now,' she said as the door closed behind Sylvia.

Oh, she thought, *is it wise to bring Theo to the party on Sunday? It will be such a family affair and he will feel awkward.* But then she changed her mind and pushed away her fears. Sylvia was right. Theo should be thrown in at the deep end. It would shake him up, get him out of his gloom and make him understand why she was so happy here. With that thought, Marian got into her car and drove to the office, the other, much bigger concern turning her stomach into a tight knot.

Pierce was preparing for the meeting with John Peters when Marian arrived at the office. 'Great news,' he said when she walked in. 'I got a review and an interview with *The Irish Times* at the end of September and also a possible slot on both *The Morning Show* on RTÉ and *The Late Late Show* the following week. I also have an interview with Pat Kenny on Newstalk the week after that, and then some book signings in some bookshops in Dublin and a possible launch with Dubray in Grafton Street just before that.'

Marian stopped and stared at him. 'Wow, you have worked hard. How on earth did you manage all that?'

'I pulled a few strings,' he said, beaming. 'Old mates from college here and there and then I cashed in on a favour I was owed.'

'Well done,' Marian said and clapped him on the back. 'This means John Peters can't possibly refuse to change the date of his publication. And that will buy us time to...'

'To what?' Pierce asked, sitting down at the desk. 'Try to make him rewrite the story so the family secrets won't be exposed?' He shook his head. 'I doubt he'll agree to that. Authors can be very difficult to steer in the right direction, especially if they self-publish. Have you looked at his social media platform? He has thousands of followers on Facebook and Instagram. Then there's TikTok and Bluesky and maybe even X, which I haven't looked into yet.'

'But if he has all that, why does he need us?' Marian asked.

'He wants to get into the Irish market with printed books, and he can't do that on his own,' Pierce explained. 'He needs someone with media contacts to create a buzz. TV and radio still work here as people in Ireland generally still watch TV and listen to the radio. He has managed to get popular around here and in Cork for some reason but now he needs to spread the word around the country.'

'Oh, I see,' Marian said. 'So that's what he's after. And, of course, since the novel is based on a true story, as he says in his book description, it will be hugely popular all over the country.'

'But that's what we want to try to stop, or at least change,' Pierce said. 'The story, I mean. To make the connection with Magnolia Manor and the Fleurys less obvious.'

'I know,' Marian agreed. 'The question is – how?'

'We just have to play it by ear.' Pierce gestured at the table in front of the little sofa where mugs and a plate with a cake had been laid out. 'And ply him with coffee and Karina's strawberry cake with whipped cream. That should do the trick, don't you think?' he joked.

'Absolutely,' Marian said with a wry smile. She suddenly realised that Pierce had no idea that she knew John Peters. She hadn't wanted to explain her connection with the author in case she accidentally revealed what had happened on the plane. *I'd better tell him right now*, she thought, *or it will come as a huge shock.* 'But before he comes, I should tell you that I—'

They were interrupted by a knock on the door and then it opened and Sean peered in. 'Hello,' he said. 'I was told to come here by a very nice lady wearing an apron.'

'My sister,' Pierce said. 'She's a professional cook.' He held out his hand. 'Hello and welcome. I'm Pierce and this is Marian, my assistant.'

'Oh,' Sean said, looking surprised. 'Hi there, Marian. So this is where you work?'

'You know each other?' Pierce asked, looking taken aback. 'Why didn't you say so, Marian?'

'I was about to,' Marian stammered. 'I forgot I hadn't told you.'

'How do you know each other, then?' Pierce asked, looking put out.

Marian stared at Sean, willing him not to reveal the whole truth. 'Well, we...'

'We met when we were travelling together on a plane,' Sean said. 'From Australia to Dubai. But Marian only knows me by my real name and she hadn't a clue that I'm an author and that I write under the pseudonym John Peters. My real name is Sean Duvivier. My father was French and my mother Irish. From Tralee, as a matter of fact.'

'Oh,' Pierce said. 'I see. Well, that's quite a lot to take in, I have to say.'

'I suppose I should have said all that in my email,' Sean said apologetically. 'But I preferred to tell you in person.'

'What do I call you, then?' Pierce asked, still looking confused.

'Call me by my real name,' Sean said. 'Then we can talk about John Peters like a product we're marketing.'

Pierce smiled and nodded. 'Good idea. Unusual, but I like it. Please sit down and we'll have coffee and cake while we talk.'

'That cake looks delicious,' Sean said. 'I didn't have breakfast, actually.'

'No breakfast?' Pierce asked. 'In what B&B are you staying?'

'I'm not in a B&B, but in a dilapidated cottage on the edge of town,' Sean said as he sat down. 'The cooking facilities are limited there, to say the least. My mother left it to me in her will and I'm here to see what can be done with it. I used to spend my childhood summers there, but that was a long time ago. I didn't know it had got so rundown. It needs a huge amount of work that I don't have the energy to even think about. In the end, I suppose I'll sell it. Someone else can have the pleasure of doing it up.'

'That sounds like a good plan.' Marian cut a slice of the cake, put it on a plate and handed it to Sean while Pierce poured coffee into the mugs and helped himself to cake.

'So,' Pierce said as they all started on the cake, 'I have some news about the media coverage for your new novel. But first, I would like to ask you if we can read the novel before publication, and then, if you would consider publishing it a little later than you had planned?'

Sean glanced at Marian while he took a bite of cake. 'Why would I do that?' he asked. 'The readers who preordered the book will be very disappointed.'

'Yes, but all the media publicity I've lined up for you won't happen around that date. It was impossible to schedule anything at such short notice,' Pierce explained. 'I managed to arrange some interviews for late September, which was the earliest they could do. We have *The Late Late Show*, Newstalk with Pat Kenny, *Ireland AM*, and both a review and an interview in *The Irish Times*.' He drew breath and looked expectantly at Sean.

Sean looked from Pierce to Marian. 'Well, that's quite a

line-up. I must say I'm impressed. But would it matter if the book had already been published for a while when I go on stage, so to speak? I realise I should have contacted you earlier, but I hadn't planned to hire a book publicist until now.'

'If the book has been out over a month, it'll be old news,' Pierce said. 'Launching it to coincide with all the media coverage is the best way to go, believe me.'

Sean nodded while he took another bite of cake. 'Maybe you're right. This is delicious, by the way. Just like my mother used to make it.' He put the plate on the table and shot Marian a glance. 'This idea of pushing for a later publication date is not because of the content of the novel, is it? I know about Marian's relationship with the family that the novel is based on, so...'

'I... Well, of course I'm worried about the similarities of the fictional family in the novel to the Fleurys,' Marian replied. 'And how people around here will react once they read the novel and make the connection.'

'I knew that,' Sean said.

'But that's not why we want to delay the publication,' Marian cut in. 'It's about the timing of the media coverage.'

'Their schedules were already full for August,' Pierce interjected. 'It was impossible to get anything around that time. In fact, we were lucky to get what we got for late September. In any case,' he continued, 'September is a better time to publish books. Lots of people are still on holiday in August, so they don't pay much attention to new publications.'

'I would have thought they'd want something to read on the beach,' Sean argued in a pleasant tone, despite the cold look in his eyes.

'But your books are hardly beach blanket reads,' Marian countered. 'I read your latest novel, and it's not at all a light read for the deckchair.'

'You read *A Stranger Comes Home*?' Sean looked at Marian in surprise.

'Yes, and I loved it,' Marian said. 'It really resonated with me.'

'Oh,' he said, looking pleased. 'That's good to hear. I'd love to discuss it with you sometime.'

'I'd be happy to,' Marian said. 'And I can't wait to read *Family Secrets*.'

'Neither can I,' Pierce said. 'So how about that for starters? Can you send it to us in some kind of format so we can read it onscreen?'

'Of course,' Sean said. 'If you have Kindles, you can send a Word doc to your account and then it will be easy to read.'

'Great,' Pierce said, pushing a piece of paper and a pen across the table. 'So if we can sign this agreement, then I think we will go forward with everything. If you agree to change the publication date to late September, of course. Otherwise I don't think we can go on.'

Sean looked at the agreement for a moment and then at Marian and Pierce in turn. 'I only want to do this one book with you. And then we'll see.'

'That's fine,' Pierce said. 'We can change the agreement accordingly and you can sign once we've done that.'

Sean nodded. 'I'll have to go on my social media platforms and apologise to my readers. But I'm sure they won't be too annoyed.'

'I'm sure they won't,' Marian soothed.

'I just want to make one thing clear,' Sean said with a steely look in his eyes. 'I will not, under any circumstances, change a word in either the description or the plot.'

'Well, of course we were hoping we might persuade you,' Marian confessed. 'But I realise that was a bit of a long shot.'

Sean nodded and got up. 'Good. I'll be off now to rearrange the timings. In any case, my editor will be happy to have a little extra time to finish the proofreading, as will I. Nice to meet you,

Pierce. Marian, we have to meet up to discuss your take on *A Stranger Comes Home*.'

'I'd love to discuss the plot of *Family Secrets*. Who told you the story of the Fleurys?' Pierce asked.

Sean shot another glance a at Marian, who stared back at him, waiting for him to reveal everything. 'Well,' he started, 'that's an interesting question.'

Marian held her breath. *This is it*, she thought. *The end of my stay here and this enjoyable job. And what will Claire say when she finds out? And Sylvia and my cousins? They'll hate me forever after this.*

SIXTEEN

After a brief pause, Sean shook his head. 'As a journalist, I never reveal my sources and that applies to my role as author too. So that will remain a secret between me and my informant.'

'I see,' Pierce said, looking disappointed. 'I thought that might be a good backdrop to your interviews, that's all. The story of the story, so to speak.'

'I'm afraid I'll have to pass on that particular detail, even though it's quite an interesting tale on its own,' Sean said, standing by the door. 'Goodbye for now, Pierce.' He shook Pierce's hand. Then he kissed Marian on both cheeks, walked out the door and ran down the stairs, leaving Pierce and Marian staring at each other in shock.

'Well, that was not at all what I expected,' Pierce said, sitting down again.

'Nor me,' Marian said as her knees gave way and she sank down on the sofa, heaving a secret sigh of relief. *At least nobody will know my part in this mess.*

'Marian?' Pierce said, looking at her with concern. 'You're suddenly very pale. Are you not feeling well?'

'I'm grand,' Marian said. 'Just a little overwhelmed by every-thing. I think my blood sugar is a little low too.'

'You didn't have any cake,' Pierce said and slid the plate with her untouched slice of cake towards her. 'Have some now and I'll make another cup of coffee for you in the Nespresso.'

'Thanks, Pierce.' Marian picked up the plate with the cake and took a bite. It was truly delicious and she started to enjoy it, feeling much better about everything. 'It went well, don't you think?' she asked as she finished her slice of cake.

'Yes,' Pierce replied as he busied himself with the coffee machine. 'At least we've bought a bit of time. Now we have to read the book and then assess what to do about whatever secrets it reveals.'

'All the misbehaviours of my great-grandfather's brother, for a start,' Marian said. 'It's hinted at in the description, anyway.'

'That's bad enough, of course,' Pierce said. 'If the stuff about the feud and the gambling debt comes out, it's going to create a stir. But it happened so long ago. It's Sylvia's "dubious past" we have to worry most about.' He handed her a steaming cup. 'Here, a fresh cup of coffee.'

Marian smiled at him as she took the cup. 'Thanks, Pierce. I'm feeling much better now.'

'Good.' He sat down again and smiled back at her. 'You were looking really peaky there for a while. Now, where were we?'

'Sylvia's frolics in the sixties,' Marian said with a chuckle. 'I'd say it's something racy, whatever it was.'

Pierce nodded. 'Possibly. But whatever it was, we have to stop it coming out or the gossip and the finger pointing will never end. Sylvia might have a lot of friends but there are people in town who resent all the power she has in all the committees. She also has a lot of clout in the County Council and has been involved in many a row about planning and other things they decide.'

'It's amazing she does all that at her age,' Marian said.

'She's a real powerhouse,' Pierce said. He shook his head and sighed. 'I wish I knew who told John Peters all that stuff in such a way that he got interested. Must have been a long and detailed conversation.'

'Yes, wherever he heard it,' Marian agreed, her heart beating at the lie. She finished her coffee and stood up. 'Anyway, he'll sign the agreement and we've got him to delay the publication, so that's a good start. I'm glad you didn't tell him that you're my brother-in-law.'

'That might have made him pull out of dealing with us altogether,' Pierce said.

'But I think I told him I was working for my brother-in-law the last time we met,' Marian said as the memory of the lunch in Anascaul popped into her mind. 'But he doesn't seem to remember that.'

'I hope he never does,' Pierce said. 'Now all we have to do is get him to rewrite bits of the novel so nobody knows who he's writing about,' he remarked, his voice heavy with bewilderment. 'How do we do that? Any ideas?'

Marian shrugged. 'Not at the moment. I'll think about it.'

'So will I,' Pierce said. 'Maybe you could have a chat with him on your own? He seemed to like you.'

'Maybe,' Marian said. 'We'll see. In the meantime there's your party and my husband, who has just arrived. Sylvia said to bring him so he can meet everyone and I've invited him. But...' she paused, 'we're in the middle of a bit of a crisis at the moment, so I'm not sure that was a good idea.'

'Yes, Claire told me,' Pierce said. 'But why not? It might be good for the two of you to have a little fun. Forget your troubles for a while in all the chaos of the Fleury family barbecue with kids and dogs, beer, burnt food and all sorts of other mayhem.'

Marian smiled. 'That sounds like a lot of fun, I have to say.

Kids, dogs, beer, food, chaos. That could be just what we need to shake us up. Okay, I'll have a chat with Claire and then I'll tell Theo we're definitively going.' She picked up her bag. 'I'll see if she's still downstairs in Karina's office.'

'She is,' Pierce said. 'We're going home together. Anyway, I'll finish up here. Go and talk to Claire.'

'I will,' Marian said. 'See you Sunday.'

'Bye, and thanks for coming in. Let me know if you have a brainwave about John Peters,' Pierce said.

'Okay. But don't hold your breath.'

Marian went downstairs and found Claire in Karina's office, busy at the computer. She turned around as Marian knocked on the open door. 'Hi, how lovely to see you. I was just going to see if you were still upstairs. I heard you have a very exciting new client.'

'Yes,' Marian replied. 'You'll be excited to hear that it's John Peters.'

Claire's eyes widened. 'Wow, that is fabulous. You must be so thrilled to work with him.'

'Yes, well, in a way. But there are some problems we need to sort out,' Marian said. 'But that's not what I wanted to talk to you about. We haven't spoken for a few days so you might not know that Theo has just arrived.'

'Sylvia told me,' Claire said. 'How do you feel about him arriving out of the blue like that?'

'I'm not sure,' Marian said. 'In way I wish he hadn't come just now. But he's here and I have to deal with our problems. What I wanted to tell you was that Sylvia thinks I should bring him to your party on Sunday. Would that be okay?'

'Of course,' Claire said and got up from her chair. 'If you want to. It'll be fun, I think. A good way to see how he fits in with the family. A real baptism of fire,' she added with a chuckle.

'He's Australian,' Marian said with a wry smile. 'He's used to heat.' She sighed. 'But okay, I'll bring him.'

'Don't look so glum,' Claire said. 'We'll cheer you both up.'

'That'll take you a while.' Marian couldn't help smiling at Claire's enthusiasm. 'But thanks. I didn't want to ruin your happy moment, that's all.'

'Nothing can,' Claire said. 'I know I've kept you away from the house while we were doing all the work, but now that it's finished, I can't wait for you to see it. It's a small house with a huge garden, as you'll discover. Plenty of lawn for all the Fleury kids to run around on and lots of flowerbeds for me to weed.'

'I'm so looking forward to seeing it all,' Marian said. 'But now I'm going home to have a bit of a break before I see Theo tomorrow.'

'Okay,' Claire said. 'I have a few things to do here and then Pierce and I will go home together.'

'See you Sunday, then,' Marian said and left, walking out of the house feeling happier than before. Sunday would be a nice day. But first she had to get through Saturday.

She stood for a moment on the doorstep, looking down the leafy street at the view of the ocean and then up at the sky where clouds were drifting across the sun, changing the light from time to time. She breathed in the fresh, salt-laden air and wondered if Theo would one day feel as at home here as she did. Or would he always long for the intense tropical heat and humidity of Queensland? She knew that he was more adaptable than she was and usually settled in quickly in a new environment. He'd liked living in Dublin, but would he take to the wildness of Kerry where the weather was so unpredictable? She hoped he would and that the Fleurys would be as friendly and welcoming as they had been to her. But if they found out how she had given away all their secrets, they might not be willing to have either of them stay around. That thought was worrisome, but she pushed it away as soon as it appeared and closed the door behind her.

Someone was waiting for her in the front garden. Having been lost in her musings, Marian gave a start as Sean emerged from behind the rhododendron bush beside the gate.

'Marian,' he said, touching her arm. 'I want to talk to you.'

SEVENTEEN

Marian squinted at Sean in the late-afternoon sunshine. 'About what?'

'A few things,' he replied, his brown eyes slightly wary as he looked at her. 'Would you have time for a drink? Maybe somewhere on the Strand?'

'Oh,' she said, trying to recover from the shock of seeing him there. 'You gave me a fright, popping out from behind the bush. But yes, that would be great because I want to talk to you too.'

'Wonderful.' He beamed at her and opened the gate, ushering her through. 'After you, pretty lady.'

She couldn't help smiling at him as his eyes twinkled and a little smile played on his lips. 'You're very gallant all of a sudden.'

'I want to make up for my behaviour,' Sean said.

'That'll take you a while,' Marian remarked drily. 'I have already given out to you about recording me and then using what I said for the plot of your novel, so I'm not going to go on about that. It was sneaky and mean but you already know that.'

'I do,' he agreed cheerfully. 'So now I'll buy you a drink hoping you can forgive me sometime in the future.'

'You mean when hell freezes over? I will when you rewrite the story to erase any trace of likeness to the Fleury family,' Marian said as they started to walk down the street.

'That's a lot of rewriting,' Sean said. 'But maybe you could read the novel before you decide to hate me forever.'

'I intend to,' Marian said, beginning to enjoy herself. 'Read the novel, I mean,' she added with a chuckle, 'not hate you forever.' It gave her a little thrill to see the flirtatious look in his eyes. It made her feel both young and pretty, something that hadn't happened for a very long time. She was angry with him for what he had done, but she decided to put all that aside for now and simply enjoy his company. He seemed to be taking everything in his stride, not stuck-up at all about his success. And she liked that.

'I should hope not,' Sean said. 'I'd be very sad to think you hated me forever.'

'Forever is a long time,' she quipped as they arrived at the Strand, the street that ran along the harbour. She looked up at the blue sky where seagulls glided around, then out across the glittering water, and sighed happily. 'It's a lovely afternoon so let's forget about hate and problems and just enjoy it.'

'I agree,' he said and looked around. 'How about a drink at that restaurant over there with a terrace that has lovely views of the bay?'

'Yes, that's a very good choice,' she replied and turned to the left, walking towards the restaurant in question. 'They have great seafood there too.'

'Then we might stay for dinner,' he suggested.

'We'll see,' Marian said, laughing.

They went up the steps to the terrace and sat down at a small round table near the railings. A waitress appeared straight away and Sean ordered two glasses of rosé, asking if it was a French wine.

'Yes,' the waitress replied. 'It's from the South of France somewhere.'

'Hopefully Provence,' he said. 'Okay with you, Marian?'

'Yes, but just one glass,' she said. 'As I'm driving.'

'You're very well behaved,' he remarked. 'Not like that woman I met on the plane.'

'Oh her,' Marian said. 'I think I've left her behind. She was getting on my nerves, actually. Feeling sorry for herself, drinking too much wine, and telling family secrets to a perfect stranger.'

'I'm glad you think I'm perfect,' he quipped.

'Trying to trip me up, are you?' she asked. 'Like you did then.'

He folded his arms and looked at her. 'No, I'm trying to make you smile. And it worked. I like to see you smile like that.'

Marian's smile widened into a grin. Being with him like this, just chatting idly, made her feel so good. She knew she should be angry with him, but his good mood was so contagious. 'I'm not always glum, you know. It's just that life's been hard for me for a while.'

'Yes, I know. But I'm happy to hear that you have left that woman I met on the plane behind. You seem a lot more cheerful now. As if you've finally landed in a place called home.'

Marian laughed. 'Gosh, you're very poetic. You should write a book.'

'I don't know,' he shot back. 'It seems like a lot of hard work.'

'I'm sure it is,' Marian said. 'I wouldn't know where to start. And then doing all that editing and publishing all on your own. Your last novel, the one about a stranger coming home, really moved me. You're such a talented writer. It's quite amazing that no publisher has picked you up yet.'

'Oh, they have,' Sean said. 'I'm approached all the time. By publishers and agents. But I love being my own boss; I always have. I even thought that asking a publicist to do the marketing for me was kind of lazy. But I need to get my work out there more and not just be a local talent. So Pierce seemed to fit the bill as I heard he had great contacts where it matters most.'

'He does,' Marian said. 'He's been editing and publicising non-fiction books for a long time, so he's built up quite a network in Ireland.'

'So I gathered,' Sean said as the waitress arrived with their drinks. 'Thanks,' he said to her. 'Could you bring us some menus? Just in case we get hungry.'

'Of course,' she said and walked away.

'Not that you have to stay,' he said to Marian.

'I might, though,' Marian said and picked up her glass of chilled rosé. She lifted it up. 'Here's to your continued success.'

'And yours,' Sean said and clinked his glass against Marian's.

'My success at – what?' she asked when she had taken a sip.

'At life,' he said. 'At being happy again.'

Marian put down her glass. 'I'm not sure how to succeed at that. Right now, this moment, I'm enjoying myself, but there is some stuff I need to sort out before I can feel better about myself and my life.'

'And your marriage?' he asked softly, looking at her with sympathy.

'Yes, that's what I'm struggling with,' Marian admitted. 'But I don't want to talk about it.'

'In case I put your story into a novel?' he asked. 'I get that you wouldn't trust me with anything confidential again after that episode on the plane. But I would never put someone's marriage problems into a book. That's a personal tragedy I would never reveal. I've been through some heartbreaking things myself, so I have plenty to draw on without stealing anyone else's misery.'

'You have?' Marian asked, noticing that the light in his eyes had suddenly gone out.

'Yes,' he replied. 'So I know what you might be going through. I was married for over twenty years. Happy years,' he added. 'Until it all ended in tears – mostly mine.'

'I'm so sorry,' Marian said. 'That sounds a lot worse than what I'm going through.'

'Oh, I don't know,' he said. 'Why compare things that make us sad? It's like comparing the plague to cholera. Which is worse?'

Marian smiled at the comparison. 'You're right. No need to compete about who's suffering the most. Let's forget that for tonight.'

'You're right, we should.' Sean picked up the menus that the waitress had just put on the table and handed one to Marian. 'Will we stay on for dinner? God knows I could do with some decent food.'

'Oh, me too,' Marian said, pleased to see he was looking more cheerful. She picked up the menu and studied it for a while. 'Oh, look, they have sole on the bone. I'll have that. The fish here is very good, I've heard.'

'Great choice,' Sean said. 'I'll have that too.' He waved at the waitress and placed the order when she arrived at their table. Then he turned back to Marian. 'So,' he said, 'tell me about how you're finding Kerry.'

'It's truly wonderful,' she said. 'My family came from here but I had never been here before, as I told you.'

He nodded, looking amused. 'Because of that family feud, right?'

'Yes. That's what kept me from coming here. It's thanks to Claire that the two families connected again. And now, here I am, with my own little flat at Magnolia Manor and I love it.' She paused for a moment as the waitress arrived back with cutlery, napkins and a carafe of water. 'But now,' she continued when they were on their own again, 'my husband has arrived and he wants us to try to get back together. I think he's going to try to talk me into going back to Australia.'

'But you don't want to leave Kerry?' Sean asked gently. 'Now that you've discovered what a wonderful place it is.'

'Exactly,' Marian whispered. 'I'm only beginning to settle in, to get to know the family and to find roots I didn't know I had.'

'Do you still love him?' Sean asked.

Marian pondered the question for a moment. 'I do,' she said. 'But so much has changed. I don't know how to explain to him that this is where I want to live. Or to make him want to stay here too.'

'Make him discover the magic of this place,' Sean said. 'Let him see what makes it so special and why you love it so much.'

'Why do I love it? It's hard to put a finger on it,' Marian said. 'Kerry is so many things all at once.'

Sean nodded. 'Yes, that's very true. I wrote about what this place does to me in that novel, the one that's about to be published. I tried to put it in a nutshell.'

'What did you write?' Marian asked.

'I can't remember exactly, but it was something like this.' Sean leaned forward and said in a low voice: '"Kerry is not just a place. It's the hush between raindrops, the light in a stranger's smile, the lifelong friendship with people you know and love, and the wild heartbeat of the sea, whispering stories into the wind."'

'That's so beautiful,' Marian said, feeling tears well up at his words. 'It feels like a gift. Thank you.'

'You're very welcome,' he said and straightened up. 'But here is our dinner and it looks delicious,' he added as the waitress approached with two plates loaded with sole on the bone, new potatoes and vegetables that she carefully put in front of each of them.

They both started to eat, enjoying the delicate flavour of the fish, the buttered new potatoes and vegetables that came with it. Then Sean looked up from his plate and fixed Marian with his gaze. 'You said you wanted to talk to me. About the family secrets?'

'Not the family secrets as such,' Marian said when she had dabbed her mouth with her napkin. 'It's about Sylvia and what you found out about her. Or did you? I know she had some adventures in Paris when she was young, but then I wondered if you've made stuff up?'

He put down his knife and fork. 'I haven't made anything up, just changed things around to fit the plot of the novel.'

'That doesn't sound very reassuring,' she said.

'Oh, Marian,' he declared, his eyes boring into hers, 'I want you to understand that my novel is a declaration of love. For Kerry, for a family that is so embedded in the history of this town, and for my mother's family and her connection to everything in it. You'll see what I mean when you read the novel. I'm sure you will, because you said *A Stranger Comes Home* resonated with you. Your story inspired me, that's true, but there are so many other elements in the book as well. So much of it is part of me and my own memories. My childhood visits to my grandparents' little cottage that I now own and all that is part of me and my growing-up years.'

There was such passion his eyes that Marian forgot what she was going to say. His words had moved her in a way she hadn't expected. 'I think I'll have to read the novel as soon as possible,' she said. 'I have to try to grasp what you're trying to express. I have a feeling it's much more than a story written for effect, or to destroy the reputation of a family everyone knows and loves.'

He nodded. 'That's what I want you to discover. So can we leave this alone until you've read the story to the end?'

'Okay,' Marian said. 'If you promise that the secrets about Sylvia aren't detrimental.'

'Of course,' Sean said. 'I tried to be as respectful as possible. You'll see when you read the book. As soon as I get to my laptop, I'll send you the manuscript and you can check for yourself.'

Marian smiled, relieved, believing what he said.

'So, I think we'll finish our dinner and I'll go home and send it to both you and Pierce, who I think also has a vested interest in the book.'

'In more ways than one,' Marian said and got up. 'Thanks for dinner, Sean.' She waved at the waitress. 'I'll pay for my meal, of course.'

'Of course not,' Sean protested. 'Dinner is on me and no arguments,'

'I won't argue,' Marian said. 'Thank you again. It was lovely. I'll be in touch when I've read the novel.'

'Bye, Marian.' Sean rose and kissed Marian on both cheeks. Then he backed away. 'Sorry, I'm so used to the French way of saying hello and goodbye. It's not meant to be anything else.'

Marian smiled. 'I know. Arnaud, Sylvia's fiancé, does it all the time. I think it's charming.'

'That's good to know.' Sean smiled back at her. 'I enjoyed the evening. And I feel as if a very special friendship has started between us.'

'I think you're right,' Marian said, warmed by how his eyes sparkled when he looked at her. 'Despite everything. Bye for now.'

'See you soon, I hope,' Sean said, sitting down as she walked away.

Marian continued up the street to where she had parked her car, her mind full of everything that had happened tonight. The sun was slowly slipping into the sea, colouring the sky in a riot of red, pink and orange and the breeze gently ruffled her hair. What a lovely evening it had been, despite her concerns.

As she drove off all she could think of was what Sean had said about Kerry.

It is not just a place, it's the hush between raindrops, the light in a stranger's smile, the lifelong friendship with people you know and love, and the wild heartbeat of the sea, whispering stories into the wind.

Beautiful words and such a gorgeous description. But how could she make Theo see and feel it in his bones the way she did?

EIGHTEEN

Despite being exhausted, Marian couldn't go to sleep. Her conversation with Sean earlier that evening was going through her mind over and over again, especially what he had said about her marriage to Theo. She still felt a deep love for him, and she knew that would never go away. But the way he had acted since they moved to Australia had been both selfish and inconsiderate.

I was also at fault, she thought. *I could have tried harder and not complained so much. We were so in love at first, so united in everything we did. Then the children arrived and we were a happy family until the children left home. Was that what wrecked our relationship? Not being a family any more, just two people with separate needs and dreams?*

She wrestled with her thoughts and feelings until she finally fell into an uneasy sleep and woke up a few hours later, still unsettled and worried. Giving up on sleep, she sat up in bed and checked her emails and saw that Sean had sent the novel in Word format. Excited, she sent the document to her Kindle address and then picked it up to start reading. She felt she had to read at least the first chapters before she could reassure herself that the story was not too damning for the family.

Marian turned on her Kindle and clicked on the book with the title *Family Secrets* and it opened at the first chapter. She was soon so engrossed in the story that she knew she wouldn't be able to put it down.

The first chapter opened with a family party, and the birthday of the matriarch in the story, called Mary-Ellen Finegan, head of the Finegan family, who lived in a big country house on the edge of a cliff with views over Inch Beach and the surrounding countryside. The family was similar to the Fleurys, only there were more grandchildren who were boys and girls and not just three girls like Sylvia's granddaughters. It was sweeping saga and much of what had happened at Magnolia Manor was described in the novel in such a way that it would be obvious to anyone in Dingle whose story this was based on.

'Holy moly,' Marian muttered when she came to the bit about the gambling debt that would threaten the ownership of the country house, which, thinly disguised, was so obviously based on the real manor. And then the story about the twin brothers and the question of who was the rightful heir also came up, making Marian wince. But then she forgot to compare the two families, as she was transported to the world Sean had created, and the love affair he had with Kerry and its people.

It was a wonderful novel – full of intrigue, conflict and drama, and the descriptive passages made Marian feel she was really there, in the house and gardens, with all the characters John Peters had created, as if his pen was a brush that painted pictures so vivid that Marian felt she was seeing everything in front of her, and hearing the voices of the people in the book and feeling their heartbreaks and joy all mixed together. It was similar to the history of the Fleurys, but still different, even if some of the conflicts and problems were exactly what Marian had told Sean during that long and tedious flight when she had been so distraught and tired. The house wasn't quite the same as Magnolia Manor and the surroundings different, but it still resonated with her, as it would with everyone who knew the Fleurys. The author had included a few details to distract the reader and to the casual observer, the novel was truly fictional.

But despite all this, Marian knew this story would expose the family and all the secrets they had been so anxious to hide to the outside world. She felt so bad about her role in the whole mess that she began to cry, tears rolling down her cheeks until she was sobbing uncontrollably. She covered her face with her hands and pushed her Kindle aside, giving herself up to her grief, not just about what she had done, but also the failure of her marriage that she feared was never going to be resolved.

Will Sylvia ever forgive me if she finds out what I've done? she wondered. *And what about Theo? Will we ever be able to resolve our problems?*

The tears and grief made Marian tired and she finally fell asleep, exhausted by all the emotions. She had wanted to get to the part where the grandmother in the story went back to the memories of her youth, but sleep took over and Marian didn't wake up until late the following morning when her phone rang.

It was Theo, wondering what had happened to her. 'Weren't you supposed to call me at nine?' he asked, sounding slightly annoyed.

'Oh, no, I overslept,' Marian exclaimed. 'I'm so sorry, Theo. Why don't you come here and we'll go for a spin around Dingle? We'll take Claire's car that she lent to me and make a day of it. What did you think of Inch Beach?'

'Inch was good,' he said. 'The waves weren't like in Queensland, but I was told that surfing is really best here in the winter. Especially after a storm.'

'And then it's dangerous,' Marian remarked. *Will he ever grow up?* she wondered.

'Yeah, but you can still ride a wave or two,' Theo said.

'Come on, babe, shake a leg. Get out of bed and let's go and see the sights. Can't sit here all day.'

Marian smiled at the old nickname. He had called her 'babe' when they were first dating. 'Okay,' she said, feeling a dart of excitement that surprised her 'Give me half an hour and I'll be outside to meet you, all washed and dressed and shipshape.'

'You're a good sport,' he said, exaggerating his Australian accent.

'I try my best. See you soon,' Marian said, still smiling. Theo seemed in a good mood, which cheered her up. Whatever happened today, they wouldn't have a row.

'See ya,' he said and hung up.

Marian got out of bed and after a quick shower, pulled on her jeans and a green T-shirt with 'I love Kerry' in big white letters, just to emphasise her allegiance to the county she now considered her home. Then she pulled a brush through her hair, applied sunscreen and had a cup of tea and toast with a thick slice of cheese, and an apple. That done, she ran down the stairs, saying hello to an older woman appearing from one of the flats.

'Lovely day,' the woman said as they walked down the stairs together. 'I hope the weather holds. I'm going to Dingle to meet my grandchildren and I promised to take them to Murphy's ice cream shop.'

'I'm sure it will stay nice all day,' Marian said as they reached the front door. 'Have a lovely time with the grandkids.'

'I hope you have a lovely day, too,' the woman said before she got into her car and drove off, just as Theo arrived on foot up the avenue.

'So do I,' Marian mumbled as she walked down the steps to meet him.

'Hi,' he said and then awkwardly leaned forward to place a light kiss on her cheek.

Marian breathed in the familiar smell of lemon soap he had always used and then took a step back to look at him. 'You shaved,' she said, happy to see his smooth tanned skin and that the dark circles under his eyes were nearly gone. 'And you had a good rest. Feeling better?'

'Yes, much better,' he said, smiling.

'Great,' she said. 'So let's get going, then. My car is the red Yaris over there. Hope you won't find it too uncomfortable.'

'It's fine,' he assured her, and they got into the car, Theo squeezing his tall frame into the passenger seat with a little bit of wriggling. Then he grinned at Marian. 'Don't look so worried. I'm feeling great and looking forward to the drive. So come on, girl. Show me the sights and let's put our troubles on ice for a while, okay?'

She had to smile. His good mood was contagious and she found herself looking forward to the day ahead. 'Okay,' she said and started the car.

They were soon driving up the road towards Ventry and then Marian decided to take the Slea Head Drive, which would take them along the coast of the Dingle peninsula all the way to Ballyferriter. The views were spectacular and the sun came out of the clouds and shone on the sea that turned a deep turquoise in the bright light.

'Wow,' Theo said, looking out the window. 'Sky and sea all the way to the horizon. And the mountains plunging into the ocean and the green grass everywhere. It's all so incredible.' He rolled down the window. 'Just to feel that sea air,' he said. 'It's such a treat to have this fresh air coming at you all the time and not to have to hide from the sun. It nearly makes me feel drunk.'

Marian shook her head and laughed. 'You can have a pint of Guinness at the pub where we're having lunch. It's near Bally-ferriter on the edge of a cliff. Just wait till you see it. Then you'll be truly drunk, both from the Guinness and the stunning views.'

'You're spoiling me,' he said. 'Does this mean you think we have a chance?'

Marian slowed the car and stopped at a point that had views of both the mountainside and the ocean below. She looked at him for a moment. 'Yes, we might have a chance to get back together. But it depends on so many things. I need to keep the freedom I have found here. That is something I'll never give up.'

'You want us to live apart?' he asked, looking both confused and hurt.

'No, but...' Marian stopped. She knew she had to make Theo understand that she could only agree for them to get back together if they changed the way they lived and the way he saw her. She could no longer be his unofficial assistant who did everything while he went off to play on the beach with his mates. But it was too complicated and would take a long time for him to change his ways. 'Oh please, let's not talk about that now,' she sighed. 'You said we should take a break from our problems today. Let's just enjoy ourselves.' She started the car. 'We're nearly at the pub. They have great sandwiches.'

'Okay,' he said as they drove off. 'No more bellyaching from me. Or awkward questions.'

'Good,' Marian said, momentarily calmed. 'And tomorrow we have Pierce and Claire's barbecue.'

'When I'll be sized up by the whole Fleury family,' Theo said. 'That's a scary thought.'

'I'm sure you'll love them,' Marian said. 'They're such a fun bunch, you know.'

'Tell me about them,' Theo said. 'Just so I know what to expect.'

'I will, over lunch,' Marian promised, happy to have a safe subject to resort to instead of having to confront their marital problems.

.   .   .

When they were sitting at a table outside the little pub where the view of the Atlantic was breathtaking, Marian told Theo all about the Fleury family.

'First, there is Sylvia,' she started. 'The most amazing woman. She's in her mid-eighties but still beautiful in a patrician kind of way. Stylish, classy with a sharp eye and a wonderful sense of humour.'

'I'm in love with her already,' Theo said, biting into his ham and cheese sandwich.

'Everyone is,' Marian said fondly. 'Even if she can be a bit sharp at times.'

'That's even more interesting,' Theo remarked, taking a slug of his pint of Guinness. 'Someone who is sweet and kind all the time is not that much fun in the end.'

Marian nodded and nibbled at her sandwich with mozzarella and tomato laced with pesto. 'Sylvia is certainly not boring. Then there's Lily and Dominic,' she continued. 'Lily runs the café and garden centre at Magnolia Manor. It's behind the wall near the greenhouses. We can have lunch there sometime next week.'

Theo nodded, chewing. 'Great. And Dominic? What does he do?'

'He has a house restoration business. They do everything from building extensions to renovating, electricity, plumbing, bathrooms and so on. He also sings with a band that plays trad music in pubs on Saturday nights. '

'Must be a busy guy,' Theo remarked. 'Does he do all that himself or does he hire contractors?'

'I think he does a bit of both. Contractors and then some of his own workmen. Yes, they are very busy and are looking for staff all the time.' Marian noticed a sudden glint in Theo's eyes that hadn't been there before. But it was gone before she had a chance to analyse it. Maybe it was just that he thought Dominic would be interesting to talk to. Or was it the music? 'We could go and listen to them tonight if you want,' she said. 'They're playing in a pub in Dingle.'

'Is that The Fiddler's Elbow?' Theo asked. 'I saw some posters when I was walking past the pub near my B&B.'

'That's his band,' Marian said. 'You'll love them. What a great idea. Why didn't I think of it before?'

'Because you were too busy worrying about today,' Theo suggested, winking at her. 'You thought I'd be pressuring you to go back to Oz, weren't you?'

'I was,' Marian said. She smiled at him, sitting there, nursing a pint of Guinness, looking oddly at peace as he gazed at the lovely views and enjoyed the excellent sandwich. He looked comfortable and happier than when he had first arrived. It gave her a ray of hope. Maybe they could work out some kind of plan – or at least make peace? This thought cheered her up and she looked at Theo, feeling a more positive vibe between them.

'No pressure at all,' Theo said, closing his eyes to the sunshine, looking like a contented cat. 'This place is so relaxing. I just want to be on holiday from everything.'

'Oh yes,' Marian agreed, feeling her shoulders relax at his words. 'That's a good idea,' she said and, like him, closed her eyes to the sun. *Except I can't take a break from everything,* she thought. *I still have John Peters' novel and Sylvia's secret to worry about. And I never want to return to Australia. This isn't a holiday...*

'Marian?' a voice said in her ear.

She opened her eyes and discovered Colette, her friend from the book club, standing in front of their table. 'Hi,' she said, shading her eyes with her hand. 'What a surprise to see you here, Colette.'

'I'm here with my grandchildren,' Colette said, gesturing at two girls sitting at the next table eating ice cream. 'They wanted crisps and ice cream, so I gave them both.' She glanced at Theo, who had woken up from his trance.

Theo held out his hand. 'Hi there. I'm Theo,' he said. 'Marian's husband.'

'Oh, hi.' Colette smiled and shook his hand. 'I'm Colette. Marian's friend from the book club. Nice to meet you, Theo. So you're here on a visit from Australia?'

'That's right,' Theo said. 'But sit down and have a chat with Marian while I go in and pay.'

'Okay, just for a minute,' Colette said and sat down while Theo went into the pub. 'Well,' she said when Theo had disappeared inside. 'I just wanted to tell you something that might upset you. It's about John Peters' next novel. It was supposed to be published at the end of August, but now he has posted on his Facebook author page that he has to delay it for a month.'

'Oh,' Maran said. 'Well, I knew that. Pierce has just started working with him, actually.'

'Really? That must be fun,' Colette said. 'But that wasn't what I wanted to tell you. It's about the description of the book on Amazon. It seems that...' she paused for a moment, 'the family in the story looks *very* like the Fleury family, I have to say. There are certain details that might start rumours, you see. And then there is a hint that Sylvia – or the fictional grandmother – seems to have done things in her youth that could have caused a scandal at the time if it came out.' Colette drew breath and looked at Marian, waiting for her reaction. 'Actually,' she whispered, 'I heard people talking about it in the hairdresser's this morning. Mostly about Sylvia.'

NINETEEN

'Oh, no,' Marian said. 'So it's started, then. I was wondering when it would happen. The gossip, I mean.'

'Well, I'm not going to join in with the gossipmongers,' Colette said and got up as her granddaughters waved at her. 'I just thought you should know. I have to go. The girls want to go to Ballyferriter for a swim and they're getting restless. Oh, and your husband is very attractive,' she whispered in Marian's ear before she left. 'Okay, girls,' she called to her granddaughters who kept asking to go to the beach. 'Granny is coming. We'll chat later, Marian,' she said before she joined her grandchildren and ushered them into her car. 'See you, Marian,' she shouted through the window before she drove off.

'What was that all about?' Theo asked as he joined Marian. 'You look a little startled.'

'Just a bit of gossip,' Marian said. 'And she said you're very attractive.'

'Did she?' Theo beamed. 'What a lovely woman.'

'I knew you'd like her if I told you that,' Marian quipped, trying to push her concerns for Sylvia to the back of her mind

'But maybe we should get going too? Lots more to see and the roads are narrow and winding.'

'You didn't tell me about the rest of the Fleurys. I mean, you did before you met them, but now that you have, I'd like to hear your impressions of them.'

'I'll tell you while we're driving.'

'Great.'

They got into the car and were soon driving towards Ballyferriter, a tiny village on the tip of the Dingle peninsula. As she drove along the narrow country lane, Marian told Theo about the rest of the Fleurys. 'Tricia is the mother of the three girls. Lovely woman. Her partner, Cillian, was her late husband's best friend and they met up again after many years and fell in love. I think it must have been Fred's memory that united them or something. Anyway, they live together in Tricia's cottage and then Cillian sometimes takes off in his campervan and is gone for long periods. Seems to be an arrangement that suits them.'

'Wouldn't be my cup of tea,' Theo remarked.

'I know,' Marian said, tempted to comment that he liked to be waited on hand and foot, but she bit back the sour comment. No need to get into that kind of argument right now. 'Then there's Rose and Noel,' she breezed on. 'Rose runs the Magnolia business with the flats and the events and all that. Noel is a solicitor and works in Dingle. Rose is very nice, but a bit of a control freak, I think. She's very like Sylvia in character. Noel is a darling.'

'And the actor duo?' Theo asked.

'Vi and Jack,' Marian filled in. 'Gorgeous couple. Their twin boys are two and a half, so they're kept busy all day long. They take turns to stay at home with them as they have to go on location sometimes, especially Vi. Jack has switched from acting to writing screenplays and directing.'

'Interesting,' Theo said. 'But Lily and Rose also have kids, right?'

'Yes. Lily has two children. Naomi, who's nearly ten and Liam, who's five and a half. I think Rose and Noel's children are seven and four or something. But you'll meet them all tomorrow at the barbecue.'

'I'm a little nervous about it, I must confess,' Theo said. 'I don't like being scrutinised.'

'Ah, they won't scrutinise you,' Marian assured him. She knew she was the one who would be questioned, if Claire found out about the letter she had come across. But Theo wouldn't be silly enough to mention it, then tell Claire the reason why she'd fled to Ireland in the first place. 'They'll give you a beer and clap you on the back and ask you what sports you like. Don't worry about it.'

'Okay,' Theo said, not sounding convinced. 'I am looking forward to the trad music event in the pub tonight, though.'

'Yes, that'll be fun. And you'll meet Dominic and then you'll at least know him. I'll tell him to have a drink with us afterwards.'

'Great,' Theo said. 'That's someone I'll be interested to meet.'

Marian glanced at him. 'Why him particularly?'

'No reason,' Theo said, looking coy. 'Just something that occurred to me about him.'

'I see,' Marian said, her mind drifting to what Colette had said.

The gossip has started, she thought. *How long will it take before it's all over town? I'd better tell Sylvia tomorrow. I could reassure her about what Sean said. Maybe the secret he is writing about isn't as scandalous as I fear.*

Marian was still on edge that night as she made her way to the pub on a bike she had borrowed from Rose. This way she could have a drink without having to use her car. Theo would meet her there as his B&B was nearby. After bumping into Colette earlier, she knew she had to get Sylvia on her own tomorrow and tell her what was going on in town. She might already know, of course, as by now everyone must be talking about what was in the description of that book. There had been one or two hints from people she knew when she popped into the local grocery shop on her way back from their drive, but she had shrugged and said she had no idea what it was about.

She was sure the pub would be alive with the story, but as Marian entered, all eyes were on her and Theo, and she realised that they would be the subject for discussion tonight.

'Why is everyone staring at us?' he muttered in Marian's ear.

'Because they haven't seen us together yet,' she replied. 'And now they're wondering who you are and if we're an item.'

'Are we?' he asked, looking curiously at her.

She took his hand and kissed him on the cheek. 'For tonight, yes. I'll introduce you to a few people as my husband and then they'll all know within minutes.' She pulled him along with her and stopped at a table with three couples she knew. 'Hi,' she said in a loud voice to make herself heard in the noisy pub. 'I don't want to interrupt, but I just want to introduce you to my husband, Theo. He has just arrived from Australia.'

The group smiled and waved and shouted: 'Hi, Theo, welcome to the Kingdom.'

'Thank you,' Theo shouted back over the din of many voices laughing and chatting.

'Enjoy the music. They're a great band,' a woman called.

'I'm sure I will,' Theo replied, beaming at them.

There was a buzz in the pub while they sat down and waved and smiled at everyone and then ordered two pints of Guinness and crisps and olives to nibble on.

Then everyone seemed to have forgotten about them as The Fiddler's Elbow arrived on the small stage at the end of the pub and started to play. The music was so amazing that Marian forgot all her problems as she clapped and stamped her feet in time with the beat of the jigs and reels. Dominic's voice rang out across the silent, enthralled crowd, singing both sweet ballads in Irish and popular songs in English.

Marian watched as Theo was completely entranced by the music and Dominic's singing, so moved that he had to wipe a tear from his eyes, and squeeze Marian's hand so tight it hurt. She felt suddenly so close to him and realised that she had started to enjoy his company the way she used to in the old days. Then, when the band took a break, she went to the stage and introduced Theo to Dominic and then went to join two of the women from the book club while the men had a chat.

It was Tricia's friend Maggie, and another woman who introduced herself as Phil. She explained that they were there to listen to Dominic's band. 'Your husband is very handsome,' Maggie said before the conversation moved to the new gossip in town: the forthcoming book by John Peters and the connection with the Fleury family.

'It's all over town,' Phil said. 'And everyone is wondering if that gambling debt story is true and then trying to guess what Sylvia was up to in the sixties.'

'I don't think anyone knows that,' Marian said.

'Well,' Phil said. 'My mother went to school with her and she remembered when Sylvia came back from Paris, newly engaged to Liam, who she had met somewhere in France. They got married very soon after that, and everyone wondered why the wedding was so rushed.'

'I can imagine what they thought,' Marian said, amused.

'Yeah, well in those days, when someone got married, everyone counted the months between the wedding and the birth of the first child,' Phil said with a smile. 'But then, my mum said, Fred was born a whole ten months after that so the gossip died down and Sylvia was soon a very respected member of the Fleury family. In fact, she ran the place nearly straight away, Mum said.'

'But now they're all wondering what happened in Paris,' the woman called Maggie interjected.

'Maybe it should stay in Paris?' Marian suggested.

'Ah, but the cat is out of the bag now,' Phil cut in. 'And you can't put it back in, if you see what I mean.'

Marian nodded. 'I do.' She didn't want to say too much about what she knew. 'Well, the proof of the pudding is in the eating,' she said. 'Or in this case, the reading of the book.'

'I'd say it's going to be something spectacular,' Phil remarked.

'I can't wait to find out,' Maggie said.

'Shh, they're back,' Phil said as the band reappeared on the stage.

Marian went back to her table and waved at Theo, who was slowly approaching through the crowd as the first bars of 'Danny Boy' rang out. He sat down and shot a wide smile at Marian. 'Great guy,' he whispered.

Marian was about to ask him what he had been discussing with Dominic but then all was quiet again in the pub as the band played on and Dominic sang a few ballads before they finished and bowed to the standing ovation and shouts of 'More!'

As the lights dimmed and they all filed to the exit of the pub, a lot of people came up to Theo and Marian to say hello and welcome to Theo. Marian stepped outside and breathed in the cool air, a relief from the heat and stuffiness of the crowded interior. She was happy that Theo had received such a welcome and felt it was a good omen to the rest of his stay. Maybe he would feel differently about Kerry, Ireland and her need to stay here for good. She said a little prayer to the stars twinkling above her in the dark sky, hoping it would all come true in the end – in one way or another.

'Are you tired?' Theo asked behind her.

Marian turned around and smiled at him in the dim light. 'Not really. Just enjoying the cool night air after the heat inside.'

He took her hand. 'Such a nice evening. Everyone was amazingly friendly. And the music was great. Thanks for bringing me here tonight.'

She touched his cheek, wanting to kiss him but then felt it was too soon. She didn't want to rush things. They still had so much to discuss. She knew she loved him but she had an odd feeling of not wanting to let him in just yet. She had found a wonderful freedom here and a family that had welcomed her as their own and she didn't want to lose that. 'I'm glad you enjoyed it,' she said softly.

'I really did.' He squeezed her hand. 'But now you have so much on your mind and things to resolve. And I need to think about a lot of stuff, too.'

'Thank you for understanding,' she said. His words had reminded her of Sylvia and what might be in that novel. She suddenly felt an urge to get back home and get to the part that would reveal whatever it was Sean had discovered. 'I have to go,' she murmured.

'I know,' Theo said. 'Goodnight, Marian. See you tomorrow.'

After saying goodbye to Theo, Marian cycled home so fast her legs burned. She had to read the rest of John Peters' book to see what was in it that would be so damning to Sylvia. It had to be something he had found out and then used in his story, possibly exaggerated for effect, which would make the gossip even more juicy. If it was really bad, she would have to contact him and make him delete the worst bits. How she was going to do that, she had no idea. She only knew that even though she had not said anything about Sylvia's past during that fateful night on the plane, her story had sparked his interest and inspired him to write this novel.

Once home, Marian parked the bike in the bike shed and hurried up the stairs, arriving breathless to the flat where she threw her handbag on the sofa and went into the bedroom to find her Kindle that had slipped from her bed. She picked it up from the floor, switched on her reading light and lay down, opening her Kindle and started reading. The story, although absorbing, was still not at the place where the fictional grandmother reminisced her youth, so Marian flicked through a few chapters until she found what she was looking for: a flashback to 1960. The young woman had just arrived in Paris and...

Marian held her breath while she read on. This was incredible, mind boggling and quite shocking, really. If this was true, and Sylvia had really been involved in something like this, Marian knew she had to contact Sean as soon as possible.

TWENTY

The startling content of the novel went through Marian's mind as they drove to Claire and Pierce's new house the next day. Theo had picked her up in his rented Toyota saying it was his turn to do the driving. She had tried Sean's number that he had given to her the last time they met, but it went to voicemail. She had told him to call her back as soon as he could about an urgent matter, but so far there had been no sign of life from him at all. She had also sent several text messages, but there was still no response. It made her nearly sick with nerves and she knew she had to warn Sylvia about what she had read.

Theo shot a look at her as they neared the house. 'What's the matter? You look worried. Is it me?'

'No,' Marian said. 'Nothing to do with you. Something I have to talk to Sylvia about and I don't know how to put it to her.'

'You have to try to be gentle with the old lady,' Theo said.

Marian had to laugh. 'Wait till you meet her. She's tougher than you think. I just want to make sure she doesn't find out... Oh, never mind.' Marian had been about to tell Theo about her part in the story, but stopped herself in time. He didn't need to know she had been drinking wine and talking about herself and her family with another man on the plane. 'By the way,' she said, quickly changing the subject, 'what were you talking to Dominic about last night?'

'Oh, just something we're both interested in,' he said cryptically. 'Hey, is this the house?'

Marian looked up at the bungalow on the hill that rose above them. It was whitewashed with a slate roof and the front garden had an array of hydrangea bushes in full bloom in a riot of purple, brilliant blue and white. 'It looks fabulous. What a wonderful home they have made.'

'A bit small, though,' Theo remarked.

'Yes, but it's only the two of them most of the time,' Marian replied. 'Except when Jo, Pierce's teenage daughter, comes for a visit. They have three bedrooms, so that's not a problem. And Pierce insisted that she has her own bathroom as well, so they added that in an extension at the back of the house.'

'Smart move,' Theo said. 'Remember what Rebecca was like as a teenager?'

'I do.' Marian smiled at the memory. 'She was constantly locking herself in the bathroom, so nobody could come in.'

'We had to move to a bigger house with two bathrooms. And then Conor and Rebecca used to fight about whose turn it was to be in the second bathroom,' Theo said as he pulled in at the side of the road. 'Should I park here?'

'No. Go up to the house. Claire said there's plenty of space for several cars.' Marian sat there, momentarily stunned by the reminder that they had once been a family. And mostly happy, taking everything in their stride. *We were a team then,* she thought. *So united through every storm.*

'Okay.' Theo drove slowly up the driveway and when they had reached the top, they saw that there was indeed plenty of room beside three cars that were already parked on the tarmac in front of the house.

Marian got out of the car and stood looking at the panoramic views of Ventry Harbour. She could see the wide sweep of the sandy beach, and boats swaying on the waves further out. 'Gosh, this is lovely,' she exclaimed. 'I didn't know the views were so great from here.'

'Gorgeous spot,' Theo said behind her. 'Very similar to a house I saw...' He stopped.

'You saw where?' Marian asked.

'Oh, somewhere in Dingle when I was walking around,' Theo mumbled.

'Okay. Well, anyway, let's get the housewarming gift and the bottles of wine,' Marian said and opened the boot of the car. Then she saw that besides the gift-wrapped box and the three bottles of wine, there were also some tools and two small pots of paint. 'What's this?' she asked, pointing at the items.

'Oh, that,' Theo said. 'Uh, just something I picked up for Dominic on my way to meet you.'

'Really?' Marian glanced at him, feeling he wasn't telling the truth. 'Can't he pick up his own stuff?'

'Oh, well, it's...' He stopped and pushed his fingers through his hair. 'Look, Marian, this is about something that I can't tell you about yet. But in the end, I think you'll approve.'

They were interrupted by the door opening and Claire rushing out to meet them. 'Hi,' she squealed, 'you're here at last. Everyone has arrived and Pierce has just lit the barbecue.' She glanced up at the sky where dark clouds were drifting in, hiding the sun. 'We have to get started before the rain begins.' She hugged them both in turn and then went back up the steps and held the door open. 'Have a quick tour of the house and then we'll go out to our new deck.'

'Great,' Marian said and followed Claire into a bright hall with a wooden floor and walls painted a light green. There was an antique hallstand, a shelf for hats and an umbrella stand. Then they went down a corridor to the bedrooms which were all cosy with colourful rugs and walls hung with prints of landscapes and seascapes of Kerry. The kitchen had an island in the middle and a wood-burning stove opposite the cooker and fridge. A kitchen table stood under the window that had lovely views of the mountains. Then they went into the large living room furnished with a mixture of old and new.

'Some of the furniture came from Magnolia Manor,' Claire explained, showing them a chintz sofa with two matching armchairs.

'It's gorgeous,' Marian said and handed Claire the parcel. 'This will go well with your décor.'

'Thank you, Marian.' Claire tore the wrapping from the parcel and discovered a throw in shades of green, turquoise and navy. 'How lovely,' she exclaimed and draped the throw on the arm of the light green sofa. 'The colours of the sea. It matches my colour scheme perfectly.'

'I had to guess,' Marian said. 'But I knew what colours you like, so it wasn't that hard.'

'You're the best sister,' Claire said. 'But now we must go out on the deck.'

They stepped through the French windows that opened to a deck where most of the family were gathered. The back garden consisted of a wide sloping lawn, where all the children were running around playing a game with a large beach ball, screaming and laughing.

'What a lovely space,' Marian said as she took in the views of the mountains on one side and the ocean on the other.

'Marian, welcome,' Pierce said and gave her a hug. Then he shook hands with Theo. 'Hi, Theo and welcome. I'm so glad to have an Aussie onboard. Could you give me a hand with the barbecue?' He gestured at a large barbecue emitting smoke at the end of the deck. 'I'm not sure when to put the meat on and then I always overcook it.'

'G'day, Pierce,' Theo said. 'Nice to meet you at last. I'll be happy to help out with the steaks and stuff.'

'He has to meet everyone first,' Marian cut in. 'So we'll do the introductions and then Theo can give you a few pointers.'

'Wait for the charcoal to turn white,' Theo said to Pierce before Marian led him away to meet the others.

They were all gathered around Sylvia, who stepped forward to greet Theo. She shook his hand and beamed her most charming smile at him. 'So this is the Aussie hunk,' she joked. 'I must say I'm not disappointed. You're a sight for sore eyes, Theo. I hope you're enjoying your stay here.'

'So far it's been brilliant.' Theo smiled back at Sylvia, who looked at her most stylish and youthful tonight wearing blue linen slacks and a flowing blue and green paisley silk shirt.

Arnaud, standing beside Sylvia, smiled and took Theo's hand in a warm handshake. 'Welcome,' he said. 'We've heard so much about you.'

Rose was next, followed by Vi and Lily and they all surrounded Theo, asking him about Queensland and the surfing scene there. Then the men joined them and Theo soon found himself surrounded by the whole Fleury family.

The children were making so much noise it was hard to hear what anyone was saying. But the voices and screams receded into the background as Marian stared at Sylvia, thinking about what she had read in Sean's novel.

Sylvia met Marian's gaze and went to her side. 'What's the matter?' she asked.

'The novel,' Marian said. 'Is it true?'

'Is what true?' Sylvia asked in a low voice.

'I've just read the whole story,' Marian explained. 'I mean, that novel on Amazon. Pierce is doing the publicity, so the author made it available to us before publication. And now I've read the part which was inspired by your... I mean, what he must have found out about you and then exaggerated to put in his book to make the story even more exciting.'

'So what did this fictional woman who was modelled on me do that was so exciting?' Sylvia asked with an ironic twist to her mouth.

'Well, she—' Marian started but was interrupted by Rose, who had joined them.

'Are you talking about all the gossip that's going around?' Rose asked. 'That novel is up on Amazon and I've been told the blurb hints at some kind of shocking facts that are going to be revealed once it comes out.'

'Yes,' Sylvia said. 'Marian seems very worried about it.'

'Aren't you worried, too, Granny?' Rose asked. 'The guessing is getting wilder and wilder.'

Sylvia shrugged. 'Am I worried? Yes and no. I don't know what's actually in the novel. Marian was about to tell me.'

Rose stared at Marian. 'You've read it?'

Marian nodded. 'Yes. Last night. We're doing the publicity, you see.'

Rose stared at Marian. 'You're doing the publicity? For a book that will reveal all the family secrets? This seems really weird to me.'

'I know,' Marian said. 'To me as well. But we figured that this way we might be able to have things changed. We've already managed to have the author push the publication to late September.'

'And you're hoping to have talked him into some rewrites by then?' Rose enquired.

'Well, yes, if we can,' Marian said.

'So what is it that's so bad?' Rose asked. 'Will it cast a shadow over our family?'

'Well, of course it's fiction and the author has a disclaimer at the beginning of the book,' Marian started.

'Not worth the paper it's written on,' Rose said with a snort.

'Ask Noel; he's always saying that a disclaimer doesn't mean anything. You can sue, Granny, if it turns out that the content in the book is untrue and damages you in any way.'

'Yes,' Sylvia said. 'But what if it isn't?'

Rose stared at her grandmother. 'You mean... it might all be true?'

'I have no idea,' Sylvia said. 'As I haven't read the novel yet.'

'But I have,' Marian said. 'Last night. So I know what's in it, and if all that is true, I have to say I'm impressed.'

'With what?' Rose asked, looking from Marian to Sylvia.

'With the young woman who came to Paris and...' Marian stopped as Sylvia put a finger to her mouth.

'Not yet, Marian,' Sylvia said. 'I will tell everyone the true story and what I'm going to do about it in a minute. Let's enjoy the dinner first, and then I'll make a speech afterwards.'

'Okay, Granny,' Rose said with a resigned sigh. 'We'll do it your way.'

'Don't we always?' Sylvia said over her shoulder as she walked away.

Rose laughed and nodded. 'Oh yes, we do. Come on, Marian, I forgot about dinner and everything but now I see that Theo and Pierce have cooked up a storm at the barbecue. And it smells divine.'

Marian had to agree. The smell of barbecued meat and sausages was so enticing that she had momentarily managed to forget Sylvia's secret and her promise to reveal all. It also brought her back to their own back garden years ago, the Sunday barbecue and the family gathered around the table on the deck on a summer's evening. She remembered what a lovely dad Theo had been when the children were small, weaving magic into everyday things: blowing on a dandelion and telling the children they were blowing wishes into the wind, looking for shapes of animals among the clouds and even making a daisy chain and gently putting it on

Rebecca's dark blonde hair when she was three. And now she watched him handing the Fleury children bread rolls with sausages, telling them to eat them carefully because they were hot, and making sure every one of them were served before the adults.

'Theo has a great way with kids,' Lily said to Marian when they were sitting down at the table with loaded plates. 'He must have been such a good dad.'

'Yes, he was,' Marian said, looking at Theo with a dart of affection close to love that surprised her. She suddenly saw the gentle, caring side to Theo that she had forgotten about. It was a reminder that they would one day have grandchildren and that Theo would be a wonderful granddad. But if they were to separate, the grandchildren would have to deal with grandparents that were at odds with one another, and that would not be a good way for them to grow up. *If only*, she thought, *we could come to terms with what is dividing us and settle down in this beautiful place. He has to reveal his feelings too, instead of keeping it all to himself. Then and only then can we be happy. Why can't he see that?*

When everyone, including the children, had finished and the plates had been cleared away to make room for dessert, Sylvia stood up and clapped her hands. 'I'm going to make a little speech,' she said when everyone fell silent. 'Before the rain starts and we have to run inside.'

'Can we have ice cream first?' Naomi, the eldest of the children, asked.

'With sprinkles,' her cousin Sophie said.

Sylvia nodded. 'Yes, serve all the children ice cream and then they can eat it while I talk. With sprinkles and wafers and whatever they want.'

'Good idea,' Lily whispered to Marian. 'That way, they'll be quiet for a bit.'

The children were quickly given ice cream topped with

sprinkles and they started eating at once, looking at Sylvia with big eyes.

'Are you going to tell us a story, Granny Sylvia?' little Liam asked.

'That's right,' Sylvia said. 'I'm going to tell you a story about a young girl called Sylvia, just like me, who went to Paris a very long time ago to learn French, see the world and have a little fun.'

Marian stared at Sylvia standing there, looking so composed, as she waited for the revelation and wondered if it matched the plot of the novel. But as Sylvia began, Marian knew that the real story was much better than any fiction.

'I will tell it like a story, or fairy tale, if you like,' Sylvia started. 'Because that's what it was like for me. Ever since I had landed in Paris, I felt as if I was in some magical fantasy. Paris was so amazing, so beautiful and so big to me, a country girl. The buildings were so huge and beautiful, all that Haussmann architecture, the wide streets, the beautiful squares were all so overwhelming with its grandeur. I was employed as an au pair girl with a wealthy family who lived in a huge apartment near the Champs-Élysées. I was in charge of two small girls of nine and seven and I was expected to give them breakfast, take them to school and pick them up and mind them until their parents came home.'

'What were their names?' Naomi wanted to know.

'Anne-Marie and Clothilde,' Sylvia replied. 'Nice girls, if a little spoiled. But this story is not about them. I only stayed with that family for about five months.'

'Why?' Sophie asked.

'Because I found something more exciting to do,' Sylvia said. 'I was only twenty years old and minding children soon became a little tedious. I hadn't planned to leave, but something happened – or I should say someone did. I met a woman who changed my life forever. If I had not been at the Irish College in Paris that night, my life might not have taken the direction it did.'

'The Irish College?' Rose asked. 'What's that? Some kind of Irish cultural centre?'

'Something like that,' Sylvia replied. 'It was called the Irish College then. In any case, I had been taking Irish dancing lessons there in my free time and our class did a Christmas show. And that night, there was a woman in the audience who offered me a job in her dance troupe. Her name was Margaret Kelly and she was—'

'I know,' Vi exclaimed. 'She started the famous Bluebell Girls dance troupe. I just read an article about her somewhere. She was such an amazing woman.'

'That's right,' Sylvia said. 'But I had never heard of them, being a country girl just out of Kerry. In any case, she told me about it after the show over a cup of tea. She said she had watched me dance a few times at the college and she was looking for new dancers. I was tall, had good legs and showed talent as a dancer, she said. Then she asked if I'd like to come and audition at the Lido the next day. I didn't even know where the Lido was or what kind of dancing they did there, but I soon found out.'

'I bet you did,' Vi said with a wink.

'Yes,' Sylvia said, her eyes shining. 'I entered a world I didn't know existed. That theatre was like an Aladdin's cave of glitz and glamour. It was all so seductive. I auditioned in front of Margaret Kelly, her assistant and the manager of the Lido. They asked me to kick as high as I could, to do a twirl and a split and a few other moves and then I was offered a job as a dancer with the Bluebell Girls. I was over the moon and immediately left the family and moved into a tiny flat with one of the other girls. Her name was Ciara and she was from Kerry like me. I started rehearsals the very next day and was fitted for a costume, and then that was it. I was a Bluebell Girl dancing at the Lido.' Sylvia paused and looked around the table, where everyone was silent, staring at her in shock.

'You were a Bluebell Girl?' Rose said in a hoarse voice. 'Dancing nearly naked?'

'Yes,' Sylvia said. 'But not that naked. There were a lot of sequins all over my body. And feathers in my hair.'

'Wow,' Vi whispered, her face pale. 'That is so cool.'

'Incredible,' Dominic said.

'Fabulous,' Rose agreed. She raised her glass of wine. 'Here's to our granny, the Bluebell Girl.'

They all cheered and clinked glasses while Arnaud stood up and kissed Sylvia. 'My wonderful fiancée.'

'Did you know, Arnaud?' Lily asked.

'*Mais oui*,' Arnaud replied. 'Sylvia told me just before we got engaged. Like you, I thought it was incredible. But I agreed not to tell anyone. It had to be kept a secret until Sylvia chose to tell you. It is, after all, not my story.'

'I've been to the Irish Cultural Centre,' Noel cut in. 'It's in a beautiful eighteenth-century building. It was a seminary for priests from the sixteen hundreds or so in another place and then they moved to this one, near the Pantheon in the eighteenth century. I forget the whole story but that's what I remember.'

'Margaret Kelly's story is also quite amazing,' Sylvia interjected. 'She was such an inspiration to all of us girls. And she was very strict with all of us. No drinking, no socialising with male guests. Any girl who broke the rules was fired on the spot.'

'Strait-laced exotic dancers,' Dominic said with a laugh. 'What an oxymoron.'

'Margaret Kelly was a dancer herself,' Vi said, looking at her phone. 'She was in the Folies Bergère and then formed her own dance troupe called Les Blue Belles Paramount Girls, who danced during the intervals at cinemas in the early thirties. And she married a musician who was Jewish and arrested during the Second World War. Her husband was imprisoned in a camp for Jews in the Pyrenees. He escaped and she hid him in a Paris attic until the Occupation ended. She survived interrogation by the Gestapo, a gunfight between black marketeers in a night-club and a shoot-out between the Resistance and the Germans. Wow.' Vi drew breath. 'Wouldn't it be a blast to get to play her in a movie?' She turned to her husband. 'Hey, Jack, how about writing a screenplay about this woman?'

'I'd rather write a screenplay about Sylvia,' Jack replied. He turned to Sylvia, who was still standing, waiting for the excitement to die down. 'Let's hear the rest of the story. I have a feeling there's more.'

Sylvia nodded. 'Yes, a little more.'

'It's about Granddad, isn't it?' Lily asked.

Sylvia smiled wistfully. 'Yes. It's about how I met him.'

'On a train,' Rose said. 'I always thought that was so romantic.'

Sylvia nodded and took a sip of wine. Then she sat down. 'It was romantic and sweet and it felt so right.'

'But why were you on a train?' Lily asked. 'And where was it going?'

'The dance troupe had performed in Nice and we were all on the way back to Paris,' Sylvia said. 'We sat in the bar of the train while our beds were being organised in the *couchettes*. Those are the cheapest form of sleeping compartments on French trains. You sleep on a kind of shelf, six in each compartment. Not very comfortable but better than sitting up all night. While we were waiting, I started to talk to a young man sitting beside me in the bar who told me he was from Ireland. He was tall with reddish-blond hair and sparkling green eyes. When we started chatting, I discovered that he was from Kerry like me, but from the other side of Dingle. I grew up in a little village called Camp overlooking Tralee Bay. Of course, when he introduced himself I realised that he was one of the famous Fleurys from Magnolia Manor that I had heard so much about.'

'But why was he on a train from Nice to Paris?' Lily asked.

'He was on holiday. He said he always wanted to see the French Riviera, so he had gone there early in the summer when he had just finished college. And now he was on his way to Paris to see the sights and then he would go home to Kerry to take up his duties running the family business. His father, Cornelius, was not well and his mother had died two years earlier, so he was needed at home. "Just a few days in Paris," he said. And then he asked what I was doing on a train to Paris from Nice. I said I was a dancer with the Bluebell Girls at the Lido, which he thought was fascinating.'

'Was he a little shocked to hear where you worked?' Rose asked.

'No. Funny,' Sylvia said, 'when I think about it, his reaction to what I told him was so calm. There was no shock-horror, winking or suggestion that there was anything wrong with what I did, or that the girls I was with were in anyway sleazy. He asked me about my work and I told him about the long, hard rehearsals for many hours each day. I also told him about Margaret Kelly and her story and he was so impressed with her courage. The we talked about growing up in Kerry and where we went to school.' Sylvia stared into the near distance, her eyes misty. 'We sat down on a window seat and stayed there all night while everyone went to the sleeping compartments. I think I went to sleep for a while with my head on Liam's shoulder. I woke up when the train rolled into Gare St-Lazare and our eyes met. Liam took my hand and said he wanted to see me again. So I asked him to come to the Lido to watch me dance and then we could go to dinner afterwards at an all-night restaurant.'

'And then what happened?' Naomi piped up. 'Did Granddad Liam come to see you dance and take you to dinner?'

Sylvia smiled and nodded. 'Yes, he did. All of that. And then he had to go back to Ireland and I had to stay and work out my contract. He asked me to marry him just before he left. We had only known each other a few days, but I knew that we were meant to be together for good.'

'You must have felt so sad to have to part,' Vi said, looking very moved by Sylvia's story.

'I was heartbroken,' Sylvia replied. 'But after he had left, I talked to Margaret Kelly and she agreed to release me. She said that when you meet the love of your life, you have to follow him and not let him get away.'

'A very wise woman,' Theo said with a knowing look at Marian, who blushed.

'She was right,' Sylvia said. 'I knew that as soon as she said it. If I didn't go back to Ireland, I would lose the man I knew I would love all my life. So I got on the first plane to Dublin and then took the bus to Dingle and phoned him at Magnolia Manor. The old butler who was still there answered the phone. He was an awful snob and didn't approve of girls asking to talk to the young master late at night. But he did finally agree to deliver a message and then Liam called me back at the guest-house where I was staying. And then the next morning, he arrived in his little sports car and took me to Magnolia Manor and introduced me to his father. We got on like a house on fire straight away. And to cut a long story short, we were married as soon as it could be arranged. Of course everyone thought there was a baby on the way, but that was not the reason we got married so soon.' Sylvia drew breath and looked around the table. 'So that's the real, true story. I don't know what's in that book, but I'm sure Marian can tell us.'

Marian looked at Sylvia, trying to think of an answer.

TWENTY-TWO

'It's similar to your story, but not in any way as exciting,' Marian said, still trying to recover from the shock of Sylvia's revelations. It was such a wonderful romantic story and John Peters' novel paled in comparison. 'The woman in the novel isn't anything like you. She did join a dance company, but not the Bluebell Girls. It was at the Moulin Rouge and not the way Sylvia told it. And then the woman did meet a man on a train, but the details are very different.'

'That's a relief.' Sylvia smiled. 'Well, my story should raise a few eyebrows before that book comes out.'

'In what way?' Marian asked.

'My plan,' Sylvia said, 'is to publish my memoirs – or autobiography, if you prefer. I have been working on it for a long time, you see, and the manuscript is now finished. I wasn't quite sure when to announce it, but when I heard about that novel, I decided that now was the time to go public. So I urged my editor to finish and we're now ready to get it out there.'

'What?' Rose said, looking surprised. 'You've been working on your memoirs? So that's what you've been doing all afternoon when you were pretending to be resting.'

'Resting?' Sylvia repeated with a derisory snort. 'Who needs a rest when you can be writing? But yes, I have been telling a little fib here and there so I could have some peace and quiet. I've been writing this for the past two years.' She shot a tender look at Arnaud. 'My dear fiancé suggested it after I told him the story. He's been reading it along the way.'

'It's wonderful,' Arnaud said and kissed her fingers. 'So well written.'

'But what about editing and proofreading?' Marian asked. 'Have you been able to do all that yourself?'

'No,' Sylvia replied. 'I have a brilliant freelance editor who's been helping me to put it all together, photos and letters and so on. And I plan to publish it very soon.'

'How clever,' Pierce exclaimed. 'And you know I can help with the publicity free of charge if you want.'

'No thanks,' Sylvia said sternly. 'Pierce, you have agreed to do the publicity for John Peters' novel. You can't do mine at the same time. In any case, I'm going to do it all on my own.'

'On your own? But what about all the media coverage and Facebook and Instagram and all that?' Pierce protested. 'Can you manage all that?'

'I can and I will,' Sylvia retorted. 'I have my first radio interview on Tuesday.'

'What? Where?' Vi exclaimed.

'Kerry radio at eight p.m.,' Sylvia replied. '*At Home with Noreen*. Everyone in Dingle listens to that show.'

'Oh,' Lily said. 'That's a great move. It's a very popular programme. It will put an end to all the guessing and gossiping.'

'And it might kill John Peters' novel as well,' Pierce said glumly. 'At least around here where he has been doing so well.'

'I should hope so,' Sylvia snapped. 'Serve him right after all the trouble he's caused.'

'When will we be able to read your book, Granny?' Rose asked. 'We could do a launch at Magnolia Manor and invite everyone. And sell tickets to that event,' she added, looking excited.

'No, that's not going to happen, Rose,' Sylvia said sternly. 'I don't want to sell tickets for people to come to the launch. That is simply not done.'

Rose looked suddenly contrite. 'I know. Sorry, Granny.'

'But a launch in the manor would be a good idea,' Sylvia said. 'And the book could be on sale then, of course, and I could donate part of the profit to the coffers as we seem to be running a little short this month because of the leak in the basement. In any case, the memoirs will be published on Amazon in Kindle format on Wednesday, the day after the radio interview. The paperback will be available for sale through something called POD.'

'Print on demand,' Pierce cut in. 'That's a good thing to do.'

'I can order a number of copies for the launch,' Sylvia said. 'I have someone doing all the social media things for me. In fact, I have hired a book designer who will do all the uploading on Amazon and the other Internet book things, whatever it's called. Her name is Jane and she lives in England. Charming woman.'

'Ebooks,' Rose said. 'For all other outlets like Apple and so on.'

'That's right.' Sylvia shot Rose a smile. 'I don't know all the terms or the techniques. But there are a lot of willing helpers out there.'

Marian looked thoughtfully at Sylvia while she took all this in. What a genius Sylvia was to have organised all this all by herself. Marian felt a surge of admiration for this elderly woman who had the guts and brains to fight back against someone who had tried to ruin her reputation for his own gain. Whatever was in John Peters' novel would not be of any importance after this. She was sure the Radio Kerry interview would be noticed nationwide and it wouldn't take long for Sylvia's story to go viral. Sylvia had no issue being totally honest with the whole world about her story, while Marian had been lying by omission to the family who had welcomed her with open arms. But she had felt a sense of shame about betraying the Fleury family's secrets, just as Sylvia must have felt when she arrived back in Ireland, not being able to tell anyone about her adventures in Paris. And then Marian had also kept quiet about her problems with Theo. She wished she could finally stop lying to everyone, especially to Theo.

When Sylvia ended her tale, Marian exchanged a look with Pierce, who shrugged and smiled, as if to say, 'What can we do?' while everyone started talking at once and the children, having been lulled to near sleep by Sylvia's speech, woke up. Fat raindrops suddenly fell from the leaden sky, turning swiftly to torrential rain, and everyone rushed inside, carrying plates and glasses, cushions and small children, arriving in the living room dripping and laughing at it all.

Theo joined Marian as she helped put everything into the kitchen. 'What a party,' he said. 'And what a woman.'

'I know.' Marian put the stack of plates she was carrying on the table. 'I really didn't expect all this. Even though it was hinted at in that novel. The woman in the book isn't half as adventurous, even if the blurb suggests it. I think it was meant as a tease rather than a real description.'

'That's sneaky,' Theo remarked. 'And also inconsiderate.'

'Yes,' Marian agreed. 'That's exactly what I thought too.' *It was more than sneaky*, Marian thought to herself. *He used me and then he used Sylvia, too, just to get noticed.*

'But you have to work with him,' Theo said. 'How are you going to cope with that?'

'I could always quit,' Marian said. 'But I love the job, so that will be a hard decision.'

'You'll have to speak to Pierce,' Theo said. 'Maybe he won't want to work with that author either.'

Marian thought for a moment. 'Maybe. Nothing has been

signed, so it's up to Pierce to decide what to do. The problem is all his media contacts. It's all set up now, so it would be difficult to cancel everything.'

'Let's not worry about that now,' Theo said, smiling at Marian. 'We'll help with the tidying up and then I'll drive you home.'

'Yes, good idea,' Marian agreed.

They started to load the dishwasher and then went back into the living room where everyone was preparing to leave. The rain had eased to a drizzle and the children could be brought to the cars. Sylvia chatted with everyone for a while before she and Arnaud left.

Marian hugged Claire and thanked her for a wonderful party. 'Quite a surprise party in the end,' she said.

'That's putting it mildly,' Claire replied. 'I think Pierce is still reeling from the shock.'

Marian turned to Pierce, who was chatting to Theo. 'What are we going to do about John Peters now?' she asked.

'I don't know,' Pierce said. 'I think we should just carry on and do what we planned. I know it seems strange for us to handle that novel, but it's now going to be published a whole month after Sylvia's interview. All the hype about it will have died down by then and his book will not be that sensational any more.'

Marian nodded. 'Yes, I suppose you're right. And it's a good thing we will not be involved with Sylvia's memoirs, otherwise Sean will suspect we had something to do with her interview and social media coverage.'

'Clever move by Sylvia, though,' Theo interjected.

'Very,' Pierce agreed. 'Her memoirs will be a sensation. And she's only doing one radio interview, which will go viral before long. I mean, that Bluebell story will be the talk of the town.'

'Some older people will find it hugely shocking,' Marian remarked. 'But most of them will, like Vi, think it's so cool.'

'It is,' Claire said, smiling. 'Incredibly cool. I'm sure at the time it would have caused a near scandal, but the Bluebell girls were so glamorous. Had it been any other dance troupe at the Lido or the Folies Bergère, it would have been a lot less acceptable. But Margaret Kelly was such an inspirational woman. Her dancers were sexy in a classy way, and I believe they were the best dancers in Paris at the time.'

'How do you know?' Marian asked.

'I saw the TV series. It was shown on RTÉ a while back,' Claire replied. 'It was made over forty years ago, though, so I don't think it will be shown again.'

'What a pity. I would have loved to have seen that,' Marian said.

'I had no idea that Sylvia was one of those dancers,' Claire remarked. 'She shook us all up with that revelation, I have to say. Can't wait to hear that interview.'

'We'll all be glued to it,' Theo interjected.

'But now we have to go,' Marian said. 'I'm sure you're tired.'

'Just a little,' Claire confessed. 'But Theo did a great job with the barbecue and you were a huge help, too, Marian, with the tidying up and loading the dishwasher.'

'Ah sure, that was nothing,' Marian said and hugged Claire. 'Thanks for a great party.'

'I should thank Sylvia for the floorshow,' Claire joked as she hugged Marian back. Then she hugged Theo and whispered something in his ear that Marian didn't catch.

They waved goodbye to the Fleury sisters loading their offspring into cars and got ready to leave. As they drove down the hill, Marian glanced at Theo in the evening sunlight and thought about the past day and how he had fitted in so seamlessly with the whole family, from small children to the older generation.

If only he could see how lovely it is to be part of this family, she thought, *and if Rebecca finally moves to Dublin and Conor comes for visits from London, we can somehow be a family again, even if the children are adults with their own lives.*

But before that could happen, she had to be honest with her husband about how she felt, how she had been feeling for all those years. She looked at him, at his sharp profile, high cheekbones and those grey eyes fringed with black lashes. He had aged well; his fair hair, now with a few grey strands, was still thick, and his body toned and fit after all the surfing. But there was a secretive streak in him she found hard to deal with.

Theo shot Marian a glance that was full of questions. 'What are you thinking about?' he asked. 'Building castles in the air as usual?'

'Yes, I suppose I am,' she said with a smile. 'A bit of wishful thinking that soothes me.'

'I know,' he said as they drove through the gates of Magnolia Manor. 'Well, we'll see. Maybe some of your dreams will come true. One day,' he added cryptically.

Marian looked at the gatehouse and the light in the upstairs windows, imagining that Vi and Jack were putting their little boys to bed. 'I only know one thing,' she mumbled.

'You'll never leave this place,' he filled in, his voice soft. 'I already knew that the minute I saw you again. There is a light in your eyes, a kind of happiness of someone who has finally come home. Strange, as you had never been here before.'

Marian was shocked. All this time she thought he couldn't see it. He'd always been able to read her, and it seemed that now he saw her in Kerry, he finally understood how much she belonged here too.

'Maybe I was in an earlier life?' Marian suggested as Theo pulled up in front of the manor. 'That's how I felt, anyway.'

'Or it's in your genes,' he suggested. 'A kind of memory that's handed down through time.'

'I like that idea, even though it's far-fetched.' Marian started to get out of the car. Then an idea suddenly struck her. 'Come up to my flat and have a cup of tea,' she said, leaning into the car.

Theo stared at her. 'Do you mean it?'

'Of course I do,' Marian insisted, surprised by his reaction.

Theo hesitated. 'Well, I'd love to see this house and your flat, of course. But...'

'But what?' Marian smiled. 'Come on, don't be shy. I think you need to discover the magic of Magnolia Manor.' She felt suddenly nervous but then a kind of excitement at asking him to come inside what felt like her own fortress, the walls of which had kept her safe from him and his demands. Then she told herself not to be ridiculous. 'It's just a cup of tea,' she said. 'Barry's, your favourite.'

Theo laughed and switched off the engine. 'How can I resist? I'll just park the car.'

Marian waited while Theo drove over to the parking place and then joined her at the entrance door. She looked at him, feeling this was a watershed moment which could end either badly or be the start of something new and wonderful between them. She knew she had to be honest and stand her ground, but would he be able to break down her barriers? She swallowed nervously and pushed the door open.

TWENTY-THREE

They went inside the vast hall and continued into the large lobby where Marian stopped at the bottom of the staircase.

'We could take the lift up to the second floor and then walk up to my flat. But maybe you'd like to see all the rooms down here first?' she asked.

'Yes, I would,' Theo said. 'I want to see everything.'

'Okay.' Marian took his hand. 'Come with me.'

They walked down the corridor, lined with old paintings, and went into the ballroom, where Theo looked in awe at the painted ceiling where cherubs and nymphs floated around among the clouds, the crystal chandelier from the early eighteen hundreds, the parquet floor and the tall windows overlooking the grounds and the rose garden. There was a faint smell of candles and flowers after the wedding party that had been held here the day before.

'What a beautiful room,' Theo said. 'There is a real sense of history here. Of balls and parties and other celebrations through the centuries.'

'Yes, it's amazing to think it's been here like this for over two hundred years,' Marian said, touched by how taken he was with the atmosphere of the ballroom.

They continued through the dining room with its walls hung with old portraits and the large Regency dining table and chairs, to the library that still had some of the old books in the bookshelves lining the walls, the leather sofas and chairs sitting on the old Donegal carpet, the colours faded but still beautiful. Theo didn't utter a word until they arrived back in the hall.

He looked at Marian, his eyes sparkling. 'Wow,' he said. 'I had no idea the rooms were so beautiful and still so intact.'

'They have been restored with a very gentle hand,' she agreed. 'The tenants of the flats are also very respectful and love the rooms the way they are. The library is especially popular as they can sit on the sofas and read or play cards or just chat and have a cup of tea. It's like a large sitting room for them to use. But now I'm going to take you upstairs and show you my flat. We can take the lift if you like.'

Theo looked up at the wide staircase with its carved oak banister. 'No, I'd like to walk up these stairs and imagine what it was like in the eighteen hundreds. I assume all the bedrooms were on the first floor?'

'Yes,' Marian said. 'And now they have been turned into studio flats.' She started to walk up the stairs, Theo trailing behind her, running his fingers along the beautifully carved banister.

They arrived on the top floor, panting while Marian searched in her handbag for the key. She opened the door and Theo followed her into the tiny hall.

He stepped into the living room and immediately sat down on the sofa in front of the fireplace, looking out the window. 'Lovely view. And the flat is nice but a bit like a doll's house. How do you cope with this tiny space?'

'I manage very well,' Marian replied. 'It's perfectly fine for just one person. And just look at that view,' she added, making a sweeping gesture at the window where the vista of the gardens and the ocean were especially beautiful in the golden light of the setting sun.

'It's the best part of this flat,' Theo said, trying to make himself comfortable. But with his tall frame, the sofa was clearly too small for him.

'I'll make some tea,' Marian offered, slightly put off by his negative attitude.

'I'll move to the table instead,' Theo suggested, and went to sit down at the table beside the kitchen. 'This is better,' he said once he had settled on the kitchen chair while Marian busied herself making tea for them both.

'There you go,' she said as she put two steaming mugs in front of him. Then she sat down on the chair opposite Theo.

Theo grabbed one of the mugs and took a sip. 'Good tea.'

'Of course,' Marian said and smiled fondly at him. 'Nothing better. You used to love a cup of Barry's.'

'Still do,' Theo said. He drank some more tea and then put his mug down, fixing her with a serious expression. 'I get it now,' he said.

'Get what?' Marian asked.

'This house, the family, this whole area. The endless sea, the sky, the wind, the waves, the ocean. The mild air, even the rain and then... the people of Kerry.' He drew breath. 'How can I possibly compete with all that?'

'You don't have to compete,' Marian said softly. 'I'm not saying I've landed in some kind of paradise either. There are days when it never stops raining and the wind is howling. There are tedious things like getting up early, going to work and paying tax. People in Kerry are not always lovely; some are rude and grumpy, just like anywhere. But... This is where I want to live despite all that.'

'Because now you feel you have a family,' Theo filled in. 'You never had much of a family before, except your great-aunt and your sister. I think Claire feels the same. I've seen how they have welcomed you and been there for you and how they close ranks when any of them is in trouble.' He shook his head and laughed. 'The Fleury women, eh? I often wondered where you got your strength and resilience from, but now I know. You've become even stronger since you arrived here, even more determined. Australia was not for you, but you stuck it out and tried your best.'

Marian nodded. 'I did but then I just couldn't cope with everything, especially when I found that letter.'

'That didn't help, I suppose,' Theo said with a resigned sigh. 'We've drifted apart during the last year or so, I think. There's no denying that.'

'No, but...' Marian stopped. 'I have a feeling you're more comfortable with this place than you ever were when we were living in Dublin.' *It's strange*, she thought. *Could it be that the magic of Kerry is working without me having to persuade him?*

'In what way?' Theo asked, looking intrigued.

'I've seen you here, with the family and how they like you a lot already,' Marian explained. 'And I've watched you slowly coming around to the idea of living in Ireland again. Or maybe I'm mistaken about that,' she said, meeting his eyes.

'Not really mistaken,' Theo said, looking thoughtful. 'But I'm not ready to decide about the future yet. I just want to have a holiday, really. A break from worry and tensions. And this is a lovely place for a holiday. I feel so relaxed here.'

'Oh yes, me too,' Marian said with a surge of happiness and hope. 'It's the peace and tranquillity that I love the most.'

'That's it.' He took her hand. 'Let's not discuss this any further. I'll go back to the B&B when I've finished the tea. And then we can have dinner tomorrow night, if you like.'

'Or you could stay here?' Marian suggested, her heart beating. 'The sofa folds out to a sofa bed, or...'

'Or what?' he whispered, still holding her hand in a tight grip.

'Or we could sleep in my bed,' she whispered and leaned across the table, placing a light kiss on his mouth.

He slowly rose and pulled her up into his arms. 'Are you sure?'

'Yes,' she said, melting into his embrace. She suddenly felt so close to him. There seemed to be a new understanding between them that had never been there before. Then she stepped away, looking into his eyes. 'This doesn't mean that I'll be coming back with you. I want you to understand that.'

He gently pushed back her hair from her face 'It doesn't have to mean anything except that you love me enough to ask me to stay tonight.'

'That's a step forward, though,' Marian said, as the vibes from him told her that he was beginning to come around to the idea of them living in Kerry together. It felt like a sweet victory and at the same time a new kind of love, better and stronger than ever before. Then, in the early days, and even the first few years in Australia, it had been all about the children and their family. But now it was only about Theo and Marian, two people who had fallen in love on a beach in France many years ago and now found themselves on another shore where maybe they could start afresh.

TWENTY-FOUR

Marian woke the next morning to the sound of the kettle boiling. Theo must be up already. She stretched and smiled, remembering the evening before that had ended in such a romantic way. They had made love as if it was the first time and then gone to sleep in each other's arms, comfortable despite the narrow bed.

She sat up and smiled at Theo as he carried in a tray with a mug of tea and two slices of toasted soda bread with marmalade, a bowl of yogurt with granola and a glass of orange juice, just as she liked it. 'Oh, how lovely. Thank you. But what about you?' she asked. 'Don't you want breakfast in bed too?'

Theo placed the tray on Marian's lap. 'In this bed? Are you mad? I was hanging off the edge of it all night.'

'When you weren't hanging off me,' Marian said, laughing. She held out her arms. 'Oh, come here. It was such a romantic evening. Don't you feel we're getting back something we lost?'

Theo bent over and kissed her. 'I think we did. I also think we're on our way to something even better.'

'Yes. Maybe we are. A bit to go yet, but it was a lovely start.' She suddenly noticed that he was dressed. 'Are you off already?'

'Yes. I had a shower in the teeny-tiny bathroom. Sorry if there is a bit of water on the floor. There just isn't enough space for a bloke with shoulders like mine.'

Marian smiled, but she felt a tinge of disappointment that he was rushing off so soon. 'I can imagine. Don't worry, I'll dry the floor. Where are you off to?'

'I have an appointment in town,' he said with a mysterious look.

'What kind of appointment?' she asked, intrigued.

'I can't tell you what it's about. Just someone I need to talk to about... things.' Theo stroked Marian's cheek, but she felt herself flinch, thinking immediately about Helen and whatever had been going on between them. 'I'll be in touch about tonight. Dinner and a walk, weather permitting?'

'Lovely,' she said. 'I have to go to work and then I'll be free around four or so.'

'Great. Enjoy your breakfast.' Theo smiled, threw her a kiss and then disappeared.

Marian sipped her tea while she listened to Theo's footsteps as he ran down the stairs, her mind full of what had happened last night, and what he had said. He was definitively coming around, she felt, and clearly becoming enchanted by both Dingle and Magnolia Manor. The family seemed to have done their best to make him feel welcome which, Marian suspected, was Sylvia's doing. Who would not be charmed by such a family with such a fascinating history? But she wished he wouldn't hide things from her. If they were going to rebuild their trust for each other, this wasn't the way to do it.

Is he meeting Helen and reporting back to her? Marian wondered, feeling an increasing niggle of worry.

But she would have to get up soon or she'd be late for work. Pierce needed her to put everything together for John Peters' publication and media coverage. Then there was Sylvia's interview on Tuesday which, Marian was sure, was bound to cause a sensation in town. How strange that she had kept this secret for so long, and that Arnaud knew about it.

She finished her breakfast and then had a quick shower before she mopped the water from the floor and hung up the towels Theo had left on the radiator. That done, she got dressed, ran downstairs and rushed out the door to her car. But before she had a chance to drive away, someone called from the top of the steps. It was Rose.

'Marian,' she shouted. 'Hang on a sec, I want to ask you something.'

'Yes?' Marian said, wondering what was so urgent.

Rose reached the car and stuck her head in the window on the driver's side. 'Just wondering if it's true that you were on a date with that author the other night. What's his name, John Peters?'

'A date?' Marian shook her head. 'Of course not. It was a working dinner. We're doing all the publicity for his book. And he wanted to discuss some details of the campaign,' Marian explained, feeling her face flush at the thought of what they had talked about. It hadn't been a hundred per cent professional and the banter between them had been flirtatious, to say the least, most of it coming from him. 'Who told you?' she asked.

'Mum's friend Maggie,' Rose replied. 'She seemed quite envious. She also said you kissed him as you were leaving.'

'Kissed him?' Marian repeated. 'Oh, no. That was just one of those French things. He's half French and he's used to kissing female friends on both cheeks as a greeting. You know, like Arnaud does.' Marian drew breath and mentally crossed her fingers that Rose would believe her.

'Oh.' Rose stared at Marian for a moment. 'I see. Well, I'm afraid that particular story is out now. I hope it won't get in the way of your reconciliation with Theo. Lovely guy, by the way. The kids are already mad about him.'

'He loves children,' Marian said fondly. 'I'm sure he won't

believe I was on some kind of date, though. But I'd better tell him about it, so he's prepared.'

'Good idea,' Rose said. 'But he didn't seem like the jealous type anyway.'

'I don't think so,' Marian said, hoping she was right. 'Thanks for letting me know, though.'

Rose nodded. 'Just thought I should warn you. But hey, Granny's story will make everyone forget all about it. Can't wait to hear the interview.'

'Looking forward to it,' Marian said and started the car. 'See you soon, Rose.'

Rose said goodbye and Marian drove off, thinking about what Rose had told her. She chastised herself for being so careless, having dinner and with Sean in such a public place which finished with him kissing her on both cheeks. It had seemed innocent to her, but anyone watching would think there was more than friendship going on between them. And now she wasn't sure she even liked him as she had discovered how he had used her just to get the story out of her. She didn't know how she could work with him, now that she had discovered what he had done. She hoped fervently that he would never reveal her role in his novel to anyone. At least not to Theo.

Later that day, when Marian was just about to go downstairs to have lunch with Claire and Karina, her phone pinged with a message from Sean.

Great news. I think I have a buyer for the cottage. How about a drink to help me celebrate?

Marian stared at the message, wondering how to reply. She couldn't agree to see him in private and had to make sure they only met professionally. In any case, now that she and Theo were beginning to rebuild their marriage, there was no way she could go out with another man, even on strictly friendly terms. She thought for a moment and then sent a reply.

Glad to hear it! I'm sure you're relieved. Sorry, but I'm busy right now with family. See you in the office tomorrow in any case.

Marian sent the text, hoping Sean would understand what she really meant. She had to put him off in a friendly way and not show her dislike for him after what she saw as a kind of betrayal. There was no reply, so she assumed he accepted her refusal. Then she joined Claire and Karina in the kitchen for a quiche and salad that Karina had just made.

'This is divine, Karina,' Claire said, as she put another piece of quiche in her mouth. 'Best ever, I think.'

'Yes,' Marian agreed, patting her mouth with a napkin. 'I agree. What did you put in it that made it so extra tasty?'

'Local cheese,' Karina replied, looking pleased. 'There is a new cheesemaker in Dingle and he only uses local milk. This one is a take on the Dutch Leerdammer but with a slightly different flavour. I love the way it melts into the egg and ham mixture. And then I added some spinach, sundried tomatoes and chopped herbs.'

'Brilliant,' Claire said. 'I suppose you're putting the recipe into the new cookbook for autumn?'

'Yes,' Karina said. 'It's going to be called *Karina's Comfort Foods*.'

'We're preparing the publicity for that one,' Marian cut in. 'I think it'll do very well. The last one was a huge success, Pierce told me.'

'I'm also doing a video for my YouTube channel,' Karina said. 'It's a new thing for me but I like a challenge.'

'That's exciting,' Marian said, admiring this sixty-something woman who wasn't afraid to test her skills. Her cooking was legendary and her connection with Magnolia Manor had helped Claire get in touch with the Fleury family when she was what she had called 'working undercover'. Now she was such an integral part of the family it was as if she had grown up with the Kerry Fleurys. Marian felt the same way, wondering how it was possible to have bonded with her third cousins in only a few months. But she had and there was no way she was going to leave, even if Theo put pressure on her. But she had an odd feeling he wouldn't and that they would come to a solution in the end.

'You look happy,' Claire said when Karina was tidying up.

Marian smiled. 'Yes, I am. I have a feeling Theo will eventually want to stay here. But we have a long way to go yet, so I'm not counting any chickens.'

'Just keeping your fingers and toes crossed?' Claire said. 'I hope you're right, though. I'd love for you to stay here permanently. Both of you, I mean,' she added.

'I hope so too,' Karina said from the kitchen counter. 'Pierce is so happy to have you working with him. He says his office has never been so tidy.'

'I do my best,' Marian said, 'but sometimes I wonder if a whirlwind has been there over the weekend. I love the job, though. It's so varied and interesting.'

'It seems to suit you,' Claire said.

'That's what Theo said,' Marian told her. 'And he seemed happy for me. I hope that's a good sign.'

'Do you think your husband might want to stay in Kerry?' Karina asked, putting the plates into the dishwasher.

'I hope he'll come around to that idea,' Marian said. 'But I don't want to put pressure on him. It would be wonderful if he came to the conclusion all by himself.'

'But I thought you were separated. And that you're dating

that author.' Karina looked suddenly awkward. 'Sorry, but that's what I heard at the butcher's only this morning.'

'Oh, no,' Claire exclaimed. 'That's terrible. Those gossipy women are at it again.'

'In any case, it's not true,' Marian interjected. 'Yes, I had dinner with him, but it was about work and not anything more than that. Someone must have seen it and come to the wrong conclusion. But what can I do about it? I only hope Theo doesn't hear this.'

'He probably won't,' Claire soothed. 'He's not likely to meet any of those women. They usually spread the rumours at the hairdresser's and the shops. In any case, I saw him walk up the hill this morning when we drove to the office. Must have been going for a walk or something.'

'I saw him near Noel's office a bit later,' Karina said. 'Maybe they're meeting for lunch?'

Just then, Marian's phone pinged. 'Oh, it's a text message from him,' she said.

'Who?' Karina asked. 'The dishy author?'

'No, my husband.' Marian opened the message. '"*Could you come to Noel's office?*"' she read out loud. 'I wonder what that's about.'

'There's only one way to find out,' Claire said.

'I know.' Marian texted 'okay' to Theo and got up. 'I'll just tell Pierce and then I'll go and see what he's up to.'

'Sounds mysterious,' Claire said. 'Let me know as soon as you come back. I'm dying of curiosity.'

'You're not the only one,' Karina chimed in. 'Do let us know if it's something exciting.'

'I will,' Marian promised. Then she rushed up the stairs and stuck her head into the office where Pierce was typing on the computer.

'Hi,' she panted. 'I have to go out for a bit. I'll be back in about half an hour or so.'

Pierce nodded, his eyes on the screen. 'Okay. But then we need to sort out a few of our clients' media coverage. I'm just looking at it now and sending a few queries.'

'No problem,' Marian replied. 'I'll be back as soon as I can.' Then she ran downstairs and out the door, stopping for a moment to catch her breath, wondering why on earth Theo wanted her to come to Noel's office. Was it something to do with splitting up, or even... divorce? She knew Noel often handled such cases. But they had had such a romantic evening and fallen asleep in each other's arms and then Theo had served her breakfast in bed and they had parted with a promise to see each other that evening. Marian had felt she was falling in love with Theo all over again and that they were now on the way to a much better relationship than ever before. A relationship where they were equals and could find a new harmony and peace. That couldn't be just wishful thinking.

But... Then a thought struck Marian. Had Theo heard the gossip about Sean and how they might have been on a date? Could that have made Theo so angry that he turned to Helen for more advice and then she had told him to get Noel to... *No, no, no*, Marian thought as she hurried down the street towards Noel's office which was only a five-minute walk away. *We can't lose this new feeling between us before it has even started.*

Marian arrived, breathless, at the building, trying to still her beating heart. She opened the door and went inside with a feeling of impending doom.

'Hi, Marian,' the receptionist said with a wide grin. 'Go right in. They're expecting you. The documents are all ready so all you have to do is sign.'

'Sign what?' Marian asked and opened the door to the office without waiting for a reply. Once inside, she found Theo and Noel sitting opposite each other at the desk with a stack of papers in front of them.

So this is it, she thought as she walked towards them. *The end of my marriage. What else could it be?*

TWENTY-FIVE

'Hello, wh-what is all this about?' Marian stammered, looking at the two men.

Theo smiled and held out his hand. 'Don't look so scared, sweetheart. Come and sit down and I'll tell you what I've done.'

'I think you'll be pleased,' Noel said.

'Okay,' Marian said, and, her knees shaking, sank down on the chair beside Theo, feeling confused as she tried to return Noel's smile. 'Please explain what's going on.'

'I'm buying a house,' Theo said. 'And I want it to be put into both our names.'

Marian blinked and stared at him. 'You're buying a house? How? I mean, where? And what kind of house? How can you afford it?' she babbled on, trying to take in what he had just said.

'I'm selling the business in Brisbane,' Theo explained. 'Frank wants to buy it. That was already in the pipeline when I left, actually, but I hadn't decided yet. But now that I've been here a while and—'

'You've been here less than a week,' Marian protested. 'How can you decide anything in such a short time?'

'I know it seems a rushed decision,' Theo agreed. 'But I've

been thinking about it for a while. Before you left, as a matter of fact. I know how homesick you've been and I also know you've tried your best to settle down in Australia. But that didn't work and you've been miserable. Then, when you left, I realised you never wanted to come back, so I decided to follow you here and see if it would be a place where we could both be happy.'

'And you found that it is?' Marian asked.

'Yes,' Theo said and took her hand. 'I hadn't planned to buy a house or anything; I thought I could rent something and then if we managed to patch things up between us, we could look for somewhere. But then I got a tip about this little house for sale that seemed so perfect. I thought it wouldn't do any harm to take a look. So I did and I was completely bowled over by it.'

'Where is this house?' Marian asked, still taken aback by Theo's swift turnaround. She had feared he was about to talk her into coming back to Australia with him, but now he was buying a house in Dingle?

'It's on the top of the hill, above town,' Theo replied. 'Within walking distance from here. The views are heavenly.'

'I can imagine,' Marian said, trying to understand what was happening. 'So now you want to stay?' she asked. 'With me?'

'Of course,' Theo said, squeezing her hand in a tight grip. 'When I arrived you were so on your guard and ready to fight for your rights to stay here. I was going to stand my ground and give you an ultimatum. But then... last night, we...' He stopped and glanced at Noel. 'We got back together, you see.'

Noel cleared his throat. 'Er, I think maybe I'll go and get myself a cup of tea and leave you to discuss this. I have a feeling you need a little privacy right now.'

'Yes, maybe,' Theo agreed. 'Thanks, Noel.'

'I'll be outside,' Noel said as he got up. 'Give me a shout when you're ready to sign.'

When the door closed behind Noel, Marian turned back to Theo. 'Are you really serious about staying here and buying a house and all that? If you do, it has to be for good. I don't ever want to move again. If you want to go to Australia for a visit, I'll come with you. But you know I can't ever be happy there. You have always been impulsive, jumping into things without any plan or safety net, so that's why I'm a bit hesitant about this.'

Theo kissed Marian's hand. 'I know all that, my darling. You know me so well. But this is not based on some wild impulse; it's a feeling I've had for some time, you see. Helen, you know, my friend who's been giving me a lot of advice—'

'Oh, please, let's not bring her into this,' Marian exclaimed and snatched her hand from Theo's grip. 'Whatever she said has nothing to do with me.'

'Well, in this case she made a lot of sense. But I won't mention it if it upsets you. I'm a little tired of her, to be honest,' Theo confessed. 'She's just a wannabe psychologist, really. So we can forget about her from now on.'

'That's a relief,' Marian said. 'Now let's get back to you and the house. Can you show me a photo or something?'

'I have some pictures of it on my phone,' Theo said and picked up his mobile from the desk and showed Marian a photo of an old house in the middle of an overgrown garden.

She looked at the photo for a moment, then swiped to see the interior of the house, which was charming but not in a very good state of repair. 'It needs a lot of work to make it comfortable,' she remarked.

'I know. But I can do a lot myself, as you know,' Theo replied.

'Maybe.' She studied the photos for a while and understood immediately why Theo had fallen in love with it. The little house was a cottage with a slate roof, some of which were missing. The windows were old fashioned and she could see that they would have to be replaced and the façade repainted. There was a front garden with a gnarled apple tree and hydrangea bushes. The grass was knee-high and the weeds poked through

the gaps in the concrete path that led to the red door where the
paint was flaking off. The house, judging by the plan, had two
bedrooms, a living room and a kitchen large enough to become a
kitchen-diner. And when Marian saw the photos of the old
cupboards and the flagstone floor, the larder, the bedrooms, the
largest of which had a bow window with stunning views of the
town, the harbour and the ocean beyond, she was just as smitten
as Theo had been. She handed the phone back to him with a
brilliant smile. 'Now you have me nearly in tears. It looks
fabulous.'

He leaned over and kissed her cheek. 'I knew you'd love it.'

Marian chuckled. 'Of course you did. I'm a sucker for cute
old houses. And that view is to die for. The work to do it up will
be hard, but fun. I know how good you are at that sort of thing.'

'It's going to be so great for us both,' Theo said. 'Remember
the old apartment we lived in when we were first married and
had no money?'

'Yes,' Marian said, as the memory of their very first home
popped into her mind. The flat in the least fashionable part of
Dublin had been the only one they could afford. 'You worked so
hard to make it comfortable.'

'So did you,' Theo reminded her. 'Despite being pregnant.
But you really helped a lot with painting and decorating. We
were such a team then, and now we'll do it again.'

'We're a little older, though,' Marian pointed out. 'I'm not
sure I can cope with a lot of hard physical work.'

'Of course you can,' Theo countered. 'You look very fit. And
you'll be fitter still by the time the house is finished.'

'Or dead,' Marian joked.

'We'll survive. So what do you think?' Theo asked. 'Will we
buy this house? It's going for a song, so we can well afford it.'

'It's a wonderful new start for us.' Marian leaned over and
kissed Theo, suddenly overwhelmed with a new-found love
for this man who was willing to sacrifice everything for her –

even his country. That was not something she could do but Theo was different. He had that enterprising spirit and was not afraid to try new things or live in another country. But then Ireland and Kerry were much easier to cope with. The friendliness of the people and the mild climate were things that made moving here a very soft landing for any stranger wishing to settle in. 'Just one thing before I agree to sign this contract.'

'What?' Theo asked.

'I'd like to see the house. Just to find out if I get the feel of home.'

Theo smiled. 'Yes, that's a good idea. Of course you must see it as you'll be part owner. Silly of me to think you'd sign just like that before you've even been there.'

'Yes, but you were so carried away by it,' Marian said. 'I know that's what happens with you when you get enthused by something. I love the idea of us buying an old house and doing it up. I think it's the only way we can get back what we had all those years ago. I also love you for being willing to sell the shop and move back to Ireland. It's our only chance, I think.'

Theo nodded. 'Yes, that's what I figured out too.' He rose from his chair. 'Come on, we'll tell Noel you want to see the house. We can sign the contract later.'

They went out to the reception area where they found Noel making tea in the kitchenette. 'Oh,' he said. 'You've finished your chat. Do you want tea?'

'No thanks,' Theo said. 'But Marian wants to see the house before she signs anything. So we'll go and take a look and then make another appointment for the signing.'

Noel nodded. 'Of course. I thought it a little odd that Marian hadn't seen it. Give me a shout when you're ready.'

'We will,' Marian said. 'Come on, Theo. Lead the way. Is it far?'

'Only five minutes on foot,' Theo promised.

'Five minutes for you means fifteen minutes for anyone normal,' Marian said, laughing.

She was right. It took them a little more than fifteen minutes to reach the top of the hill where the little house stood in the garden with the old apple tree that had a lot of fruit hanging from its branches.

'What a crop,' Marian said and plucked an apple from the tree and then bit into it. 'Very sweet,' she said, munching.

Then Theo opened the door which creaked loudly. 'Please come into our castle, my queen.'

'Oh,' Marian said, surprised. 'Are we allowed to go inside without the agent being here?'

'The door wasn't locked,' Theo said. 'I was here this morning for a viewing and she said I could come back if I wanted. The owner lives abroad, but he's staying here at the moment. She said he had gone to Cork for a few days, though, so we won't disturb anyone.'

'Okay,' Marian said and stepped inside. 'If you're sure it's okay.'

'I swear.'

Marian found herself in a small porch with wainscoting on the walls and an old hallstand with a cracked mirror and hooks for coats and umbrellas. 'I hope we can keep that,' she said. 'I'd love to do it up.' She continued into the living room where the floorboards creaked with every step she took. She went to the window and looked out at the view which was even more stunning in real life. She sat down on the old window seat and kept looking out to sea, then turned and looked around the room that had a sagging sofa in front of the period cast-iron fireplace. She sat there for a while, breathing in the slight smell of damp mixed with a flowery smell from a dried flower arrangement that was falling apart on the mantelpiece. The room had a tranquil atmosphere and she felt a calm come over her, as if the house was whispering 'welcome home' into her ear. 'Oh,' she said, looking at Theo. 'I get "the feel" here. A kind of peace that seems to settle on my shoulders.'

'I know,' Theo said looking happy. 'I felt it, too, when I was here this morning.'

Marian got up from the window seat. 'I'll just take a look at the kitchen and then we can go. No need to see the bedrooms if the owner is still living here. We can see them later.'

The kitchen turned out to be charming even though it needed a serious update. But Marian loved the flagstones, the solid oak doors of the cupboards, the larder, the little wood-burning stove and the view of the small back garden through the old window. The tap was dripping into the old basin and there was a smell of cooking from the old gas cooker that had seen better days. The Formica-topped kitchen table seemed to be from the 1950s and the old fridge older still. Dishes drying on the old sink confirmed that someone was living here despite the decrepitude of the house. She spotted a brochure on the floor as Theo walked away. Thinking that he must have dropped it, Marian picked it up, deciding to look at it later.

'Are you sure you don't want to see the bedrooms?' Theo asked as she walked out of the kitchen.

'Yes,' Marian said, feeling suddenly uneasy about prowling around someone's house, even though they were planning to buy it. 'I think we should go. I love the house, though. It's perfect for us, I think.'

'So you want us to buy it?' Theo asked, looking anxious.

'Yes,' Marian said. 'I do.' She went to his side and put her arms around his waist, hugging him tight. 'It'll be a new adventure for us.' She felt a surge of joy as she saw the light in his eyes. This house felt like a gift that would rekindle their love for each other and give them a project to work on. It wouldn't be easy and they would have many arguments but it would be exciting and new. 'I'll stay in the flat and come over and help you after work,' she suggested.

Theo nodded, holding her tight. 'Yes. I can live here while we're working on it. And here's another bit of good news. I have a job. Only part time at first but once the house is up and running, it'll be full time.'

'A job?' Marian asked. 'Doing what?'

'Plumbing,' Theo replied with a grin. 'I'm a qualified plumber, after all. I'm going to work for Dominic. He says he's in desperate need of a plumber. I'm starting next week.'

'Oh, that's so perfect,' Marian said, near tears with happiness. 'All my wishes coming true at last. I'm nearly scared something is going to ruin it.'

'Nothing can,' Theo assured her. 'Now let's go and arrange to get that contract signed and pay the deposit.'

'I can't wait,' Marian said, taking his hand and pulling him along with her out of the house. She stopped just outside the door as a car pulled up by the little gate.

'That must be the owner arriving home,' Theo said. 'Maybe we should say hello?'

'Yes,' Marian said. 'Why not?'

But she froze as she saw the man getting out of the car. *Oh no*, she thought, her heart contracting. *Not him. Why didn't I realise whose house this must be?*

TWENTY-SIX

Marian stood rooted to the spot as Sean walked towards them.

'Hello,' he called. 'Are you the nice people buying my house?'

'We are indeed,' Theo replied.

Sean smiled and then, when he came closer, he spotted Marian. 'Oh wow, it's Marian, my muse,' he exclaimed. 'And this must be the missing husband? I see you've found each other again.'

'Yes, well...' Marian started.

'This is quite a coincidence,' Sean said. 'Like a plot twist in one of my novels. Strangers meet on a plane and their paths cross again and again. I should write it down so I can remember the details. Reality meets fiction yet again.'

'We've had quite enough of that,' Marian snapped. 'We don't need any more.'

'I suppose,' Sean said apologetically. 'But can I still call you my muse?'

'How can I stop you?' Marian asked, with a sense of impending doom.

'I beg your pardon?' Theo cut in, looking confused. 'Marian

is your muse? And what's that about me being a missing husband? And you met on a plane? How did that happen?'

Sean shook his head, laughed and held out his hand. 'I'm sorry. I should have introduced myself first of all. I'm Sean Duvivier, also known as John Peters, and this is my house.'

Theo reluctantly shook Sean's hand. 'I'm Theo Watson. So this is your house? How come you have two names?'

'I'm an author,' Sean explained, ignoring Marian's warning look. 'And I write under the pen name John Peters. I met Marian on the plane from Sydney to Dubai and we chatted through the night over several glasses of airline plonk. She told me all about the Fleury family which sort of inspired my latest novel.'

'Did she now?' Theo said, shooting a suspicious glance at Marian. 'And what else did she reveal?'

'Oh, nothing much,' Sean said. 'Just that you two were separated. But now I see you're back together and buying a house – my house. That's great news. I'm delighted you're brave enough to take it on. It needs a lot of work.'

'Yes it does,' Theo said and backed away from Sean. 'We haven't quite decided if we'll buy it, though. It might not suit us right now, actually.'

'Oh?' Sean said, looking disappointed. 'That's a pity. Well, let the estate agent know what you've decided.'

'I will,' Theo said. 'But now we have to go. Goodbye.'

'Bye for now,' Sean said pleasantly. 'See you at Pierce's office, Marian. I really enjoyed our dinner the other night. Must say, you and Pierce did a fabulous job with the media coverage. Can't wait to get started.'

'Thanks,' Marian said as Theo pulled her away. 'Bye, Sean.'

They walked down the hill in silence and Marian could see that Theo was fuming. When they were out of earshot, Theo stopped suddenly and glared at Marian, folding his arms.

'So,' he said. 'I think you have a lot to explain.'

'I suppose I do,' Marian said, trying to think of way to tell him what had happened on the plane that would appease him. 'Well, as you know I was upset when we said goodbye and I left for Sydney to catch the plane to Dubai,' she started.

'Yes, we were both a bit upset,' Theo agreed. 'But is that an excuse to blab about our problems to a complete stranger ON A PLANE?' he shouted.

'Please, don't shout,' Marian begged, looking around to see if anyone had heard him. But the street was deserted and she calmed down. 'I was so tired and then we had a few glasses of wine, so I wasn't really thinking straight. He was so nice and charming and asked about me and my life and so on. I started talking about myself and then I just happened to mention that I was sad about what we were going through.'

'You just "happened" to mention that we were separated as well?' Theo asked in a scathing tone. 'I never felt we had gone that far. But you obviously had a different idea.'

'I suppose I did,' Marian mumbled. 'That's how I felt then. But then I couldn't go on about it so I started to tell him about the family instead and all the old stories came out.'

'All those old scandals that everyone is now gossiping about all over town?' Theo enquired. 'Dominic told me about that. And that story about Sylvia that has upset her so much she's forced to go public about it? Was that your doing as well?'

'No,' Marian argued. 'I never mentioned Sylvia. That was something he made up all by himself. I had nothing to do with that.'

'But your story sparked his interest, I bet,' Theo remarked. 'He wouldn't have started digging if he hadn't met you, that's for sure.'

'Maybe not,' Marian said with a sad little sigh. 'I know it's all my fault. So there you are, the whole truth all laid bare for you to see.'

'Except one thing,' Theo said, his eyes full of pain. 'You had dinner with him the other night? On some kind of date?'

'No, it wasn't a date,' Marian protested. 'We just happened to bump into each other and then he invited me for a drink and we stayed for dinner. It wasn't what you might think. I was trying to get him to rewrite the novel so that my family wouldn't have all their secrets exposed.'

'I see.' Theo paused for a moment. 'And you were upset about a letter from an old flame I hadn't been in touch with for a long time? That doesn't begin to compare with the damage and hurt you're causing me and the whole Fleury family right now.'

'That letter seemed quite recent,' Marian argued. 'So I thought you were still in love with this woman. Helen, I mean.'

'It wasn't recent,' Theo snapped. 'And I wasn't in love with her. Well, you must see that now, when I've flown all the way across the world to be with you.'

'Yes,' Marian whispered, 'I do see that now.' She averted her eyes from his angry glare and glanced at the brochure she had found, suddenly noticing the message scribbled at the bottom of the first page. '"*This house looks great. Go and have a look and let me know what you think, love, Helen,*"' she read out loud. Marian stared at Theo. 'Helen?' She looked at him and then everything seemed to make sense. 'What's going on?' she asked. 'Did Helen give you the tip about the house?'

Theo looked suddenly awkward. 'Oh, okay. Yes, Helen told me about it. That's what I was trying to tell you but you didn't want to hear it. She works for Lisney estate agents in Dublin but she spotted this house for sale in Dingle in their lists and told me about it. That's all.'

'That's all?' Marian asked, her voice hoarse with shock and indignation. 'You said you hadn't been in touch with her for a long time.'

Theo sighed. 'I hadn't. But then when I told her I was here in order to patch things up with you and I was willing to settle down here, she gave me this tip. It was just to help us, really. Can't you see that?'

'Not really.' Marian took a step back. 'I only see that you seem to run to Helen for help whenever we're having problems.'

'She's a good friend, nothing more than that.' Theo stared at Marian. 'But we're getting away from the real problem here. Your involvement with that author and your behaviour on the plane.'

'That's worse than your relationship with your old flame?' Marian asked.

'Much worse,' Theo said, his eyes cold. 'You must see that what you've just told me has changed things for me. I don't think I want to go ahead with the house now.'

'Neither do I,' Marian snapped. 'Why don't you move in there with Helen?'

'Don't be ridiculous,' Theo retorted. 'But you know what? I need to be on my own for a bit. I had no idea you were hiding all this from me. That has shaken me up, big time.'

'I was going to tell you,' Marian said.

'When?' Theo asked, his eyes boring into hers.

Marian squirmed. 'Soon,' she said. 'But then you surprised me with this house-buying plan and the job with Dominic and everything. I was so amazed by all of it that everything slipped to the back of my mind. It seemed so perfect all of a sudden. I'm sorry about everything. I don't want to argue like this. Why can't we forget about Helen and Sean and just try to get back what we had? Last night, when you were so loving and you gave me breakfast in bed, I was beginning to feel we were going to be okay.' She tried to take his hand.

'It's too late for that.' Theo snatched his hand away from her touch. 'I'm going back to the B&B to check out now. And then I'm leaving.'

'Where are you going?' Marian asked, feeling tears well up in her eyes.

'I don't know yet,' he said and then started to walk away from her down the hill. 'Tell Noel the whole thing is off,' he said over his shoulder. 'Bye, Marian. I'll be in touch about what we should do next.'

Marian watched him go, feeling all her hopes and dreams that had seemed so perfect only minutes ago crumbling to nothing.

TWENTY-SEVEN

Marian couldn't bear to face Noel, so she sent him a text saying that they had changed their minds about buying the house and she'd explain later. She was too upset to get back to work, so she also sent Pierce a text that she wasn't feeling well. Then she went back down the hill and got into her car and drove to Magnolia Manor with tears streaming down her cheeks. She just wanted to get home and go to bed and pull the duvet over her head and cry. She was sure that Theo now despised her and that there was no hope of them getting back together. He would probably run to Dublin and into the arms of that woman. She had been in a kind of dream these past few days, with Theo coming back and them slowly finding a common ground as he seemed to fall in love with Kerry and all the Fleurys. He had seemed so in tune with them and they, in turn, had instantly seen what a nice, dependable man he was.

I was so stupid, Marian thought as she sat in the car outside the manor, too tired to get out and go upstairs. *So stupid and selfish, only worrying about me and my feelings. What about his feelings?* she asked herself. *Did I ever consider them?* She hit the steering wheel in frustration and self-loathing, wishing with all her heart she could wind the clock back and undo all the things she had done and said from the moment she stepped on the plane.

'Marian?' a voice said outside the car as a figure leaned over and peered into the window.

Startled, Marian wiped her tears away with her hand and stared through the windscreen. It was Tricia. *Oh God, what must she think?* Marian wound down the window. 'Hi,' she croaked. 'I'm a little...'

'You're upset,' Tricia said, looking concerned. 'What's happened?'

'I...' Marian started. 'It's all so terrible,' she said and burst into tears. 'I'm sorry,' she sobbed. 'I've done something awful and my husband has left me just when we were getting back together. But then he found out what I've done and he left.' She shook her head. 'Oh, I'm making no sense at all. It's all such a mess and I just want to go up to the flat and go to bed.'

'You shouldn't be alone in that state. I think you need a friend,' Tricia said. 'Come on. Get out of the car and come with me to my house and I'll make tea and you can tell me all about it.'

'Tea?' Marian let out a sad little laugh. 'Oh yeah, that'll fix it.'

'Of course it won't,' Tricia said as she opened the door of the car. 'But it might make you calm down and then see things differently. In any case, you should not be on your own if you're that upset.' She took Marian's arm in a firm grip and pulled at her. 'Come on. A walk in the fresh air will be good for you too.'

Marian got out of the car and stood there for a while trying to steady her nerves. 'What were you doing here anyway?' she asked.

'I was helping Rose with the accounts,' Tricia said. 'Cillian is on a dig just north of Galway, so I had time to kill.'

'Dig?' Marian asked, confused. 'Oh yes, he's an archaeologist, of course. Interesting job,' she said in an attempt to sound normal.

'Yes,' Tricia said. 'Very interesting. But now it's about you.' She gently closed the door of the car, put her arm through Marian's and started to walk down the gravel path that ran the length of the garden towards her cottage. 'You have everything?' she asked. 'Your bag and stuff?'

Marian held up her small handbag. 'That's all I have, with my phone and keys.'

'All you need, then,' Tricia said. 'I'll provide any other necessities.'

'Like tea and sympathy,' Marian said, feeling hugely grateful for the shoulder to cry on. She needed a friend and Tricia was the best choice as she was not a Fleury by blood and could look at everything from a neutral angle. Marian knew that Tricia and Sylvia had not been on the best terms for a while but had forgotten all their old animosities and become friends when Tricia moved back to Dingle after an absence of many years. There had been huge rivalry between Sylvia and Tricia, as Sylvia was the grandmother of the three Fleury girls and Tricia their mother. But all that had disappeared after Vi and Jack's wedding when Vi had worn Tricia's wedding dress and Sylvia's veil, a great compromise that had ended the battle of whose dress she was to wear. Ruffled feathers were smooth again and troubled waters calm as Tricia let Sylvia be in the spotlight most of the time, taking a back seat whenever she had to. It didn't bother Tricia at all, she had said to Marian; she was happy to let Sylvia be the queen of Magnolia Manor and the belle of any ball or event.

'Here we are,' Tricia said as they arrived at the lovely garden that surrounded the cottage with hydrangeas and roses in full bloom and apple and plum trees heavy with ripe fruit. Bees buzzed around the flowers and butterflies fluttered around the trees and shrubs and all was so peaceful that Marian felt as if transported to an oasis where she could forget all her troubles for a little while.

She breathed in the smell of flowers and fruit, felt the warm sun on her back and listened to the birdsong. 'Heavenly,' she said with a sigh. 'This place always seems to soothe my spirits.'

'Mine too,' Tricia said and opened the door. 'I thank the stars and heaven above for giving me my forever home.'

'Your forever home,' Marian repeated wistfully. 'That sounds so wonderful. I thought I had found mine today. But then it all came to nothing through my own stupidity.'

'I'm sure it's not all your fault,' Tricia soothed. 'Go into the living room and sit on the sofa. I'll go and make tea and cut up the brownies I made this morning as a treat for Sophie and Naomi, who were supposed to come over. But then the weather turned so nice that they decided to go to the beach instead and I was left with a whole tray of brownies to eat all on my own. I think they're the best remedy for a broken heart.'

'Thanks, Tricia,' Marian said, trying to smile through her misery. 'Not that it'll mend my broken heart, but it's so nice to have a friend who's willing to listen.' She went into the cosy living room and sat on the green velvet sofa by the window that overlooked the garden. The room was beautifully decorated with colourful rugs on the wooden floor and framed prints of flowers and trees mixed with family photos and a lovely seascape over the fireplace that had a mantelpiece made of driftwood.

Marian stared out the window, going over everything that had happened only an hour or so ago. Sean's sudden arrival had startled her and then what he said had frightened her even more as he revealed how they had met on the plane and then repeated every single thing she had said to him. And then his mention of them having dinner together recently had finally ended her new-found happiness with Theo. She had a sneaky feeling Sean had done all that on purpose. But why?

Tricia coming into the room with a tray loaded with two steaming mugs of tea and a plate with brownies cut into Marian's thoughts. 'Oh you shouldn't have gone to all that trouble, Tricia,' she exclaimed.

Tricia put the tray on the coffee table in front of the sofa. 'It's no trouble at all. And to be honest, I need it as much as you do after struggling with the accounts all afternoon.' She sat down beside Marian and handed her a mug. 'Here, hot tea and plenty of it. Then help yourself to a brownie and then talk if you want to, or not if you don't.'

'I don't know where to start,' Marian said, taking the mug and holding it close to her chest, breathing in the fragrance, its warmth giving her a sense of comfort.

'Well, the beginning of it all would be good,' Tricia said and took the other mug from the tray.

'Yes,' Marian agreed. 'The whole thing started during the flight from Sydney...' Between sips of tea and bites of brownie, the story slowly came out, from her disenchantment with her marriage to her inspiring an author to write the novel that was causing the Fleurys so much trouble. Tricia didn't interrupt her once, only listened intently, her eyes wider and wider with shock and amazement.

'Holy mother,' Tricia said when Marian had come to the end of her tale of woe. 'That is some story all by itself.'

'I know,' Marian said and hung her head. 'And I know I'm to blame for all the gossip that's going around town right now. I reneged on the family rule of not blabbing to outsiders about the Fleurys. I suppose you think that's unforgivable. I do, too, as a matter of fact. I hate myself for doing it.'

Tricia put her hand on Marian's. 'Don't hate yourself. That's so destructive. I know, because I have felt that way myself. Hurting other people because of something you said or did happens to us all at one time or another. So you had a drink or two that loosened your tongue and then you blabbed secrets to a stranger on a long flight. Was that such a major sin? I'm sure you never thought you'd see him again or that he would even remember what you said.'

'No, I didn't,' Marian agreed, feeling only slightly better. 'I was sure the whole conversation would be completely forgotten and that the man I was sitting beside would just disappear. How wrong I was,' she said bitterly.

'You couldn't have known. What a weird coincidence that you happened to sit beside John Peters on that plane,' Tricia continued. 'And then his mother being from here and him spending his summer holidays in this area as a child.'

'His real name is Sean Duvivier,' Marian said. 'John Peters is his pen name. Did you know him when he was a little boy coming here for his holidays? Isn't he around your age?'

'I think he's a bit younger,' Tricia replied. 'But no, I didn't know him at all. I grew up nearby, but I didn't even know Fred until we met at college in Dublin. I don't think he would have known John Peters either. He played with his school friends when he was a child, not with summer visitors.'

'I suppose not,' Marian remarked. 'Well, I'm glad you don't hate me for what I just told you.'

'Of course I don't,' Tricia assured her. 'It was an unfortunate accident. I don't think anyone in the family will hate you either.'

'Maybe. But Theo does, that's for sure. He left in a rage,' Marian said glumly, deciding not to go into Theo's relationship with Helen. She had probably blown that up out of all proportion anyway. Theo couldn't possibly be in love with his former girlfriend, Marian told herself. 'I don't know where he went. He was absolutely furious.'

'Oh, I'm sure that was just a fit of jealousy,' Tricia said. 'I'd say he'll be back.'

'You don't know Theo,' Marian said. 'He can stay mad for a very long time. And what about Sylvia? How will she react now that her story will be out in the open? She might think I spilled the beans on her, too, when she finds out what I did.'

'Sylvia?' Tricia let out a laugh. 'She's revelling in all the attention. Now she will be the supercool star in everyone's eyes. I think she has been waiting for the perfect moment to reveal all about her Parisian adventures. She couldn't tell anyone at the time; that would have been too shocking and she would have been thought of as the scarlet woman. But now? It will be seen as the most daring, exciting thing any woman ever did.'

'You don't think it will cause scandal?' Marian asked.

'Maybe in some people's eyes. Those holier-than-thou women on the Tidy Towns committee or wherever they hang out. But Sylvia won't care. She can handle them.'

'Yes, I'm sure you're right,' Marian said, feeling a little more cheerful.

'She might even be grateful to you for forcing her hand,' Tricia remarked, smirking. She held out the plate with the brownies. 'Here, have another one. They're very therapeutic, don't you think?'

'They certainly make me feel more hopeful,' Marian said, taking another brownie. 'Not so much about Theo, but about my role in the creation of that novel. I think Theo is a lost cause. I've wrecked every chance of a reconciliation.'

'If that's true, maybe he doesn't deserve you,' Tricia said. 'If he has any sense at all, he'll see what a wonderful woman you are and forgive you. If there really is anything to forgive, I mean,' she added, helping herself to another brownie.

'Oh, I think what I did was awful,' Marian said with a deep sigh. 'Careless and stupid. But maybe not telling him straight away was the worst bit.'

Tricia leaned forward and looked at Marian. 'How did you feel about John Peters? I mean, when you were having dinner with him? Great-looking guy, I have to say. I bet he has a bit of that French charm, too.'

Marian felt her cheeks flush. 'He's very attractive, I give you that. But what he did was very underhand and mean. And then that he had no sympathy at all for the Fleury family was a bit of a turn-off for me.'

'Just a bit?' Tricia asked, raising an eyebrow. 'So you do still find him attractive?'

Marian shook her head. 'Not any more. Not after the way he talked to Theo. It was as if Sean went out of his way to make Theo suspect that there was something between him and me. And of course Theo believed that and then we had a row and he walked off. I'll never see him again.' Marian buried her face in her hands. She started to sob, tears streaming down her cheeks, a feeling of hopelessness and deep sadness overwhelming her.

Tricia put her hand on Marian's shoulder. 'Have a good cry. Let it all out and then...'

'Then what?' Marian asked, lifting her tear-stained face to stare at Tricia.

'Then move on,' Tricia urged. 'Go back to work, do the things you enjoy and above all, make peace with yourself. All that self-loathing is very destructive.' Tricia took a paper napkin from the tray and handed it to Marian. 'Here. Dry your eyes and then try to think of something positive. Something you're looking forward to.'

'I'm not sure there is anything,' Marian mumbled as she wiped her eyes and blew her nose.

'Well, I'm looking forward to Sylvia's interview tomorrow,' Tricia declared. 'And the reaction in town after that. It'll be fun to hear what people will say in the pubs and cafés.'

'Yes,' Marian agreed, trying her best to think of something other than her misery. 'I'm looking forward to that too. But I don't know what to do about my work with Pierce. Should I quit? I don't want to work with John Peters. I don't even want to see him again.'

'I think you should have a chat with Pierce and tell him

what happened. He might take you off the John Peters campaign. I'm sure he'll understand how you feel.'

'Yes, you're right. That's what I should do. I'll call him in a minute. I'm going to tell him everything,' Marian announced. 'It's not fair to keep him in the dark about my role in the novel.'

'Maybe it would be best if you went to Claire and Pierce's house tonight?' Tricia suggested. 'Then you can tell them both. Claire needs to know too. After all, she's your sister.'

'Yes, you're right,' Marian said, feeling a pang of guilt at not having shared everything with Claire. 'I should have told her a long time ago and I should have spent more time with her instead of being so preoccupied with my own problems.'

'Oh, she was busy being on her honeymoon and then doing up their house and everything,' Tricia said. 'So please don't feel bad about not telling her.'

'Thanks, Tricia. You're a darling,' Marian said with a surge of affection for Tricia, who had been such a friend from the moment they met.

'You're welcome,' Tricia said. 'Come on, wipe your tears, have another brownie and then call your sister and ask if you can come over tonight.'

Marian laughed and took the last brownie on the plate. 'They should be recommended by doctors for depressed people.' She stuffed the whole brownie into her mouth and then took her phone from her handbag. 'I'll call Claire right now,' she said when she had swallowed her mouthful.

'Excellent.' Tricia got up and put the mugs and the empty plate on the tray. 'I'll put this in the kitchen while you call.'

Marian clicked on Claire's number and waited for an answer.

'Hi, Marian,' Claire said almost immediately. 'Where are you? Pierce said you ran off just after lunch and didn't come back. Something about Noel's office and Theo. And then you told him you weren't well.'

'I'm at Tricia's house,' Marian replied, suddenly feeling that what had happened with Theo was a long time ago.

'What are you doing there?' Claire asked. 'And where is Theo?'

'It's a long story,' Marian said. 'We had a row and then I was too upset to come back to the office. I was wondering if you and Pierce are home tonight? I'll tell you everything then.'

'Yes, we're home,' Claire said. 'Why don't you come over straight away? I'm just putting a chicken in the oven to roast and we can't eat all of it. We'd love to see you.'

'Thanks, that sounds lovely,' Marian said. 'I'll just go home and tidy up and then I'll be over at your house in about forty-five minutes.'

'Perfect,' Claire said. 'See you then.'

Marian got up from the sofa just as Tricia came back. 'I'm going to Claire's,' she said. 'She just invited me to a roast chicken dinner. Not sure I can cope with food after all the brownies, though, but I have to try.'

'By the time you sit down to dinner, you'll be hungry again,' Tricia said. 'Great that you get to talk to them both. I know it won't be easy, but Claire will understand. After all, she was hiding her real identity for months last year and then we were all shocked to hear the revelation about your side of the Fleurys.'

'I know but at least she didn't tell anyone outside the family,' Marian said. 'Now I have to confess that I was the instigator of all the gossip.'

'Like I said, I'm sure Claire will understand,' Tricia said.

'I hope you're right,' Marian said without conviction. Claire might be able to accept Marian's story. But what about all the other members of the Fleury family? Would they be able to forgive her, or would she have to leave Magnolia Manor in disgrace?

TWENTY-EIGHT

Claire welcomed Marian with open arms, enveloping her in a bear hug as they stood in the doorway. 'Oh, I'm so glad you came. We haven't been together much lately and I've missed you.' She stepped back. 'But come in. Dinner is nearly ready and the table laid in the kitchen. And Pierce is doing the veggies.'

'Oh, great,' Marian said, touched by the warm welcome. She followed Claire into the kitchen where Pierce was standing by the counter opening a bottle of wine. The delicious smell of roast chicken made Marian feel quite hungry despite all the brownies she had eaten earlier.

'Hi, Marian,' Pierce said. 'Welcome. Are you feeling better now?'

'Yes, I'm fine. I told you a bit of a fib because I was upset. I'll explain later.'

'I see,' Pierce said. 'We can talk about it after dinner. How about a glass of wine before we eat?'

'Lovely,' Marian said and went to the table that was laid for three. 'Will I sit down here?'

'Yes,' Pierce said and proceeded to pour red wine into the glasses on the table while Claire joined Marian.

'We decided not to eat on the deck,' Claire said. 'It's going to rain later and we didn't want to risk it.'

'You were right.' Marian took a sip of the wine and then put the glass down and looked at Claire. 'Well, as I said on the phone, I have something to tell you.'

'About you and Theo?' Claire asked in a gentle tone. 'Something has happened. I can tell by the sad look in your eyes.'

'Yes,' Marian said with a deep sigh. 'I think we've broken up for good.'

'Oh no,' Claire exclaimed and put her hand on Marian's. 'I'm so sorry. That's awful. But are you sure it's for good? Maybe you can talk about whatever it is and...'

'No,' Marian said. 'It's over. I know it is. I never told you, but I came here when I found a heartbreaking letter from an ex-girlfriend.'

'What?' Claire looked shocked. 'Theo had an...?'

'No,' Marian exclaimed. 'He hasn't been having an affair, he was just confiding in her, but it was the straw that broke the camel's back, which made me come here on my own. I wanted to tell you, but I was embarrassed and I didn't want to burden you when you were so happy. It all seemed like such a failure. Then, when Theo arrived here, we were beginning to get close again, but he found out about something I've done. And now I don't think we'll ever get back together after this.'

'Is that why you left the office in such a hurry?' Pierce asked, sitting down on Marian's other side.

'No, that was because of something I thought would make us happy,' Marian said. 'But it ended in a row and then he stalked off and said he was leaving.'

'You have to tell us everything,' Claire urged. 'Not bits and pieces like this.'

'I know,' Marian agreed. 'It's a long story that started on the plane on the way to Ireland. Well, to Dubai, to be precise.'

'I'd better serve dinner before you start,' Pierce said. 'Then you can tell us everything.'

'I hope it won't ruin your appetite,' Marian remarked.

'I'm starving, so I don't think anything could,' Claire said.

Pierce got up and started to cut up the chicken he had just taken out of the oven. Then he put a drumstick and a piece of the white meat on a plate, added vegetables and potatoes and handed it to Marian. 'There. Hope you'll like it. There is gravy in the sauceboat.' Then he heaped two more plates with food and brought them to the table before he sat down.

Claire picked up her knife and fork. 'Please start eating and then we'll talk.'

They ate in silence for a while and Marian tried her best to enjoy the succulent chicken, the carrots and potatoes laced with gravy. It was all delicious but she found the food stuck in her throat. But Claire and Pierce ate with great enthusiasm while Marian poked at the food on her plate.

Claire finally put down her cutlery and took a swig of wine. Then she looked at Marian. 'I think we're ready,' she said.

Marian pushed away her plate. 'Okay. I'll tell you everything,' she said and launched into her tale that started with the encounter with Sean on the plane and ended with Theo walking down the hill, saying he was leaving. She finally drew breath and drank some wine.

Claire and Pierce looked at each other in stunned silence when Marian had finished. 'Well,' Pierce said. 'That has changed things considerably.'

'I'm sure you don't want me in the office after this,' Marian said. 'So I'll quit and save you the trouble of firing me.'

'God, no,' Pierce said, looking appalled. 'Of course I'm not going to fire you. I'm going to fire *him*. I don't want to have him as a client after what he's done. It's not so much about him using what you said to him on the plane, but about what he said to Theo that caused him to take off like that.'

'Oh, but I don't want you to cancel everything,' Marian protested. 'It was just that I can't work with him after this. I think you should go ahead. Your media contacts will be annoyed if you tell them the deal is off. They might not want to work with you any more after this. In any case, after Sylvia's memoirs, his novel won't be as sensational after all. Just a pale version of the true story.'

'Hmm,' Pierce said. 'I have to think about this.'

Claire, who had remained silent, suddenly spoke up. 'Marian is right, sweetheart. It wouldn't be good for your business if you cut him off.' She turned to Marian. 'I wish you had told me all this earlier. I can't imagine how hard it must have been for you to carry all this on your own.'

'I didn't want to worry you,' Marian said. 'And you had your hands full with the wedding and the house and everything. And then I was sure you'd think badly of me,' she added in a low voice full of shame. 'I've been lying to you all this time.'

Claire shrugged. 'I know how that feels. Lying to people you love, I mean. I've been there myself. It's an awful thing to have to do. But I understand why you had to.' She paused for a moment. 'You know what? I don't think you should tell anyone else about it. What difference does it make?'

'I told Tricia,' Marian said. 'She was shocked at first but then she seemed to understand.'

'Of course she did. You were tired and emotional and a little drunk,' Claire said. 'So you shared your story and that of the family with someone you thought you'd never see again. I don't see that it was a major crime, somehow.'

'Nor do I,' Pierce cut in. 'And nobody else needs to know.'

'Sean, I mean John Peters, might talk,' Marian suggested with a shiver. 'He's good at that sort of thing.'

'I'll make sure he doesn't,' Pierce said grimly.

'How?' Claire asked.

'I have my ways,' Pierce said. 'But now we should forget all about him and enjoy the rest of the evening. You girls go and sit down in the living room and I'll tidy up here. And then we'll have dessert and a little cognac to round off the evening.'

'But I'm driving,' Marian protested. 'In fact, I'm sure I shouldn't have had any wine.'

'Stay the night,' Claire said. 'I'll lend you pyjamas and you can sleep in the guest room that we just finished decorating. It has an en-suite bathroom and everything,' she said proudly.

'You can have tomorrow morning off,' Pierce offered. 'I'm sure you're tired after all this. And I'll take you off John Peters' account. You can start on the media campaign for Karina's new cookbook.'

'Oh, that'll be fun,' Marian said. 'She told me about it. Thank you for understanding, Pierce. I'm sorry I didn't tell you about the John Peters thing before, but I just couldn't.'

'Pierce forgave me for lying to him all through the winter last year,' Claire said. 'Your lies are a mere whisper compared to mine.'

'You Fleury girls are as tough as old boots,' Pierce joked as he started to clear the table.

'We are,' Claire agreed with a laugh as she got up. 'Come on, Marian, let's go and chill in the living room.'

Marian rose, smiling, feeling relieved and nearly happy. Things seemed a little more hopeful and she felt that at least her problems concerning Sean and his novel were now on the way to being resolved. She knew the heartbreak over her marriage would take a long time to heal, but if Theo didn't come back – and she was now sure he wouldn't – she could at least try to heal in a lovely place surrounded by family.

'I can't wait to listen to Sylvia's interview,' Claire said as they came into the living room and sat down on the sofa. 'And then I wonder what the reaction will be. Can you imagine

Father O'Malley's face as he greets her after mass on Sunday? I'd go to church just to see that.'

'He'll probably be all for forgiving and forgetting,' Marian said.

'With a raised eyebrow,' Claire said with a giggle. 'After all, Sylvia does the flowers for the church every week. And she does a lovely job. Nobody else could match her. Father O'Malley couldn't manage without her.'

'Sylvia is such a powerhouse,' Marian said fondly. 'I wouldn't want to be in her bad books.'

'I know,' Claire said. 'I love her fighting spirit.'

'We should listen to her interview together,' Marian said. 'I could stay until tomorrow evening, if you'll have me.'

'Of course,' Claire said. 'We were planning to listen here with the girls anyway. I mean with Lily, Rose, Vi and Tricia. I was going to tell you about it before you came. We're going to send out for pizza and the men will mind the kids. A Fleury girls' get-together.'

'A real fright for us men,' Pierce said as he came into the room carrying a tray with slices of chocolate cake and a bottle of brandy.

'Oh, you can take it,' Claire said, looking adoringly at her husband. 'Don't tell me you don't love the Fleury girls.'

'I love them passionately,' Pierce said.

TWENTY-NINE

Marian stayed with Claire that night and went to the office with them both in Pierce's car the next morning, despite Pierce giving her the morning off. Karina's new cookbook was a project she wanted to start straight away. She felt a lot better about everything except the lingering sadness about Theo. But she knew that the divorce proceedings, which she was sure were imminent, would break her heart and take a long time to get over. But she decided to try to live in the moment and deal with whatever was the outcome of Sylvia's revelations which she was sure would be dramatic. She was happy to start work on Karina's new book and got stuck into the campaign straight away once she sat down at her desk. She felt that marketing and publicity was what she wanted to do and that she was good at it. It was fun to see her efforts on social media with ads and posts having an effect and she loved learning and testing new methods of promoting books.

'You're a natural,' Pierce told her over coffee later that morning. 'I hope you'll stay working with me. We're a good team.'

'I'd love to stay here,' Marian said. 'You're a great boss. And we're family after all.'

'Everything good rolled into one,' Pierce said, beaming.

Later that evening in Claire's house, the Fleury girls squashed onto the sofa with their slices of pizza and glasses of wine and turned on the radio to listen to Sylvia's interview.

'This is so exciting,' Lily said, just before the show was about to start.

'I'm nervous,' Rose said. 'I hope Granny is doing the right thing.'

'She's been waiting to tell her story for years,' Vi said.

'Sylvia is having a ball,' Tricia said.

'Shh, it's starting,' Claire said as the familiar voice of Noreen O'Connor came on the air.

'Hello, this is Noreen,' the presenter said. 'And tonight I have a very special guest in my studio. Her name is Sylvia Fleury and she is about to publish her memoirs. This interview will give you all a taste of what's to come. Hello, Sylvia, and welcome to the show.'

'Thank you,' Sylvia said, sounding just a little nervous. 'I'm so happy to be here. I listen to your show every Tuesday.'

'Wonderful,' Noreen said. 'So,' she continued, 'tell me a little about your memoirs and how you got the idea to publish them.'

'Oh,' Sylvia said. 'I had been thinking about it for quite some time. I felt that as I'm getting on in years, my story might be of interest to my granddaughters. But then the editor I hired to help me put the story together told me she thought it should be read by the general public out there, as it's a kind of living history.'

'I'm sure it is,' Noreen replied. 'Especially the part about the early nineteen sixties that was a real watershed, for women especially. That was the era when women were finally free to do their own thing, wasn't it?'

'Not in holy Catholic Ireland,' Sylvia remarked with a little laugh. 'But in Europe generally, yes.'

'Especially Paris, I believe,' Noreen said. 'You spent a little over a year there, you said. Could you tell us about that period in your life?'

'Oh, it was wonderful,' Sylvia said dreamily. 'I was finally free to do what I wanted without anyone looking at me over their shoulder. No Legion of Mary or parish priest or any old aunt or nun from school lecturing me about straying from the straight and narrow. And the city with its elegance and all that new fashion in every window. Short skirts and bright colours everywhere. A dream come true for me, a country girl just out of my dreary school uniform. I took to Paris straight away.'

'But you kept in touch with Ireland all the same?' Noreen asked. 'You told me that you went to the Irish College in Paris where you met someone who changed your life.'

'Yes,' Sylvia replied. 'Margaret Kelly.'

'Here it comes,' Vi whispered, chewing on her pizza.

'Shh,' Rose ordered. 'I don't want to miss a word.'

They stayed silent while they all listened to Sylvia's story. How she had become a Bluebell Girl and danced in the chorus line at the Lido wearing feathers and sequins, loving every moment, even though it had been demanding both physically and mentally. How she had shared a garret room with two other dancers, both Irish and then... The story continued with a twist nobody had known about until now.

'I was introduced to one of Margaret Kelly's friends,' Sylvia continued. 'A man called Hubert de Givenchy. He was a fashion designer and had designed clothes for both Audrey Hepburn and Jackie Kennedy. He asked if I'd be willing to model for him if Margaret would agree to part with me for a week or two. He needed models for his spring collection and I seemed to fit the bill somehow.'

'So you said yes?' Noreen asked.

'Of course,' Sylvia replied. 'Wouldn't you?'

'Like a shot,' Noreen said with a little giggle.

'Who'd refuse such a request?' Sylvia enquired. 'I was given a few items from the collection too. But the modelling assignment only lasted a few weeks, and then I went back to the chorus line at the Lido. We were rehearsing for a show in Nice.'

'So you went to the French Riviera?' Noreen filled in. 'And then, on the way back, you met someone special.'

'That's right,' Sylvia said. 'But that is all I'm going to say about that. The rest of the story is in my memoirs that will be published tomorrow. And we're doing a launch next Tuesday evening to mark the publication. It will be in the ballroom at Magnolia Manor. Everyone is welcome. But they have to promise to buy the book. The proceeds will go partly to the Simon Community for the homeless and partly to the upkeep of Magnolia Manor, which, you must agree, is a very important cause.'

'Of course it is,' Noreen agreed. 'Magnolia Manor is an important landmark in this area. Thank you so much for appearing on my show, Sylvia Fleury. Your book, *My Path to Magnolia Manor*, will be for sale at the book launch, and then in the bookshop in Dingle. I love the cover, by the way. You in front of the manor is the book in a nutshell.'

'Thank you,' Sylvia said graciously. 'And thank you also for inviting me on your show, Noreen.'

'It was my pleasure,' Noreen said warmly. 'So this is the end of tonight's show,' she continued. 'I hope it has been enjoyable. Don't forget to tune in next week when we will hear from another local author who is about to publish his sixth novel. Until then, *slán agus beannacht de leath*.' Then there was the signature tune of the show, followed by a string of commercials.

Claire turned off the radio and looked at everyone sitting, stunned, on the sofa, forgetting to eat their pizzas, the row of wine glasses untouched on the coffee table.

'Wow,' Vi finally said. 'Granny was a fashion model for Givenchy as well as a Bluebell Girl.'

'I always thought there would be something like that in her past,' Marian remarked. 'That poise and grace and the way she still walks even at her age. Not something you would have learned in the Kerry countryside.'

'Incredible,' Rose said.

'So the launch is in the ballroom at Magnolia Manor next Tuesday,' Vi said. 'How come we didn't know it would be that soon?'

'Because she didn't tell anyone,' Lily said.

'Not even me,' Rose said. 'I just saw that the ballroom was booked for a big event that day, but I had no idea by whom. Typical Granny stunt,' she added with a laugh.

Tricia held up her glass. 'A toast to Sylvia. Our very own queen.'

'To Queen Sylvia,' everyone said in unison and clinked glasses with each other. Then they all had cold pizza and more wine before it was time for the husbands to bring them home.

Marian, sitting on a chair beside the sofa, looked at the chatting, laughing women, all so happy with their lives and their partners. She suddenly felt as if she was stuck on an island of misery, the divorce looming in the near distance. Her marriage was broken and there was no way to fix it.

It wasn't all my fault, she said to herself. *Theo was also to blame, both for his connection with another woman, which I suspect was not all in the distant past. And then, when we were on our way back to each other, he walked away through a fit of jealousy.*

'Marian?' Tricia touched her shoulder. 'Are you okay? You looked so sad there all of a sudden.'

'I am sad,' she said. 'But not about the stuff on the plane or anything like that. It's about Theo and me.'

'I'm sorry,' Tricia said. 'Come into the kitchen and we'll have a chat.'

'I think I've done all the talking about this,' Marian said glumly. 'You're so kind, Tricia, but all the kindness in the world won't fix this.'

'I know,' Tricia said. 'But I just wanted to tell you that...' She stopped. 'Oh, come on. Follow me,' she said and started walking out of the room.

Marian followed Tricia into the kitchen where they both sat down at the table littered with pizza cartons. 'Look,' Tricia started, 'I just wanted to say that I've been there just like you. A man I loved left in a huff and I thought I'd never see him again. So I went on with my life and tried to enjoy being on my own. But then, a while later, he came back and apologised and we had the most romantic reconciliation you can imagine.' Tricia's eyes sparkled.

'Was it Cillian?' Marian asked.

'Yes. He came back looking very sorry for himself. That's men for you. Once they're on their own for a bit, they realise they can't live without you.'

'I don't think that'll happen to me,' Marian said. 'But thanks for giving me a glimmer of hope.'

'I have a feeling I'm right,' Tricia said. 'But if I'm not, I'm really sorry. In any case, we're all here for you. All the Fleury girls. Even Sylvia. Especially Sylvia, I should say,' she added. 'After all she gave us strict instructions to be nice to Theo to make him feel welcome.'

'That's lovely to hear,' Marian said. 'And he did feel very welcome. I think he fell in love with the Fleurys and Kerry all at once. Only he fell out of love with me,' she added with a sigh.

'I'm sure that's not true,' Tricia soothed.

'I'm afraid I do. I think I'll go now in any case,' Marian said.

'My car is parked outside. I haven't been home since yesterday and now I feel like I want to go to sleep in my own bed tonight. I love that little flat, you know. It feels like my own little haven where I can be safe and eventually maybe even happy.'

'It's such a cute flat,' Tricia said. 'And maybe the best place for you right now. Let me know if I can do anything at all. Cillian is coming home tomorrow and we'll both be here if you need company.'

'Thanks, Tricia.' Marian leaned forward and kissed Tricia on the cheek. 'I'll slip away now. Say goodnight to everyone.' Marian smiled and left, tiptoeing down the corridor, smiling as she heard chatting and laughter in the living room and then walked through the front door and down the steps to her car.

The fresh air cooled her hot cheeks and she got into the car and drove away, looking forward to a good night's sleep, finally feeling relaxed after all the stress and excitement of the past few days. What she had said to Tricia was true. She loved her little apartment at the top of Magnolia Manor, where she would never feel really alone. Her life was changing and now she would have to learn to live on her own. She felt oddly carefree, even if the sadness of her broken relationship with Theo would linger for a long time. She loved him, but if he didn't want her, she would have to accept that and move on. It was as if all the problems and heartbreak was floating away in the slipstream of the car as she speeded up and drove down the main road on her way to Magnolia Manor.

When Marian arrived at the manor, she parked the car and entered through the big entrance doors, slowly climbing the stairs, suddenly feeling exhausted. It would be so good to sink into bed and go to sleep after all the drama and emotion. Then, as she arrived at the top landing, she was startled by someone moving by the door to her flat. She froze as a figure appeared out of the shadows, her heart beating, nearly breathless with fright.

'Marian?' a voice said.

'Yes?' Marian said. 'Who's there?'

'Me,' Theo said and stepped forward, holding a huge bunch of flowers. 'I got these for you. Can I come in?'

'Yes, but...' she stammered. 'Why? What are you doing here?'

He pushed the flowers at her and she saw they were peonies and roses, her favourites. 'I want to say sorry and a lot of other things too. But first of all, I want to ask you to forgive me.'

'Oh,' Marian whispered, fumbling with her keys. 'Yes, well... Come in anyway.' She finally manged to open the door and put on the light in the hall. Then Theo followed her inside and they looked at each other for a loaded moment, full of emotion. Marian took the flowers from Theo. 'I'll put these in water. Have you been waiting here long?'

'About two hours,' Theo said. 'I sat in the car for a bit listening to Sylvia's interview and then I thought I'd come up here and ring the doorbell. But you were out so I thought I'd wait until you came home.'

'I'm here now.' Marian walked ahead with the flowers and turned on the lamps in the living room before she went into the kitchen and found a jug. 'I don't have a vase, so this will have to do,' she said and poured water into it and then put the flowers in and placed the whole thing on the kitchen counter. 'There. They're lovely. Thank you.'

'You're welcome.' Theo joined Marian in the kitchen, took her hands in his and breathed in deeply before he spoke. 'I don't want to rake over the past,' he said slowly. 'I just want whatever was wrong between us to be right again. I love you, Marian. I don't want to lose you ever again. I'll buy that house if you want and I'll do it up for you. I'll do anything, actually, to make you happy.'

Marian saw his tears and all her feelings of resentment disappeared. She put her arms around him and looked into his grey eyes, so full of sorrow and remorse. 'Oh, Theo, of course I forgive you. And I do love you, too, you silly man. But I don't want that house. It would always remind me of that guy who nearly wrecked everything for us. I'd like for us to find some other place where we can be happy. But not yet. I think that we could live apart for a bit and go on dates and look for a house together a little later. Would that be okay?'

'I was going to suggest that, actually,' Theo said, smiling through his tears. 'I've found a place to rent in a holiday complex nearby. It's nice and comfortable and the bed is big enough for two if you want to come and stay the night from time to time. I want you to know that this place – Kerry, I mean – is where I want to grow old. With you.' He drew breath and looked at her with an expression so full of love it made her own tears well up.

'That sounds absolutely perfect,' Marian whispered and kissed him. Then she pulled back. 'Oh, Theo,' she said. 'You've made me so happy. You were right that time, when you said my dreams would come true one day. Now I feel they have.'

'Mine too,' Theo said. 'I always dreamed about a place where we could both be happy. I thought we had found it in Surfers Paradise. It seemed perfect to me. You leaving was my wake-up call. I realised then that I was the only one to be happy and you'd been miserable. You hid it well and always greeted me with a smile and a hug when I came home. But when you left, you didn't pretend any more. I knew I'd have to go to Ireland and see for myself why Kerry was so much better than Queensland. It didn't take me long to love the gentle pace of life here and the warmth and friendliness of people in Kerry. All the Fleurys made me feel so welcome and that was what made see how we could both settle here and finally both feel at home.'

He drew breath and grinned. 'Gee, that was a long speech for me.'

'It came from your heart,' Marian said. 'I'm really happy you feel like that about Kerry. But I believe the winters can be rough, with storms and torrential rain.'

'I think we can cope with that,' he said. 'Endless sunshine isn't all it's cracked up to be either.'

'That's for sure.' She looked at him and saw the dark circles under his eyes, and knew he had not got much sleep the past few nights. She touched his cheek. 'You need to rest,' she said. 'Lie down on my bed and then I'll make us something to eat. I think I can at least make a grilled cheese sandwich.'

'With mustard?' he asked.

'Yes. And I even have a jar of gherkins.'

'Brilliant.' Theo let her go and went to sit on the sofa, putting his feet on the coffee table. 'I'm good here,' he said.

She bent over to kiss him. 'You look good anywhere.' Then she went into the kitchen and made the cheese sandwich, putting it under the grill, knowing that they had finally come home. Whatever happened in the future, they would stay here and grow old together surrounded by family.

EPILOGUE

Eight months later, they stood outside their new house holding hands. It was a small cottage with three bedrooms, a living room, kitchen and a bathroom in the lean-to extension at the back. It sat on the top of the hill overlooking Dingle Bay and had stunning views of both the ocean and the islands. It had taken them most of the winter to find it and when they did, it had caused many an argument about all the work the old Victorian house would need to make it at least comfortable. The garden was also overgrown with a gnarled crab apple tree that was now, in the month of April, in full bloom, and the grass knee high.

So much had happened since last year, the most exciting event being the launch of Sylvia's memoirs. It had overshadowed John Peters' novel and nobody had paid much attention to the old secrets he had revealed. Everyone was fascinated by Sylvia's story and she was hailed as the most modern and independent woman of her generation. Her launch party was a huge success and everyone celebrated with champagne and dancing into the early hours of the morning.

Marian smiled at the memory as she looked at the house. All her troubles had finally been resolved and there was harmony within the Fleury family once more.

'Happy?' Theo asked, squeezing her hand.

'Oh yes. It's the house of my dreams,' Marian said, gazing at the sagging roof, the flaking paint and the cracked windows.

'It will be once we do it up,' Theo said. 'I can't wait to get stuck in.'

'You're mad to even consider living there now,' Marian said, looking at his two suitcases on the front step.

Theo jingled the keys in his hand. 'I'll be fine. There's electricity and water and I have a bed and a table and two chairs. What more would I want?'

'At least you're not asking me to move in with you,' Marian said, laughing.

'No, you can stay in your cosy little flat,' Theo said. 'Until I make this fit for a princess.'

'And you will come for dinner every day, of course,' Marian added. 'And sit on my sofa and watch all the footie matches on TV.'

'The perfect life for any bloke.' Theo suddenly grabbed Marian and lifted her in his arms.

'What are you doing?' she squealed.

'What do you think? I'm carrying you across the threshold, of course.' Theo walked to the front door, skirting the suitcases, and managed to put the key in the lock and swing the door open. Then he carried Marian into the little hall and put her down. 'There, your ladyship. You're in our forever home.'

'Thank God for that,' Marian said, still laughing. 'I thought you'd drop me.' Then she walked into what would be their living room and felt that homely feeling, just like the first time she'd been in the little house. 'It's as if the house has been waiting for us,' she said in awe. 'I just know we'll be happy here.' It was true despite the peeling paint, the cracked mantelpiece, the broken panes in the windows. She had liked Sean's house before she knew who owned it, but this cottage was even more special. It had a peace and calm like no other place she had ever been in. She had been happy in her little flat, but this house had the space and potential to be something really beautiful.

'I think the kids will like it too,' Theo said. 'Rebecca is coming back to Ireland and Conor will love to come for visits from London. And I'd say that we'll be grandparents one day. The garden will be perfect for the littlies, don't you think?'

Marian smiled at the Australian expression. 'Oh yes. They'll love their Aussie granddad,' she said. 'But that is in the future and this is now. We have to get started, or it'll never get finished.'

The house was finally finished a whole year later. Marian couldn't believe it was the same house, as she stood in front of it, ready to move in with her suitcases and a few boxes of belongings. Beside her were her whole family: Theo, Rebecca and Conor. The children had just arrived in Kerry to celebrate the move to their parents' new home. Rebecca had recently moved back to Ireland and Conor had come over from London for a long weekend.

'Oh, Mum,' Rebecca said beside Marian. 'It's gorgeous. Dad has really worked hard.'

'We both have,' Marian said. 'It's been a tough winter with storms and rain and power cuts. But Theo with Dominic and his team finished the roof and painted the outside before the winter. And then we did most of the indoor work together. But your dad did the bathroom, and it's like something from a five-star hotel.'

'I can believe it,' Rebecca said. 'Weren't you clever to marry a plumber?'

'Of course I was,' Marian said and put her arm around her

daughter. 'And you were so clever to get engaged to that lovely Irishman and move back to Dublin.'

'I'm a little envious,' Conor said. 'I should perhaps look for a job in Ireland, but I'm happy where I am.'

'You're not too far away,' Theo said. 'And we'll get you back to the auld sod one of these days.'

'You never know,' Conor said with a wide smile, so like his father's. 'But don't count your chickens just yet. You did the right thing, though, Rebecca. And you were lucky to find that great bloke to settle down with.'

Rebecca smiled. 'Yeah, I think I was. Eoin is not a plumber, but an economist. Which will be great when we do our tax returns.'

'Nearly as good as a plumber,' Marian said and lifted one of her suitcases. 'Come on, then, kids. Let's move in. Dad can't wait to show you around.'

Theo opened the door as they approached. 'Welcome home,' he said, beaming. 'I'd carry you all across the threshold but I've strained my back putting in the bathtub, so you'll have to take a raincheck.'

'Never mind carrying anyone,' Marian said. 'Keep the door open while we get everything inside.'

Rebecca walked to her father's side and gave him a big hug. 'I'm so happy to be here at last. What a lovely home you've made for us.'

Theo hugged her back and smiled at Marian and Conor over Rebecca's shoulder. 'Our chicks seem to have come home again.'

'Only for the weekend,' Rebecca said. 'But I'll be back very often.'

'So will I,' Conor agreed.

'That's good enough for me,' Theo said, pulling his daughter into the house.

Marian followed, with Conor in her wake, enjoying seeing father and daughter together. Then she stepped inside and closed the door behind her. She was finally home with her family.

KEEP IN TOUCH WITH SUSANNE

www.susanne-oleary.co.uk

facebook.com/authoroleary

bsky.app/profile/susanneol.bsky.social

instagram.com/susanne.olearyauthor

ACKNOWLEDGEMENTS

As always huge thanks to my editor Jennifer Hunt, who is so invested in my work and is always there with helpful hints and suggestions about plotlines and character development. I couldn't manage without her. Also Jon Appleton, who was such a huge help with the final edits, turning what could have been tedious into a very enjoyable journey. Also thanks to everyone at Bookouture for all their hard work. I couldn't wish for a better publishing team.

I also want to thank my husband and the rest of my family for putting up with living with a writer, which isn't always easy. And then... my friends who cheer me on and my wonderful readers who show me their appreciation through emails and messages on Facebook and Instagram. Thank you all so much.

PUBLISHING TEAM

Turning a manuscript into a book requires the efforts of many people. The publishing team at Bookouture would like to acknowledge everyone who contributed to this publication.

Commercial
Lauren Morrissette
Hannah Richmond
Imogen Allport

Cover design
Debbie Clement

Data and analysis
Mark Alder
Mohamed Bussuri

Editorial
Jennifer Hunt
Charlotte Hegley

Copyeditor
Jon Appleton

Proofreader
Becca Allen

Marketing
Alex Crow
Melanie Price
Occy Carr
Cíara Rosney
Martyna Młynarska

Operations and distribution
Marina Valles
Joe Morris

Production
Hannah Snetsinger
Mandy Kullar
Nadia Michael

Publicity
Kim Nash
Noelle Holten
Jess Readett
Sarah Hardy

Rights and contracts
Peta Nightingale
Richard King
Saidah Graham

Dear Reader,

We'd love your attention for one more page to tell you about the crisis in children's reading, and what we can all do.

Studies have shown that reading for fun is the **single biggest predictor of a child's future life chances** – more than family circumstance, parents' educational background or income. It improves academic results, mental health, wealth, communication skills, ambition and happiness.

The number of children reading for fun is in rapid decline. Young people have a lot of competition for their time, and a worryingly high number do not have a single book at home.

Hachette works extensively with schools, libraries and literacy charities, but here are some ways we can all raise more readers:

- Reading to children for just 10 minutes a day makes a difference
- Don't give up if children aren't regular readers – there will be books for them!

- Visit bookshops and libraries to get recommendations
- Encourage them to listen to audiobooks
- Support school libraries
- Give books as gifts

There's a lot more information about how to encourage children to read on our websites: **www.RaisingReaders.co.uk** and **www.JoinRaisingReaders.com**.

Thank you for reading.